SHADOWLANDS

KATE BRIAN

HYPERION

NEW YORK

Copyright © 2012 by Alloy Entertainment and Kieran Viola

All rights reserved. Published by Hyperion, an imprint of Disney Book Group. No part of this book may be reproduced or transmitted in any form or by any means, electronic or mechanical, including photocopying, recording, or by any information storage and retrieval system, without written permission from the publisher. For information address Hyperion, 125 West End Avenue, New York, New York 10023.

alloy**entertainment**
Produced by Alloy Entertainment
1700 Broadway, New York, NY 10019

First Hyperion paperback edition, 2013
10 9 8 7 6 5 4 3 2 1
Printed in the United States of America

This book is set in Janson Text
Designed by Liz Dresner

ISBN 978-1-4231-6525-5 (paperback)

Library of Congress Control Number for Hardcover Edition: 2012025624

Visit www.un-requiredreading.com

SUSTAINABLE FORESTRY INITIATIVE
Certified Chain of Custody
Promoting Sustainable Forestry
www.sfiprogram.org
SFI-01054
The SFI label applies to the text stock

For my mom, without whom
I wouldn't be the person I am today

THE ATTEMPT

His hands felt like ice. He rubbed them together, the dry scratching an even tempo in the otherwise quiet woods. The chill in the air was unacceptable, especially for so late in the spring. After he finished this, he would move to a warmer climate. But for now he was here, and the sun was starting to make its descent. She would be along at any moment. Then the cold would no longer matter. Soon his hands would be warm. He blew into them and hummed "The Long and Winding Road," a tune that always made him smile.

He heard a crack. A crunch. His skin began to purr. He lifted himself ever so slightly from his crouch, just enough to peer from behind wire-rimmed glasses over the craggy boulder that shielded him from view. A sigh escaped his throat at the sight of her. So small, so pert, so completely, utterly oblivious. Her blond hair lay in a thick braid down her back. It was the hair that had seduced him. So thick, so soft, so many varying shades of gold. She had no idea how beautiful it was. How beautiful she was. He loved her for it.

She was skirting the dying oak tree, about to step over the wet crag full of slick, slippery, water-worn rocks. It was time. He ensured that his gray canvas messenger bag was properly camouflaged by a pile of leaves and stepped out from behind the rock. A thin branch that had fallen from a nearby birch cracked under his heavy boot.

She froze. He could feel the fear radiating off her. She whirled around, her eyes wide, but didn't see him. Hugging herself, she took a few quick steps, her heavy backpack banging against her spine. He stepped on another branch, purposely this time, snapping it clean in two. She stopped again. Now he could *taste* her fear, and he swallowed it whole, savoring the tangy saltiness of it. She started to run. The moment she looked behind her—they always looked behind them—he stepped out into the path in front of her. When she slammed into him, he didn't flinch. She weighed practically nothing. She screamed, and his chest filled with unadulterated joy.

He put his hands on her arms, steadying her. She pulled back, her eyes wide, her skin taut, her complexion pale. Then she saw him. Really saw him. And her body sagged in relief.

"Mr. Nell! Oh my god!" Her hand was on her heart. Everything was fine. She knew him. She felt safe now. Silly girl. "You scared me! What're you doing out here?"

He let her go for that one, brief moment. Gave her that moment of confident security. Then he licked his lips.

That was all it took. The fear returned, hotter and faster this time. She took a step back, but they were right at the edge of the crag. She wobbled, just as he knew she would. Reaching out, he closed his fingers around her wrist and used her own momentum to fling her around, ripping the backpack to the ground with his free hand. She tried to scream again, but he clamped one arm around her neck and the other over her mouth. He dragged her backward off the trail, her hair, her delicious hair, brushing his lips.

She struggled, of course. They always struggled. The only variable was how long she would last. How long she would fight before she realized the inevitability of what was going to happen. Before she accepted it. Some fought until the very end, clawing, kicking, biting, slamming their tiny fists against him until he strangled all the strength right out of them. Others simply begged. It didn't matter what they did. The ending was always the same.

Rory Miller would probably plead with him. He had watched her for months and knew she was not a spirited girl. Aside from her passion for science and her ability to come in third in almost every cross-country race she'd ever run, she didn't have much fire in her. In fact, there was almost nothing special about her at all. Except for the hair. Her beautiful, golden hair.

He opened his mouth and took some of it under his tongue.

She tried to scream again, but his grip was too tight to let the sound escape. The boulder was mere inches away. He pictured slamming her temple onto the razor-sharp edge, cutting a ragged wound into her scalp. But then this would be over far too quickly.

As he reached the edge of the boulder, his heel came down on a wet leaf, and he slipped. For a fraction of a second, he fought for balance, and his grip on her loosened ever so slightly. It was the minutest of mistakes, but it was enough. She let out a screech and slammed her sharp elbow into his solar plexus.

He doubled over, trying to breathe, but the air wouldn't come. His vision clouded over. His hand pressed against the cold surface of the rock, and he blinked until his eyes began to clear. That was when he saw the jagged, broken end of a branch thrusting upward toward his face.

He heard the crack. Tasted the blood seconds before he felt the excruciating pain. His glasses flew off his nose. His knees hit the freezing mud, which quickly turned red from the river of blood streaming from his nose.

"You whore!" he screamed, blood burbling in his mouth. But she was gone.

No. No. No. This could not happen. He pulled a handkerchief from his pocket, covered his nose, and staggered forward. Twigs and brambles whipped his arms, underbrush tugged at his feet, the cold wind stung his face, but still he ran. He had tasted her already. He had to have her.

Everything was a blur without his glasses. Then, a glimpse. A flash. The white canvas lining of her hood. He ran faster. He could feel her again. Feel her terror. All he had to do was close the space between them and she would be his. His fingers stretched. They ached. Just one more inch and he would have her. Just one. More. Inch.

A blinding light flashed. A screeching of tires. He heard her scream before he realized what was happening. She'd reached the edge of the woods. She'd reached the road. And now she was either dead or saved.

Instinctively, he hit the dirt. His nose throbbed. His sweat congealed on his skin, freezing him from the outside in. There were voices. Shouts of alarm. Ever so slowly, he slunk backward. Slunk into the bushes, the woods he knew so well. He could hide here. He could disappear. He would be all right. But it wasn't enough. Because he had tasted her. He had tasted her. He had tasted her. How could he ever survive knowing how close he'd come? This need would never be sated. Not now. He knew he would never rest until he had her.

Not dead, he prayed as he slipped deeper into the oncoming darkness. *Please don't let her be dead.*

If she was not dead, there was still a chance. If she was not dead, he would find a way. He always, always found a way.

THE ESCAPE

The uneven end of a thin tree limb ripped the skin from my cheek. My lungs burned with every ragged, panicked breath. My eyes were so blurred I couldn't see where I was going. My foot caught on a tree root, and I flew forward. I screamed as I imagined him right behind me, closing in on me, grabbing me off the ground, and dragging me to my death. I pushed myself to my knees and gasped for air. His breath was hot on my neck. His fingers grazed my shoulder. I let out another scream, my throat constricting, but when I whirled around, no one was there. I forced myself up and kept running.

I shoved aside a clawlike branch and leaped over a fallen maple trunk, almost tripping again as I hit the ground on the other side. This was not happening. It couldn't really be happening. Mr. Nell was my teacher. He was a good guy. Funny. Everyone thought he was so cool in that retro, dorky teacher way. This had to be a nightmare, and any second I was going to wake up and laugh over the fact that I ever thought it was real.

I heard a twig snap behind me. A footfall. He was closing in. He'd looked into my eyes and licked his lips. He'd tasted my hair and moaned.

My throat filled with bile. I was not going to die this way. I was not going to let him have the satisfaction. I was supposed to go to college, become a doctor, get married and have kids, win awards, buy a beach house, and die surrounded by my loving family knowing I'd saved countless lives over the course of my storied career. Or, like my sister, Darcy, was always saying, I was supposed to die alone and surrounded by cats. Either way. But not like this.

With one desperate explosion of adrenaline I surged ahead, and suddenly, there were no trees. There were no leaves, no brambles, no underbrush. There was only asphalt tearing the fabric of my jeans at the knee and an SUV bearing down on me.

The last thing I saw before I flung my hands up was the

gleaming silver grille headed right for my face. There was an awful, deafening screech, and the world filled with the scent of burned rubber.

I held my breath and braced for impact.

"Rory?"

I blinked. Christopher's face loomed over me. His beautiful, perfect, startled face. His dark hair was slicked back from his forehead, wet from the school showers.

"Oh my god, are you all right?"

I looked back at the woods as he grabbed both my arms and dragged me off the road. When I tried to stand, my knees gave out and I leaned into him, gripping the sleeves of his black-and-white varsity jacket with my dirt-streaked fingers. There was blood on the back of one hand, and mud soaked the cuff of my sleeve. Every single inch of me was shaking.

"Get in the car!" I yelled.

"What?" His brows knit in confusion over his warm brown eyes. "Rory, what're you—"

"Get in the car, Chris!" I shouted again. "We have to get out of here!"

Keeping my eyes on the woods, I staggered toward the passenger-side door. The trees dipped and swirled in my vision, and the ground beneath me began to tilt. I pressed my hands against the hood to keep from going down, breathing through the dizziness. I couldn't give up now. Not when I was so close to safety.

"I've got you," Christopher said in my ear.

He helped me into the car and slammed the door. I jammed my trembling fingers down on the lock button over and over again until it finally clicked. Something moved in the corner of my vision and I seized up, but then I saw the flick of a bushy tail and realized it was just a squirrel scampering up a tree trunk.

"Rory, what's going on?" Christopher asked, getting behind the wheel. "Why are you covered in mud?"

"Just drive, Chris. Please," I begged. My body started quaking so violently it hurt. I tried to hold my breath, tried to control the shaking, but it wouldn't stop. Even when I shoved my hands under my arms, clamped my knees together, and clenched my jaw. It just wouldn't stop.

"But my house is right—"

"Please just take me home," I begged. "And call nine-one-one."

"Why?" Christopher asked. He looked me up and down, his face pale. "Rory," he said, his voice tense. "What happened?"

"Mr. Nell," I stammered through my teeth. "Mr. Nell attacked me."

"Mr. Nell the *math teacher*?" he blurted, taking the turn

at the end of his street too wide and nearly hitting a car waiting at the stop sign. My stomach swooped as the other driver leaned on his horn. My hands flung out and braced against the door and the side of Chris's seat.

Chris pulled the car over onto the shoulder. He cupped one hand over his mouth, a worry line forming just above his nose. When he looked at me, my heart stopped beating. His eyes went from stunned, to resigned, to murderous in the space of five seconds. It was only then that I understood how he really felt about me. Right there, in that awful moment, with cars whizzing by fast enough to make the car shudder.

Why had I ever turned him down? If I had just said yes, if I had just blown off Darcy's feelings like she'd done to me so many times in my life, Chris and I would have been a couple. We would have left school together today, and he would have driven me over to his house to tutor his sister. If I had just said yes, I never would have been taking that shortcut through the woods, and none of this would've happened.

"He didn't—" Red splotches appeared along Chris's neck and moved up his face. "Rory, he didn't—"

My stomach hollowed out as I realized what he was asking. I shook my head. "No." A sob escaped my throat, and I covered my face with both hands. "No."

Chris sank back in his seat. "Thank god." He reached for the Bluetooth button on his dashboard.

Suddenly, a man's voice filled the car. "Nine-one-one. What's your emergency?"

"My girl—my friend was attacked," Christopher said, his voice cracking.

"Is your friend with you?" the man asked.

"Yes," Christopher replied. "She's here. She's . . . okay."

He reached out and took my hand, clasping it so hard it hurt.

"What's your location?"

"We're in my car on Seventeen, right near Fisher's Crossing," he said. "But the guy's still out there. Mr. Nell. I don't know his first name. He works at my school. At Princeton Hills High. He's still in the woods."

"And your names?" the man asked.

"Christopher Kane and Rory Miller."

"All right, sir. Don't move. We're sending someone right to you."

"Okay," Christopher said, swallowing hard. "Okay."

Rain began to fall in huge drops, splattering across the windshield. He hit the button to end the call. For a long moment, neither one of us said a word, or moved, or breathed. Then he got out of the car, walked around to my side, and squeezed in next to me. I crawled into his lap, and he shut the door and just held me. Burying my face in his chest, I breathed in the deep woolen scent of his jacket, closed my eyes, and tried to stop seeing Mr. Nell's face. I tried to think of something else. Anything else. My mother smiling at me a few months before she died. My father taking me on my first run. My sister twirling around in a red tutu and heart-shaped sunglasses, putting on a show for the family at Thanksgiving. But the image of Mr. Nell obliterated the memories one by one. That ugly, puke-colored corduroy jacket. The chip at the top of his wire-rimmed glasses. The watery eyes. The yellow teeth. The thin, dry lips. The slick tongue. It just. Wouldn't. Stop.

I let out a pathetic-sounding groan, and Christopher held me tighter.

"It's okay," he whispered. "Everything's going to be okay."

But I knew in my heart he was wrong. Nothing was ever going to be okay again.

NUMBER FIFTEEN

The flashing red-and-blue police lights left pulsating blurs across my vision. Christopher kept his gaze straight ahead, his breaths remarkably even as he followed the patrol car down my winding street, his windshield wipers whacking back and forth, too fast for the increasingly light drizzle. He pulled up to a curb near my house, where two dozen police cars were parked and a black van was stationed half on my front lawn, half on the street.

"Whoa," he said quietly.

Slowly, numbly, I climbed out of the car. All I wanted to do was get in the shower, curl up in a ball on the tiled floor, and stay there until I felt clean again. But I had a feeling these officers had other ideas.

"Rory?" My father strode away from a crowd of uniformed police officers and severe-looking men in trench coats and stormed toward the car. His white button-down shirt was half untucked from his pants, and his threadbare tweed suit jacket flapped open. His eyes looked bloodshot, his nose red, and glistening raindrops dotted his dark hair. When he reached me, he threw his arms around me, his fingers digging into my shoulder blades.

As we stood there, dozens of strangers and neighbors eyeing us, I felt awkward and stiff. I couldn't remember the last time he'd hugged me. My dad still picked me up from school when I was sick and made our favorite meals whenever he had the time. But ever since my mom died, he'd stopped checking in to see how we were doing or kissing us good night. He'd retreated into himself, developing this angry, simmering outer layer that was constantly set to blow.

A siren blared as another police car pulled up. The hug ended abruptly. Darcy hovered nearby, her slim arms crossed over her Princeton Hills High School Cheerleading sweatshirt, the black hood up over her dark brown hair to shield her from the drizzle. Christopher started to get out of the car, but the second their eyes met, he got back in and stayed there. My dad cleared his throat.

"Are you okay?" he asked. "When the police showed up at my lecture hall, I thought . . ." His voice trailed off, and he reached out to awkwardly clutch my wrist, as though making sure I was really still there. "If anything ever happened to you . . ."

"I'm fine," I assured my dad. "I'm just—"

"What were you thinking?" he asked suddenly, pulling away. I flinched, my heart vaulting into my throat, and I took an instinctive step back. "Cutting through those woods *alone?* You could have been killed!"

Now this was the dad I knew. Quick to temper, quicker to blame. It was oddly reassuring—a normal thing in a surreal day.

"Dad, lay off!" Darcy snapped.

His face turned red and he looked at the ground, avoiding eye contact with anyone.

"Get inside," he said quietly but sternly.

I ducked my chin, tears stinging my eyes, and walked shakily toward our house. Darcy fell into step with me, so close our shoulders kept grazing while we walked. One glance back at Christopher was all I could manage. He lifted his hand from the steering wheel in a semblance of a wave, his lips flattened into a tight, encouraging smile. Suddenly, I just wanted to be back in that car, back with him, back where I felt safe. But then he revved the engine, and just like that, he was gone.

Once we were inside, my father slammed the front door behind us. Then he stopped short. Standing near the wall in the living room, next to framed photos of me and Darcy when we were younger, was a slight woman in a dripping black baseball cap and a black overcoat. Several men in blue jumpsuits were sweeping through the downstairs, running mechanical wands along the walls and counters, while another climbed the steps to the second floor.

"Who are you?" my father demanded.

"My name is Sharon Messenger." She took out a wallet and flashed a badge at us. Three bold, capital letters leaped out at me: *FBI.*

My heart started to pound painfully.

"Why is the FBI here?" my father asked, his forehead wrinkling.

The agent ignored him and turned to me. "Is this the man who attacked you?" she asked, taking out a smartphone and tapping one of the on-screen keys. Instantly, Mr. Nell's face appeared on the screen, but he was much younger, with a mustache and square black glasses instead of his gold wire-rimmed frames.

"Yes," I said, turning away. "That's him. That's Mr. Nell."

Agent Messenger pressed her pale lips together. She slid out of her rain-soaked coat, hung it on the rack, then gestured toward the sitting area. "Why don't you all have a seat?"

"Why don't you tell us what's going on first?" my dad challenged, squaring his shoulders. In his day, my dad was an athlete, a lean cross-country runner like me. But after my mother died, he'd stopped working out, stopped running, and now he just looked tired and weak.

"Dad," Darcy groused, "can we please not make a fight out of this?"

My dad's eyes flashed, but he sat down on the old recliner. I sank down on the far end of the couch, pulling my knees up under my chin and hugging myself tightly. Darcy took the opposite end, while Agent Messenger paced over the worn Oriental carpet my parents had bought on their honeymoon.

"The man you know as Steven Nell is actually Roger Krauss," she said without preamble. "The FBI has been trying to find him for over a decade." She stopped pacing and looked me directly in the eye. Her drenched black curls stuck to her neck, looking like tattoos against her milky skin. "He's killed fourteen girls in ten states. First he stalks them. Then he hunts them down and . . . You're lucky you got away."

My blood turned to ice. Fourteen girls. He'd murdered fourteen girls. And I was supposed to be next. I was number fifteen.

"No way," Darcy blurted, shoving her hood away from her face. "Mr. Nell is an actual serial killer?"

"It looks that way, yes," Messenger replied.

Suddenly, the shaking started again. For the first time, I noticed the dried leaves clinging to the undersides of my sleeves. I ripped them frantically to the floor, my fingernails tearing at the wool.

Messenger took off her baseball cap, wiping drops of water off her forehead. She had purple bags under her eyes, her cheeks were gaunt, and a few strands of gray spotted her dark hair even though she didn't look much older than thirty-five. I wondered how much of Messenger's past decade had been dedicated to finding Mr. Nell—and failing.

"Krauss is smart. Brilliant, actually," Messenger said in an even tone, like she was talking about the weather or a movie she saw last week, not a brutal killer. "He always covers his tracks and he's a master at disappearing. Every time we get close, he slips away." Messenger's phone beeped at her hip. She quickly checked the screen before tucking it back away. "We had intel that he might be here in New Jersey, and now we have our proof. Every officer and agent in town is searching for him right now."

"Good," Darcy said, looking at me. "I hope they shoot him in the face."

"Darcy," my father warned.

"Can't say I disagree with her, sir," Messenger said, raising her palms.

"Agent Messenger?" a voice called.

The man who'd gone upstairs bounded into view, a plastic bag in his hand. Nestled inside was a small black square attached to a wire. A spy camera. "We found it in the girl's bedroom, hidden in the slats of the closet door."

"Oh my god." Darcy's jaw dropped in horror as she turned to look at me.

I couldn't breathe. He'd been in our home. He'd been *watching* me. The shaking turned violent.

"Take it to the lab," Messenger said with a brisk nod. "Figure out the transmitting radius. It might feed to a location nearby."

My stomach clenched. "How long has it been there?" I whispered.

Messenger's dark eyes softened. "It's impossible to say," she said gently.

I thought of my room, with its butter-yellow walls, my microscope, and my biology books. It was where I did my homework and ran my labs, where I called my friends, where my mom used to tell me stories about a frog named Neville to help me fall asleep. It was where I woke up each morning and got dressed and . . .

I ran for the hall bathroom, slamming my knees against

the tile floor in front of the toilet. I heaved and heaved until my stomach was empty. Then I sat back against the wall and closed my eyes, blindly reaching for the flusher. Instantly, Mr. Nell's face swooped toward me, and I pressed the heels of my hands into my eye sockets, trying to obliterate the image.

If only I could erase the knowledge that Mr. Nell—the man who always wrote GOOD WORK in all capitals on my tests and underlined it three times, the guy who'd talked me into entering the statewide math competition last fall, the person I'd trusted and considered a mentor—had watched me in my bedroom and spied on the most private moments of my life. I had never felt so violated. I needed to escape. I needed a shower. I needed to get clean. I needed to be alone.

"I'm going upstairs!" I shouted on my way out of the bathroom.

"Wait."

My dad stood at the end of the hall, a concerned look on his face. He hesitated for an awkward moment before asking, "Are you okay?"

Tears instantly sprang to my eyes. My dad crossed the living room in two steps, took the agent's coat off the rack, and handed it to her. I almost couldn't believe what I was seeing. My father and I had just communicated. We'd actually understood each other.

"Well, thanks for coming by, but if you and the other officers don't mind, I think my daughter needs some peace and quiet," my father said, trying to usher her toward the door. She didn't budge.

"I'm sorry, sir, but that's not going to happen," Messenger said, folding her damp coat over her arm. "It's not safe for you to be here alone. There's a good chance Krauss isn't done with your daughter."

My heart and stomach switched places. I clutched my hands together to keep them from trembling. Not done with me? What the hell did that mean?

"We're going to place a protective detail on your house," Messenger said, turning to look me in the eye, as if she knew how badly I needed reassuring. "I don't want any of you leaving this house until he is caught and locked behind bars. That means no school, no work, no nothing."

"What about my classes?" my dad asked. His job meant everything to him, at least since mom had died. "Summer term just started."

"I'm sure the university can find a substitute," Messenger said tightly.

"I guess that means I don't have to take my bio final," my sister said with a smile.

My dad glared at her. "We'll have your school drop off all your homework."

Darcy visibly sagged, but I barely registered any of it. Suddenly, I was back in those woods, running for my life, feeling Nell breathing down my neck while Messenger's words echoed in my head, over and over.

Not safe. Not safe. Not safe.

"You'll catch him, though, right?" I said urgently, finally finding my voice. "I mean, with all those cops and everything looking for him . . . there's no way he's going to get away."

"I wish it had happened some other way, Rory, but this was exactly the break we needed." Messenger placed a reassuring hand on my arm, her dark eyes locking on mine. "With any luck, we'll have him by the end of the night."

SOON

"What do you mean, you still haven't found him?" my dad demanded.

"I'm sorry. We suspect he's still in town, but he's gone underground," Messenger said wearily. Her black pants sagged around her narrow hips. "I promise we're doing our best. It's just a little bit of a waiting game."

Waiting. That was all we ever did anymore. Seven full days had passed and here we were again, gathered in the living room, listening to Messenger tell us exactly nothing. I leaned my head on the back of the couch and looked up at the ceiling, staring at the crack I'd been studying all week long. It had actually gotten longer since last Friday, snaking its way from the corner near the front door all the way to the center of the room. Next to me, Darcy's silver-polished nails stopped clacking on her laptop's keyboard.

"So, wait," she said, slapping the computer closed and standing up. "You're telling me we *still* can't leave?"

"Yes, that's what I'm telling you," Messenger replied, rubbing her forehead.

"No. No way," Darcy snapped. "Tonight is Becky Mazrow's graduation party. I've only been looking forward to it all year. There's no way I'm going to sit here watching the Kardashians on my computer while everyone in my class is there."

"Darcy," my father said impatiently.

"What?" She raised her shoulders. "They can send me with a security detail or something," she said, looking at Agent Messenger. "Their inepticy is the reason we're holed up here like some family of fugitives."

"*Inepticy* isn't a word," I said quietly.

Darcy ignored me.

"Yeah, I don't think that's top on Uncle Sam's priority list," Messenger replied.

"I don't believe this! You said you were going to catch him 'tonight,'" Darcy cried, throwing in some air quotes. "That was a week ago!"

"I'm sorry, but—"

"Sorry for what? Sucking at your job?" Darcy shot back.

"Darcy!" my dad thundered.

She fell silent and plopped back onto the couch, her chin jutted out in defiance. But the thing was, she was right. It wasn't fair that we were stuck here. It made no sense that the entire FBI couldn't catch one guy. I just never would have had the guts to say it.

"So . . . what?" I asked, crossing my arms over my $E=mc^2$ sweatshirt. "You're just waiting for him to show himself? To make a mistake? I thought you said he was brilliant. What're the chances he actually screws up and lets himself get caught?"

Messenger didn't have to answer. The resigned look on her face said everything. I pulled my knees up under my chin and hugged myself as tightly as I could. What if the mistake he made was breaking into my room and stabbing me to death before anyone could do anything? Had anyone considered that?

"Unbelievable," my dad said, throwing up his hands. He paced over to the front window and looked out at the two police cruisers idling near the end of our driveway, a constant ever since the day I was attacked. A red light at the base of the window blinked at a regular interval, part of a complicated alarm system the FBI had rigged for the house. "I don't think I can take much more of this. My sub better give that quiz tonight," he muttered. "If she doesn't give them the quiz, my whole grading system will be entirely thrown off."

Darcy's phone buzzed, and she groaned. "It's Becky again. She's going to kill me if I miss this party."

"Enough!" I blurted, standing up. Suddenly, I felt like I couldn't sit next to her for one more second. "There's a killer on the loose and he's after *us*! I can't believe you're worried about a party!" I wanted to yell at my dad for caring so much about a stupid quiz, too, but of course I didn't. All my angry thoughts toward my father always stayed just that—thoughts.

Darcy rolled her eyes. "I know you've never been to one, Rory," she said sarcastically. "But they're actually kind of fun." Then she looked me up and down and slowly pocketed her phone. "Unless you like being under house arrest."

"I *like* being *safe*," I retorted.

"Why am I not surprised?" she shot back, rising to her feet to face off with me. "You're here practically all the time anyway, holed up in your room with your little stethoscope and all your beakers—"

"It's a microscope," I spat.

"Whatever. All I know is, it's no wonder you've never had a boyfriend."

"Darcy!" my dad snapped. "That's enough."

Darcy shot me an acidic glare.

My mouth filled with a bitter taste. As desperate as I was to keep the secret about me and Christopher, there were times, like now, when all I wanted to do was throw it in her face. Prove that she wasn't the only one with a life, the only one people found attractive, the only one who could take a chance.

As if on cue, my phone pinged with a text. I smiled slightly when I saw it was from Christopher.

Any updates?

Chris had texted a few times to check in on how I was doing. A couple of kids from the cross-country team had also reached out. They all had the same set of questions, questions they would never have asked if they actually stopped to think. Like *Were you scared?* or *Did you think you were going to die?* And my personal favorite, *Did your whole life flash before your eyes?*

No. No, it did not. What had flashed before my eyes were the things that were actually there. The leaves budding in the trees, the cloudy sky, the dirt under my fingernails. All I could think was, These are the last things I'm ever going to see. I was going to die in the woods. The very same woods where Darcy and I used to play Peter Pan and Pirates of the Caribbean. The same woods where I broke my arm when

I climbed a tree to spy on Darcy and her first boyfriend. The woods where I used to steal away and read my mom's ancient encyclopedias when Darcy's teasing got so merciless I couldn't take it anymore.

I hit reply.

Nope. Still trapped.

Then I tucked my phone back in my front sweatshirt pocket.

Darcy glanced at me sharply. "Who was that?"

"No one," I said quickly, hoping my cheeks didn't look as hot as they felt.

Messenger rubbed her eyes. "You haven't told anyone about the security measures here, right?"

"No, of course not," I said quickly, a defensive tone in my voice. I always did what I was told. For a horrible moment, I wondered if that was why Mr. Nell had picked me. Because I was so predictable, so organized, so easy to follow.

Messenger rocked back on her heels, holding her hands up in surrender. "Okay, okay. I just don't want you to get hurt again, Rory."

My heart folded in on itself and clenched until it hurt. It was a new sensation, something that started after the attack, whenever I thought about Steven Nell.

"Look, guys, I understand that this is hard. I really do.

I just need you to hang in here a little longer. Can you do that for me?"

Messenger's tone was earnest. But she didn't get it. None of them did. They didn't understand what it was like to run through the woods with a killer on your heels. The only person I wanted to be with, the only person I'd felt safe with since the attack, was Christopher. My heart gave another painful squeeze, and suddenly I felt claustrophobic, like I couldn't breathe.

Screw it. I was going to call him. Darcy would never know. If she asked, I'd just tell her I was catching up with my lab partner. Then she'd definitely leave me alone.

"I'm going to my room," I said, already clutching my phone inside my pocket.

I turned and took the stairs two at a time, my heart pounding with anticipation at the very idea of hearing Christopher's voice. The upstairs of our house opened onto a wide landing with a skylight overhead. All five doors, which led to three bedrooms, a study, and a bathroom, were shut tight. I opened the first one on the right, the one to my room, and closed it behind me, leaning against the familiar wood. I tugged the phone out, but my hands were shaking so hard I dropped it on the floor. I left it there for a second and took a deep breath. I didn't want to call him sounding all out of breath and hysterical. I needed to give myself a second to calm down.

I closed my eyes, and instantly thoughts of our first—and only—kiss flooded me. It was back when I was still tutoring him, before I started working with his little sister. We had been sitting at the desk in his room. I was on his cushy desk chair, because he'd insisted, and he was on a hard kitchen chair he'd dragged up the stairs. It was two inches shorter than mine, which put our faces about even. I'd been crushing on him for weeks, but he'd been Darcy's boyfriend forever, and I'd done a pretty good job of controlling myself by reciting the periodic table or listing the presidents whenever I wanted to stare at him. For whatever reason, though, that night I couldn't keep my gaze from traveling back to his face every five seconds. He'd gotten his hair cut, and for the first time I noticed the flecks of green in his brown eyes. It was hard to believe anyone that handsome actually existed in my school, and I suddenly felt so jealous of Darcy for getting to kiss him. She got to feel what it was like to be in his arms. She got to have him look at her like she was the only girl on Earth.

Then Christopher suddenly had a calculus breakthrough and he jumped up, cheered like he'd just hit a home run, and spun my chair around. I laughed and closed my eyes to keep from getting dizzy, which only made me dizzier. When he stopped me, I opened my eyes again and all I saw was his face as he brought his lips down on mine.

The second he touched me, it was as if something inside of me was released. Something I hadn't even known was there. But still, I pushed him away.

"What are you doing?" I demanded.

"I broke up with Darcy," he blurted, breathless.

I felt like I'd just been tipped upside down. "What? When?"

"This morning. You didn't hear?"

I rolled my eyes. It was so natural for him to think that everything about his life reached every ear in school in a nanosecond.

"No. She didn't . . . I haven't even seen her," I said.

"Well, I broke up with her because I couldn't take it anymore," Christopher said, squatting down in front of my chair like he was taking his catcher's stance. "For the last few weeks, whenever you're here . . ." He paused and reached for my fingers. "Rory, whenever you're here, all I can think about is this."

Then he leaned forward and kissed me again. I put my arms around his neck and he hugged me to him, tugging me up so we were both standing. I couldn't believe any of this was happening. Christopher liked me back. He'd broken up with Darcy for me. I'd wanted this for so long, and, unbelievably, it turned out that he'd wanted it, too.

Christopher kissed me hard, like he was hungry for it,

and I matched his every move. He tasted like Oreos and smelled like a fresh shower. When we tumbled onto his bed, I was so excited and baffled and flattered and happy. And then I saw Darcy's face and I pulled away.

"We can't do this," I said, panting for breath.

"Because of Darcy?" he said, reaching for my wrist. He clamped his fingers around it, and I realized how big his hand was and how small my wrist seemed. He shook his head. "She'll be okay. We'll just—"

I turned around and sat with my back to him, my legs hanging down the side of the bed.

"She's my sister, and she's in love with you," I said. "I can't—"

"But, Rory." He sat up behind me. "I'm not in love with her."

"Chris—"

"Rory," he said playfully. He slid over so I could see his face. "I have been trying not to kiss you for, like, two months. Every time you come over here, I get excited like it's a date or something. It's pathetic, but I actually look forward to calculus tutoring. I can't take it anymore. And yeah, it sucks that you're the sister of the girl I've been with for the last two years, but that's just the way it is." He pushed a lock of hair behind my ear. "I want to be with you, not her."

They were the sweetest words anyone had ever said to

me. Someone had picked me. Mousy, too-smart, awkward me over popular, gorgeous, witty Darcy. But Darcy was all about Christopher. She jumped whenever he texted. She wore his varsity jacket around the house even when the heat was jacked up.

So I told him no, and I got up and I left. But he still came over the next day when Darcy was at cheerleading practice and asked me to the holiday dance. And though I wanted nothing more than to go with him, I still said no. Because Darcy had spent the whole night crying in her room. And I couldn't do that to her.

The rhythmic ticking of the chemistry-themed clock my mom had bought me for my tenth birthday brought me back to the present. My breathing slowed and I felt a little calmer. Maybe I couldn't have gone out with Christopher then, but I could at least tell him how I felt now, especially considering how mean Darcy was being. If nothing else, the experience with Steven Nell was an awful reminder that life was short.

I opened my eyes, and my room came slowly into focus. Outside the window, rain had started to fall. A screen saver picture of me and my mom at the finish line of my first track meet flashed across my laptop. My blue yoga mat was unfurled on the floor from when I'd done my abs exercises, my fallen phone sitting in the center of it. A running shoe poked out from underneath my white bed skirt. Then I blinked. I could have sworn I'd left my bed unmade that morning—I'd been having nightmares ever since the attack, and it felt pointless to smooth out the sheets when I'd just wildly tangle them up each night. But now it was made with perfect hospital corners, the pillows neatly fluffed. And there, on my patchwork bedspread, was a single red rose.

For one moment, I wondered if Christopher had left it for me. A small note card was tucked beneath the rose's thorny stem. A ragged breath caught in my throat. On the card, printed in all-too-familiar capital letters and underlined three times, were five ominous words:

WE WILL BE TOGETHER. SOON.

RUN

I screamed. Loudly. My knees gave out and my butt hit the floor. I scrabbled back against the closet door and curled into a ball, sobs racking my chest.

"Rory!" My father burst into the room with Messenger and Darcy on his heels. "Rory, what happened?"

Shaking, I pointed at the bed. Instantly, Messenger was on her walkie-talkie, barking orders.

"Oh my god," Darcy breathed.

"Get her out of here," my father told her.

Gently, Darcy tugged me off the floor and into the hall-way, where we both sat on the floor. Outside, sirens wailed.

"He was here, Darcy," I whimpered. "He was in my room. He got past the officers . . . the alarm . . ."

"It's okay. You're okay," Darcy said, putting her arm around me.

"It's not okay," I said. "He's going to kill me, Darcy. He's going to kill me."

I squeezed my eyes shut and cried. Outside, the roar of a helicopter engine filled the night, and searchlights illuminated the hall.

"How could this happen?" my father demanded from inside my room. "How did he get in here?"

"The how isn't important right now. It's the fact that he did," Messenger stated, walking out into the hallway. The rose and the note dangled from her fingers in separate evidence bags. "We'd thought our measures would be enough, but clearly he's even more capable than we'd realized."

She placed her hand on her gun holster, as though checking to make sure it was still there. All of a sudden, she was like a whole new person—energized, ready to jump into action. Her phone beeped and she checked the message, then tucked it away. She looked at each of us.

"You'll need to leave for a safe house," she told us. "Tonight."

"Leave? Now?" my dad exclaimed.

Darcy got up, dragging me off the floor.

"No way," she said. "I can't just leave. I'm graduating next week!"

"A safe house?" I said. "Why?"

"There's something I didn't tell you before," Messenger explained, looking me in the eye in a way not many adults ever seemed to do—like I was her equal. "He's never failed to finish a job before. Only one other victim escaped from him, and two weeks later he broke into her house and killed her entire family." She took me by my shoulders. "Rory, I am not trying to scare you, but he will keep coming. He will never stop."

My heart executed a series of folding maneuvers that made me feel faint.

"And as for you, I'm sure they'll still give you a diploma, but are you really going to care if you're dead?" the woman asked Darcy.

"Wow. You really don't sugarcoat anything, do you?" Darcy asked.

Messenger stared her down. "Not my style. Now I suggest you all start packing. You're leaving here in fifteen minutes. No photos, no personal items or IDs. Nothing that connects you in any way to this life."

Turning her back on us and heading for the window over the staircase, she glanced out. Dozens of cops in rain gear scoured the wet lawn, the helicopters' searchlight flashing its wide beam over everything from our old swing set to the dilapidated fence around what used to be my mom's vegetable garden.

"We really have to do this? We really have to go?" my dad said through his teeth, bracing one hand over his head on the wall near his bedroom door. His face was ashen.

I saw his eyes travel to a framed picture on the opposite wall. The one professional shot of my family, taken when I was in third grade, Darcy was in fifth grade, and my mom was young, beautiful, and untouched by cancer. She smiled back at him, her blond hair gleaming, her makeup perfectly applied, her favorite pink turtleneck crisp and unfaded. It had been threadbare by the end, with sweat stains around the top of the collar and little holes frayed at the hem, but she had refused to take it off. It was her favorite thing and she didn't want to let it go.

My heart slowly tore down the middle. I wished with every fiber of my being, with every bone in my body, with every ounce of my blood, that she was here right now. And I knew he was thinking the same thing, too. My mother would have known what to say, what to do. My mother would have taken charge.

"Look, Mr. Miller," Messenger said, her tone soothing. "Hopefully it won't be forever. But it's the only way to keep your family safe."

My heartbeat pounded in my ears. My skin prickled. My feet itched to move, to run, to flee. My father looked over his shoulder at us, and our eyes met.

We have to get out of here, I wanted to scream. *Please listen to her. Please.*

"Girls," he said, his voice gravelly. "Go pack."

LEAVING HOME

In my room, I grabbed my big duffel bag, the one I usually packed for science camp, and started opening drawers, pulling clothes out at random, and shoving them inside.

I couldn't believe this was happening. I couldn't believe that Mr. Nell had found a way past the FBI into my house. That I was being forced to leave the only home I'd ever known. The house where my mother had lived. The house where she'd died.

Angry, terrified tears filled my eyes as I whirled around. Tacked to the mirror around my desk were dozens of blue, red, and yellow ribbons, awards for science and academic competitions. In the corner on my desk was my microscope, surrounded by schoolbooks, notepads, slides, and sample dishes. None of that stuff was coming with me, obviously, but I grabbed *The Merck Manual* off my shelf and shoved my iPad into my bag. It slid right out and bounced across the floor.

"No!" I screeched, releasing all my emotion on behalf of my prized possession. I knelt to pick it up, my eyes overflowing with tears as I checked it for dings and scratches. I turned it on, and it blinked happily to life. Irrationally, I laughed and hugged it to my chest.

"Rory?" my father called. "What the hell was that?"

"Nothing! I'm fine!" I shouted back, my voice breaking.

Why? Why did I have to cut through the woods that day? Why had Mr. Nell picked me? Suddenly, my tears wouldn't stop.

Just breathe, Rory. Calm down and breathe.

I sat back on my heels and silently recited the periodic table.

Hydrogen, helium, lithium, beryllium, boron, carbon, nitrogen, oxygen, fluorine . . .

Recitation was a great calming mechanism. My mother had taught me that back when she was sick, and it had helped me get through all the hospital visits, the long nights after she came back home and there was nothing to do but wait for her death. It got me through the funeral, the wake, and a thousand terrified nights since, wishing she was here with me.

"Rory! Where are my black jeans?" Darcy demanded, appearing in the doorway.

"What? How would I know where your black jeans are?" I quickly shoved my iPad into its case and turned my back to her, wiping my eyes with both hands. I glanced at the photo of me and my mom from my ninth birthday and snatched it off my dresser. I didn't care what Messenger said. The picture was coming with me.

"Because I put them in my closet this morning and now they're not there."

I shot Darcy an incredulous look. She was always doing this—accusing me of taking things I would never take from her.

"Like your jeans would even fit me," I shot back, shakily gathering up my charger and a few pairs of socks from my top drawer. "In case you haven't noticed, you have no thighs."

"Well, then where the hell are they?" she shouted.

"I have no idea! Is this really what you're worried about right now?" I cried.

"They're my favorite jeans!" she yelled back.

"Girls!"

Agent Messenger had appeared at the top of the stairs.

"What?" we both shouted at her.

Then my heart dropped. Yelling at an FBI agent was probably a bad thing.

"You have two minutes," she told us. "Get it together."

Then she turned and walked into my father's room, where he was busy slamming drawers and ripping clothes off hangers.

"I don't believe this," Darcy sputtered, yanking on the drawstrings of her sweatshirt. "I've only been looking forward to Becky's party all effing year! Everyone's going. Everyone! But guess who's not gonna be there in her favorite black jeans! Me!"

I rolled my eyes and took a deep breath. She was just venting. Just dealing. If I could scream at my iPad falling to the floor, she could ramble psychotically about some stupid party. That was all that mattered to her, after all. Her friends. Her parties. Her fun.

She stormed into the hallway and started down the stairs. Suddenly, there was a loud tumbling noise followed by a crash. Heart in my throat, I ran out of my room.

"Sonofa—"

Darcy was sprawled at the bottom of the stairs, her head back against the corner of the small dresser where we threw the mail and everything else we didn't know what to do with.

She sat forward and shakily reached for the back of her head.

"Are you okay?" I demanded.

"I'm fine."

She drew her hand out. Her fingertips were coated in blood.

"I'll get Dad," I said.

"No! I said I'm fine," Darcy shouted, shoving herself to her feet. "I'm going to check the laundry room."

She took one staggering step, then righted herself and disappeared around the corner. I glanced over my shoulder, surprised my dad and Messenger hadn't heard her fall. But then I realized they were making enough noise to drown out just about anything, him slamming around his room and her speaking loudly over the din.

Slowly, I tiptoed over and hovered near the open door, just out of sight.

"How long are we going to have to be away?" I heard my dad ask, banging a drawer closed.

"As long as it takes to find this guy and lock him up," Messenger said. "For now, let's talk logistics."

"All right, fine," my father said tersely. I heard a zip, then another slam. "So talk."

"As soon as you and the girls are ready, we'll lock up and go," she said. "The car we're providing for you is parked in the driveway. In it is a GPS programmed with your final destination, along with a packet of information on your new identities, credit cards, IDs, that sort of thing."

"New identities?" my father asked incredulously. "Is that really necessary?"

"It will be if you need to stay in hiding for more than a couple of days," she replied. "Your first names will stay the same, but you'll be the Thayer family, from Manhattan."

My father let out a rueful laugh.

"What's so funny?" the agent asked.

"I always wanted to live in the city, but my wife couldn't stand the noise."

I never knew that about my dad. He'd always seemed like Mr. Suburbanite.

"Do you always put new lives together so fast?" he asked.

"When dealing with a man like Krauss, we try to have our bases covered. We created this contingency plan as soon as we learned of Rory's attack."

"Oh," my dad said, a hard, angry note in his voice. "Was there a reason you didn't mention this to me earlier?"

"I'm telling you now," Messenger said calmly. "There was no need to worry your girls more than they already were."

There was a long pause, followed by another zip.

"All set, Mr. Miller?" Messenger asked.

"Don't you mean Mr. Thayer?" my father said, dripping sarcasm all over the place.

My face burned. Why couldn't he ever just answer a question normally? Why did everything have to be a fight?

"Girls!" my dad said, stepping into the hallway with an old black suitcase. Darcy came back upstairs with her hood up over her head and her black jeans folded in her arms. "Are you ready?" my dad asked.

"I'll get my bags," Darcy replied, ducking past him into her room. I grabbed my stuff and rejoined them, just as Darcy arrived in her doorway with her hobo bag on one shoulder, her backpack over the other, her rolling suitcase behind her, and her earbuds in her ears.

"Are you coming with us?" I asked Agent Messenger.

She shook her head. "I have to stay here. I'm the expert on Krauss," she said, gesturing to the flashing lights outside.

"Oh, okay," I said softly, a tremor of nerves running through me.

"I need your cell phones," Messenger said, holding out a palm.

"What? Why?" Darcy's eyes were wide. She was addicted to texting. I was sure she couldn't imagine the next hour without her phone, let alone possibly days.

"You cannot contact anyone," Messenger answered as I handed my phone over. "If anyone knows where you're going, it puts not only all of you, but *them* in danger as well. And when you get where you're going, you can't tell anyone who you really are or where you're from or why you're there. For your safety and theirs."

My father gave her his cell. Darcy pulled hers out and started to hit some buttons. Messenger snatched it right out of her hands.

"Hey!" Darcy shouted. "I was just deleting something!"

"Don't worry. I wasn't planning on reading your love notes," the agent shot back. "Now let's go."

We followed Messenger down the stairs. I plucked my rain jacket from its hook and trailed my family out the front door, where dozens of police cars sat silently, their lights flashing. The rain was coming down hard. I tugged my hood up to cover my hair. A big black SUV sat in the center of our driveway, its chrome hubcaps glossy from the rain.

My dad was just reaching for the driver's side door handle, when Messenger's phone let out a pealing screech. We all froze. Maybe they'd found him. Maybe we didn't have to leave.

"Yes. Yes, I understand," Messenger said. "Of course, sir. Yes. We're on our way now." She shoved the phone in her pocket and opened the car door for my dad. So much for that. "Do not stop until you are out of the state," she instructed. "Do not make any calls, don't tell anyone who you really are, and stick to your new backstories. Any questions?"

"Will an agent meet us there?" my dad said.

Messenger shook her head. "All our manpower will be dedicated to hunting this guy down. You have top security—I'm only one of a handful of agents who even knows where this safe house is and we can't risk blowing your location. I'll be in touch next week—and I'll hopefully be bringing you home then. Anything else?"

"No," he said. "No, I'm fine."

But there was fear behind his eyes, and my palms started to sweat. I hadn't seen my dad look scared since right before my mom died. Sad, yes. Angry, every day. But scared? Never.

"Good," she said. "Now hit the road."

She turned, folded her tall frame behind the wheel of her car, and slammed the door.

For a long moment, my father, Darcy, and I just stood there. All I wanted to do was go back inside, crawl into bed, and bury my head under the pillows. It was our house. Our home. I saw my sister and me playing tea party on the porch when we were little. Saw my mom planting flowers along the front walk. Saw my dad teaching me how to roller-skate in the driveway. Saw the hearse arriving to take my mother away the day she died. Saw my father weeping in my grandma's arms on the front step. There were awful memories in this house, many I'd rather forget, but there were a lot of good ones, too. My heart constricted at the thought of leaving them all behind—at leaving my *mom* behind.

As I opened the back door, I saw Darcy wipe at her eyes. She got in next to my father and hunkered down. A few of the patrol cars backed up and out of the way to make room as we pulled out of the drive. My father cleared his throat and shifted the SUV into gear, then drove down the street. When we got to the stop sign at the end of the street, I turned around to take one last look at the brick facade of my home, my fingers digging into the faux-leather seat. Then my dad took the turn, and the house disappeared behind the trees.

THE THRILL

And so she was on the run. It wasn't the way he usually did things, but he could adjust. He could adapt. That was the mark of a highly developed human being.

He crouched in the neighbors' yard, behind a child's playhouse, and watched. He watched the sister curse under her breath as she yanked open the car door. Watched the father struggling with his own emotions as he took the wheel. Those two were so predictable. It almost made him want to kill them first. To do that for her. To rid her of them before he took what he needed.

Then he watched her. Watched her flick her hood up

over that lovely hair. Watched her curl into her seat. Saw her staring at her own bedroom window, longing for it even after he had invaded it.

He waited until the SUV had pulled out of the driveway and started down the street. Then he stood up, shook the water from his police hat, and flicked on his flashlight. No one looked at him as he made his way around the side of the house, through the blooming azalea hedge and across the walk. No one blinked when he popped open the door of the idling police cruiser. He smiled and flicked on the stereo, then jammed the car into gear.

No one had a clue.

AT LARGE

"Authorities are still scouring the state for accused serial killer Roger Krauss," the radio announcer said in her nasally voice. *"The man who is believed to have murdered fourteen girls and attacked one more is still at large—"*

Darcy hit the OFF button on the radio. My dad shot her an irked look, which she ignored. I wondered if Christopher was watching the news. If he had tried to call me. If on Monday, when we weren't at school, he would realize that we'd had to run. If only I'd called him before I'd found the sick present Steven Nell had left on my bed, before Messenger had taken our phones. I would have given anything right now just to hear his voice.

It was four in the morning and we'd been driving nonstop for seven hours. We'd barely spoken, the only sounds the tires thrumming over the highway; the radio, which Darcy kept turning on and off intermittently; and the mechanical voice of the GPS, which was leading us down I-95 to our final destination in South Carolina. The roads had been nearly empty, save for the occasional sedan and eighteen-wheeler delivering cargo from one state to the next.

"This must be the most boring stretch of land in America," my father muttered through his teeth, hunching over the steering wheel as he squinted out the windshield. The rain had let up somewhere in Maryland, and now we were in Virginia, surrounded by a dense thicket of trees on either side of the highway, dividing us from northbound traffic and the farmlands to the west. It felt like the scenery hadn't changed in hours.

My body was heavy. I'd been fighting to stay awake—scared of the nightmares that I knew would overtake me as soon as I closed my eyes—but it was a losing battle. I'd been blearily watching the exits pass, one by one, counting the miles we were putting between us and the place where Mr. Nell had attacked me. Each mile made me feel safer, calmer, until my breathing grew steady and my eyelids lowered as I felt sleep overtake me.

A loud horn blared, and my eyes snapped open. The car was suddenly flooded with light. I twisted around in my seat. A huge truck was bearing down on us, its brights so blinding I could barely make out the boxy shape of the cab. My heart lurched into my throat, and my dad sat up straight, glaring into the rearview mirror.

"What's this jackass doing?"

A loud horn sounded again and I screamed.

"What the hell?" Darcy turned in her seat and squinted, lifting a hand to block the light. "Just go around, asshole!" she shouted.

"Darcy!" my dad hollered. "Language!"

And then the truck bumped us from behind. Now all three of us screamed. My father swerved, and there was a screech of tires.

"Oh my god, it's him. It's him!" I cried, curling forward, my head between my hands and my forehead to my knees. In my mind's eye, I pictured Steven Nell behind the wheel of the truck, his thin lips peeled back to reveal yellowed teeth as he bore down on my family.

The truck slammed into us again, and my head snapped forward. I pictured his cracked, dry knuckles as he clung to the steering wheel, the ugly bags under his sadistic eyes, that faded plaid shirt and awful corduroy jacket he'd been wearing in the woods.

"It's not him, Rory," my father said, sounding panicked. "It's some drunk who doesn't know what he's doing."

KATE BRIAN

The truck's engine was so loud in my ear I could have sworn we were under the tractor trailer's hood. Another crash. The car lurched. My father cursed as he struggled with the wheel.

"What!?" Darcy screeched, one hand braced against the dashboard. "What is it?"

"Our bumper's stuck to his truck."

Suddenly, the truck revved again, and our car started to speed out of control toward a looming green exit sign. My stomach bottomed out. This was it. We were going to die. My family was going to die.

"Dad! What're you doing?" Darcy cried.

"It's not me! It's him!" my father shouted, his hands off the wheel.

"Dad! Do something! Do something!" I screamed.

But it was too late. There was an awful screaming, squealing sound of tires burning on pavement. Then we were spinning. The force of it threw me against the side of the car. My skull slammed into the window. Everything jarred. Everything hurt. My shoulder. My knees. My ribs. My heart. The car spun again, rattling my insides. I felt something tug at my chest, tug at my mind. Like I was trying to float outside the car and into the ether, trying to escape what was happening. For a split second, I was hovering outside my body, looking down, watching myself cower

56

in fear. Then we spun once more, and I felt the seat belt cut into my thighs. Darcy's screams grew louder, pained, desperate. And then, all of a sudden, we stopped. There was another deafening engine growl, and the peeling of tires as the truck took off into the night. Then everything went painfully, eerily silent.

DONE

"Girls? Girls!" My father's eyes bulged as he struggled with his seat belt.

My stomach was turning itself inside out, on fire, trying to rip itself free of my body. I undid my own belt and doubled over, gasping for breath.

"Dad?" Darcy croaked. I turned my face and looked up. She kept going cross-eyed as she tried to focus and she finally closed her eyes, rubbed them, then opened them again. He reached out to touch her cheeks, turning her head back and forth slowly as she blinked at him.

"'M fine," she muttered.

58

"Rory?" Dad said.

"I'm okay," I gasped. "I think." Slowly, I began to sit up, my hand over my stomach. The pain was still there, but I was able to take a deep breath without wanting to pass out.

The truck had pushed us off the highway, and we'd come to a stop down a steep, grassy embankment, just yards from the concrete off-ramp. The highway loomed overhead, out of view and quiet.

My father swallowed so hard I heard the gulp. He opened his door with a piercing creak. "Stay here."

"Wait! Where're you going?" I blurted, grabbing for his shoulder over the back of his seat.

"I'm going to see if we still have a bumper," he said grimly, making it clear he was doubtful. "I need to see if we can still drive the car."

"But—"

"But what?" he said impatiently.

"What if he's still out there?" I asked in a quiet voice. "What if he's just waiting for—"

"It wasn't Steven Nell, Rory," my father said gently.

My eyes burned with hot tears that I barely managed to hold back. "How do you know?"

"He's right," Darcy said, turning in her seat. "If it was him, he would've stuck around to make sure the job was done, right? Do you hear anything? Do you see the truck?"

I swallowed back a sob that was lodged in my throat and looked around. It was too dark to see much beyond the dense wall of trees, but the off-ramp was silent. Even the highway was dead.

"Okay," I said, my voice cracking. I cleared my throat and looked at my dad. "Okay."

He turned off the engine, pocketed the keys, and got out. I pressed my nose to the window, trying to watch him, but there was nothing outside the windows. Nothing but blackness.

"Darcy, do you see Dad?" I said urgently.

"I'm sure he's fine," she said, picking at her silver nail polish.

A minute ticked by. Then another. My heart pounded painfully. "What could be taking so long?"

Darcy shrugged and went to open the door.

I lunged forward. "Don't go out there!"

"Rory." My sister leveled me with a controlling stare. "It's fine. I'm just going to tell him we want to get the eff out of here."

"Don't," I said, shaking my head. "Something's not right."

And that's when I heard it. The low, mournful whistle, as clear as day.

It was the Beatles song, "The Long and Winding Road."

"Darcy," I gasped.

Darcy's eyes widened, and she sat up straight.

"Oh my god," she breathed. "Mr. Nell always whistled that in the hallways."

She reached over to the driver's side and flicked on the headlights with a decisive snap. The yellow glow of the headlights caught in the misty air, illuminating the grassy expanse next to the embankment, the looming thicket of trees, and . . .

I inhaled sharply, blinking rapidly. It couldn't . . . it just couldn't be.

"Is that . . . Dad . . . ?" Darcy said, her voice barely a whisper.

Our father lay in the middle of the off-ramp, his neck bent at an unnatural angle. His mouth frozen open in a scream. His dead eyes staring straight at us.

Before I could process what I was seeing, before I could put a name to what was happening, a rock came careening through the back windshield of the SUV, shattering the glass and spraying me with debris.

Darcy and I screamed.

It was happening again. Again. Again. Again. Only this time Darcy was with me. And my dad . . . I drove my fingernails into my thighs, willing myself to act. Mr. Nell was out there. My father was dead. And in seconds, we would be dead, too. It was time to move.

"Darcy, we have to go. Now," I said through my teeth, shoving open my door.

She didn't move. My feet hit the pavement, and I dashed around the car to her side.

Don't look, I commanded myself, angling my gaze away from my father. I tore open the passenger-side door and yanked Darcy from the seat.

"Come on," I urged, but Darcy just sat there, a horror-struck expression on her face.

"Darcy! We have to run, do you hear me?" I said, grasping her hands. "Run!"

Finally, my sister snapped to focus. She grasped my fingers, and together we sprinted toward the thicket of trees separating the southbound traffic from the northbound lanes.

"We have to get to the other side of the highway," I told her through gasps for breath, a plan crystallizing in my brain. Our side of the highway was dead—but maybe there were cars going north. "We have to flag down a car."

Darcy nodded, keeping pace with me step for step.

The woods pressed in thick around us. It wasn't raining anymore, but fat droplets from the earlier downpour dripped off the leaves overhead, plopping onto my shoulders and hair. My breath was jagged in my chest. Branches tore at our skin, tattooing our flesh with angry red marks. I looked briefly behind us, and a tree branch snapped into my cheek.

Instinctively, my hand went to my face. When I pulled it away, it was sticky with blood.

"Rory Miller," a sickly familiar voice called. "Where did you go?"

The sound of footsteps thundered behind us, next to us, in front of us. They were everywhere and nowhere, bouncing off the trees with the same disembodied echo as the voice.

"Rory," Darcy panted, her eyes wide. "What if he catches us?"

"He won't!" I insisted.

I thought of my first cross-country race in fifth grade. Of my mom's smiling face, already thinned out from the treatments, as she waited for me at the finish line. I'd slowed my steps as the final marker came into view, letting the person a few paces behind me pass me and pull away. I didn't want the spotlight, even then. I wanted the shadows. I didn't run to win. I ran to free my mind.

But now I had to win. *We* had to win. Because if we didn't, if we didn't get away, if we let fear take over, we would lose everything.

A huge tree loomed ahead, and Darcy broke her grip on my hand so we could run on either side of it. I sprinted forward, but when I reached out to take her hand once more, all I grabbed was air.

"Darcy!" I whispered, not slowing my pace as I looked around. "Where did you go?"

"Rory?" a faint voice called.

"Darcy!"

"Rory?" the voice came again.

I stopped and whirled around. The wooded area dividing the highway was much larger than I'd anticipated, and I was in a clearing about twenty feet wide. There was a break in the clouds, revealing a perfect half moon hanging overhead.

"Darcy!" I shouted, suddenly not caring if it drew Mr. Nell to me. I had to find my sister. "Darcy! Where are you?"

Birds took off from a tree overhead. A squirrel scampered past my feet. A soft moan sounded in the distance. Minutes felt like hours as I whirled around and around, looking for Darcy.

Then I saw it.

A long, pale finger peeked out from a tangle of low bushes and brush. The nail was painted a shimmery silver that glowed in the moonlight.

"No," I whispered, my blood flowing like ice through my veins. "No, no, no."

Slowly, so slowly, I cut through the clearing. Dead leaves crackled underfoot. A twig snapped. Fallen pine needles rustled like sandpaper on wood, and an owl hooted in the distance. Too soon I reached the hand. Heart in my throat, I pushed back the brush. A loud sob escaped my lips.

My sister—my beautiful sister—was lying there. She was on her stomach, her arms over her head like she had been struck down mid-dive into a swimming pool. Her dark hair fanned out in all angles, hiding her face—but not the deep gash in the back of her skull.

"Oh god, oh god."

Panic swelled within me as I grabbed her wrist. Her skin was still warm, but when I fumbled for her pulse, my heart shattered. There was nothing. Nothing. Tears streamed down my face, mixing with the blood matting my sister's hair. Darcy, the girl who wore a tutu for an entire year, who'd kicked Grant Sibley when he pulled my braid in fourth grade, who'd sometimes picked on me until I cried but who I loved desperately, was dead. And so was my dad.

My family, everyone I loved, was gone.

"Rory Miller . . ." a disembodied voice whispered behind me.

I spun around. A figure was standing there, hooded and dark, a shadow come to life.

Steven Nell.

He wore the awful tan corduroy jacket over a dark blue shirt. His wire-rimmed glasses glinted in the moonlight, and he held a long knife in one hand and a bloody rock in the other. His nose was flat where I'd broken it, his cheek-bones sharp, and his ice-blue eyes were narrowed at me.

"Miss me?" he simpered.

Bile rose in my throat. "You killed my sister," I hissed, rage and grief battling in me. "You killed my dad."

Mr. Nell smirked. "I wouldn't have had to if you'd just come with me. But you didn't play by the rules." The silver knife at his side gleamed. "Are you going to be a good girl now and behave?"

Was I going to be *a good girl*? Was he serious?

Adrenaline rushed through me, and I let out a feral scream. I saw the startled look in his eyes just before I hit him, like he hadn't expected me to fight. Like he'd thought I was just some meek girl who'd gotten lucky back in New Jersey. Like I would just accept that he'd murdered my family, that he'd taken all I had left like it was no more meaningful than snuffing out a candle. Like I was going to be his fifteenth girl after all.

Sixteenth, a mechanical voice in my head said. He'd already taken Darcy.

My knee knocked into his hip with a loud crack. He let out a cry of pain, but I didn't feel anything except the rage that flowed through me like molten lava. The knife slipped from his hand, landing with a soft thud on the ground at our feet. He grabbed for my shoulder, but I ducked, taking an elbow to his stomach.

He gasped, heaving a loud *oof*, and went down.

Before I could move, his hand wrapped around my ankle. He gave it a hard tug, and I felt myself falling backward. I kicked hard, flailing my limbs, and my left foot connected with something just as my back hit the ground. I heard a crunch and looked up to see Mr. Nell crouching with his hands over his face. With grim satisfaction, I realized that I'd rebroken his nose.

"You bitch," he sputtered, blood streaming down his face. I tried to kick him again, but he caught my foot and twisted it, hard. I felt something pop in my leg, and pain exploded through my body. He pinned me down and thrust his knee against my ribs, pressing me against the ground. A moment later, two rough hands closed around my neck and squeezed.

I gasped and strained, my hands pulling at his to try to free myself from his grip, but he was too powerful. His blue eyes bored into mine, and a drop of blood from his broken nose dripped onto my cheek.

"I told you I'd have you," he said with a smile. His words were warm and sickly loving. "I told you." He squeezed harder.

Gray spots formed at the edge of my vision. I clutched at the ground, trying to hold on, and my hand felt something cold, metallic.

The knife. My fingers closed around the handle.

Summoning all my remaining strength, I arced the knife up and thrust the blade into his back.

He let out a loud roar and flew off me.

Oxygen rushed into my lungs, and I rolled over onto my side, gulping greedily. Mr. Nell contorted his body and pulled the knife from his back. Only the tip was red. The wound wasn't deep—my fading strength hadn't allowed for it.

Pain tore through me as I lay there, staring up at my would-be killer. My leg throbbed, my neck was tender, and each inhale sent needles through my chest; Mr. Nell had broken my ribs when he knelt on me.

But I still had one good leg, my arms, and my rage.

When Steven charged me again, knife in hand, I was ready for him. A second before he reached me, I swung my right leg out and tripped him, then trapped my legs in his. It was agony, but I held on.

The move was something Darcy and I had done when we used to play Crocodile in our backyard when we were little. Our legs were the snapping jaws, and we'd bring down each other and our friends when they tried to jump over us.

And just like our friends had, Steven tumbled over me, his legs trapped in mine. He twisted, trying to stay upright, but went down, landing hard on his back, his right hand pummeling down on my stomach while his left flopped uselessly against the ground. I gasped at the impact, and he let out a low groan, the wind knocked out of him.

"I told you I'd get you," he rasped once more, a small smile flitting across his bloody lips.

I blinked, confused. But as I struggled to sit up, a sharp pain tore through my abdomen. It was then that I realized that the knife was still in Steven's hand—and that the blade was buried in my stomach. Only the hilt was visible, and all around it bloomed a dark, growing stain. I noticed with an odd detachment that it was the exact same hue as the red rose Steven had left on my bed.

He was right. He had gotten me. He'd gotten my dad, then Darcy, and now me. This time, as I lay there with the evergreen trees circling me, my life did pass before my eyes. I saw my mom's laughing face as we sat at the dinner table. My dad's proud grin when I got first place at the science fair. Darcy's flashing green eyes as she snuck an extra scoop of ice cream. Christopher's sweet smile before he kissed me.

Mr. Nell had won.

Or had he? I wrapped my hands around the knife's handle, my entire body on fire. I'd taken enough biology to know that the only thing keeping me from bleeding out was the knife, and that removing it would be the last thing I did.

The second to last, I vowed.

I stared at Steven, his legs trapped in mine, his torso splayed out on the muddy forest floor. His eyes were closed behind his cracked, wire-rimmed glasses, and he was lying on his back, taking rattling breaths through his broken teeth. His tan corduroy jacket was stained with dirt and blood, the flaps open, exposing his ripped flannel shirt—and his heart.

Gritting my teeth, I pulled the knife from my stomach. I registered the pain dimly, but I was too close to the end to feel anything but my need for revenge.

Steven's eyes flicked open. His pupils were huge and as black as his soul. Then the moon came out again, spilling bright light over us, and all I could see was my own reflection in the lenses of his glasses. My hands lifting the knife. My blood dripping from the metal blade. The grim set of my lips as I swung down hard, right over Steven's heart.

When it was done, I lay back, spent, staring up at the black sky.

"Rory!" a voice yelled from somewhere. "Rory!"

Suddenly, I woke up in the backseat of our new SUV, a scream wedged in my throat. Darcy's hand gripped the front of my sweatshirt.

"Shhh! Dad's sleeping," she hissed, releasing me and twisting back into her seat next to my father. "You were having a nightmare."

"A nightmare?"

I shook my head, my heart pounding wildly. My shirt clung to my back in patches of sweat and my neck was wet under my braid. I ran my hands over the seat and over my body, touching anything real to prove that what I'd just experienced was nothing but a dream. My body was whole. My sister, very much alive, was staring at me, and on my lap was the envelope containing the story of Nick, Darcy, and Rory Thayer, which wasn't all that different than our real story. Except for the fact that we came from Manhattan and that my father was a private tutor instead of a literature professor at Princeton.

I breathed in and out slowly, trying to calm myself down and get my bearings.

"Where are we now?" I pressed my forehead against the window, the cool glass bringing me fully back to reality. The car was surrounded by fog, and my father was snoring behind the wheel. A foghorn sounded and I realized the engine wasn't even running. I squinted out the window and saw another car's side mirror just inches away, not moving. We were on a ferry, just like the one we'd taken when we went to my cousin Talia's wedding up in Massachusetts.

Darcy shrugged. "No clue. I just woke up because you were yelling."

"Have we stopped since the crash?" I asked.

"What crash?" Darcy asked, her forehead wrinkling in confusion.

I balked. "The crash at the exit in Virginia."

Darcy stared at me like I was a crazy person. "Rory, you passed out in Virginia. There was no crash."

There was no crash. As Darcy's words washed over me, I let out a sigh of relief. "Thank god."

Darcy rolled her eyes. "Okay, if you're done freaking out I'm going to sleep some more."

I nodded weakly, pulling out my iPad and clicking over to my copy of *The Emperor of All Maladies*. I was too scared to go back to sleep in case I started dreaming again. But as I stared at the glowing screen, a faint smile flitted across my lips. We were on a ferry to a safe house. We were alive. And we were far, far away from Steven Nell.

JUNIPER LANDING

My father and Darcy stirred just as the fog started to lift. To my right was dark blue water and whitecaps as far as the eye could see. There was a clatter and a shouted directive, answered by another and another. The ferry was docking.

"Are we there?" Darcy asked with a yawn, looking out the window.

My father blinked the sleep from his eyes and reached for the GPS. It let out a loud double beep and flashed to life. The white screen displayed the message no one ever wants to see: NO SIGNAL.

Ahead of us, the car ramp was lowered. A man in a blue

polo shirt with a white swan embroidered onto the breast pocket waved us ahead. My dad started the engine and sat up, clearing his throat.

"Guess we're about to find out."

He drove us off the ferry, bumping onto the ramp and into a small parking lot, where a man was handing out maps. My dad cracked his window to take one, and a warm, salty sea breeze tickled my skin. I pushed the button for my own window, too, breathing in as the fresh air surrounded me. Outside, seagulls cawed and a bell on a buoy sounded.

As my dad angled into a parking spot to look at the map, I watched the passengers disembarking onto the pedestrian walkway. It was mostly kids my age and younger adults, with a few middle-aged and elderly people peppered in. I saw two guys holding hands, the definition of opposites attract. The taller guy had dark skin and dark hair and wore a tight graphic tee and a funky straw fedora, while his boyfriend had white-blond hair and freckles, and sported a green polo shirt over shorts. But almost everyone else seemed to be alone, lost in their own thoughts. I sat up a little straighter as I noticed a carved wooden sign that was painted dark blue on the background, the words spelled out in raised white letters:

WELCOME TO JUNIPER LANDING

Above the message was a wooden swan, puffing its chest out proudly, its wings back and its head held high.

"Rory, do the pamphlets Messenger gave us have an address?" my dad asked, turning the map over.

I riffled through the papers on my lap and found a little card in the folder pocket with a house key taped to it. "Yep. Ninety-nine Magnolia Street."

My dad dropped a finger on the map. "Got it," he said. "Right on the beach."

"Nice," Darcy commented, slipping on a pair of sunglasses.

My dad pulled out of the parking lot and drove slowly into town.

The buildings were crowded close together, their wooden shingles weathered and gray, the white trim around their windows splintered in places. There were wide-plank porches; bright, beach-themed wind socks tossed by the breeze; and surfboards leaned up against doorways. At least a dozen bikes were parked all over, none of them locked up, and as we rolled by a butcher shop, I heard kitschy fifties music playing through a crackly old speaker. Every window had a flower box, and every business had a hand-painted sign and a colorful awning.

We passed everything from a bakery to a bathing-suit shop to a corner stand selling sunglasses. It actually reminded me of Ocean City, where we rented a house for a week every August. Definitely a vacation destination, which would explain all the young singles on the ferry. They probably came out from the mainland every morning to work. A place like this had to be booming in the summer.

The road opened up onto a town square and a pretty park with a stone swan fountain that spouted water into the air. A guy with long dreads and a knit cap stood in the center of one of the crisscrossing walkways, singing "One Love." He had a red, yellow, and green guitar strap that looked like it had seen better days, and his guitar case was open on the ground in front of him. He kept time by tapping his bare foot.

"Way to embrace the stereotype, dude," Darcy said under her breath.

Over his head, strung from lamppost to lamppost, was a big blue sign that read JUNIPER LANDING ANNUAL FIRE-WORKS DISPLAY! FRIDAY AT SUNDOWN!

I turned around as we passed the Juniper Landing Police Department, wanting to solidify the location of the small brick building in my memory, just in case. In the distance, I could just make out the top two points of a bridge above the wafting white clouds of the fog, which still hovered over the water.

"Why didn't we take the bridge?" I asked, sitting forward again.

Pausing at a stop sign, my dad glanced in the side mirror, then turned to look over his shoulder.

"Because the GPS took us to the ferry," he said impatiently.

My face burned. I was so sick of my dad's demeaning tone I could have screamed. But, of course, I said nothing. As always.

We started moving again. A couple of girls strolled by on the sidewalk and stared at our car like they were trying to see if there was anyone famous inside. One of them, a tall, solid-looking girl with curly red hair, caught my eye and didn't look away. She held my gaze until I finally felt so uncomfortable I turned my head and pretended to cough.

"Oh my god, check out the tall-dark-and-handsome!" Darcy hissed.

She sat forward in her seat as we passed the Juniper Landing General Store, which had a blue-and-white striped awning, a couple of white wire tables set up outside, and a big sign in the window advertising breakfast and lunch service as well as THE BEST HOMEMADE ICE CREAM ON THE ISLAND. A dark-haired, broad-shouldered, square-jawed guy leaned against the window with one foot pressed back into the glass. He was casually flipping a quarter that glinted in the sun, which gave it the appearance of gold or bronze, and laughing at something the blond girl next to him had said. His laughter carried across the road.

On the other side of him was a guy with longish blond hair, sharp cheekbones, and blue eyes so striking I could see them even from this distance. His hands were crossed behind his back, his elbows out, and he was staring at our car. As I watched, he nudged the dark-haired boy, and he looked up, too. Then the blond girl did, then the petite Asian girl next to her, then the three other kids sitting at a table nearby. They simply stopped talking and stared.

Darcy instantly sat back and looked straight ahead, trying to appear cool, but I couldn't tear my eyes from the blond guy. His gaze was locked on mine, much like the redhead on the sidewalk's had been. But somehow, this was different. He was looking at me as if he knew me. As if we knew each other. But also as if he was sad to see me.

My heart started to pound in a whole new way. Like I was on the edge of something, but I didn't know whether it was something good or something bad.

"God. He is literally the hottest guy I've ever seen," Darcy said as my father pulled the car toward a dip in the road. "Maybe this whole running from Princeton thing wasn't the worst idea ever."

I didn't answer her. Instead, I turned in my seat to look back at the crowd once more. They were still staring. And they kept right on staring until we finally dipped down the hill and out of sight.

TRAPPED

Perfection. This place was perfection. A vacation town. Residents of vacation towns were blasé by nature. They never took note of a strange face, because every face was strange. And places like this were notorious for their bumbling police forces—lackadaisical, poorly trained individuals who had no idea how to deal with anything more pressing than lost children and drunken fights on the beach. Not to mention the fact that it was an island. An island with, as far as he was able to discern, only two possible routes back to the mainland—a ferry with a sporadic schedule and a bridge at the far north end, a good half-hour drive from town.

She would not escape him. She was as good as trapped. He couldn't have asked the FBI to send Rory Miller and her family to a more opportune location.

He would have to remember to send a thank-you card when it was over.

FAMILIAR FEELING

I gazed out the window as my dad pulled up in front of a beautiful white house with blue shutters, a huge front porch, and a white picket fence. A weeping willow hung over the sidewalk, and the garden was bursting with orange day-lilies and purple coneflowers. Behind the house, the ocean stretched out toward the distant horizon. The water was a brilliant aqua near the sandy shore and deepened to navy blue beyond the breakers.

"This is it?" I said dubiously. I had been imagining a depressing gray building with three cots and one shower. Maybe the government had more empathy than I'd thought.

Maybe they figured if you were on a run from a serial killer, you deserved a little pampering.

"It's number ninety-nine," Darcy sang happily, popping open her car door.

I got out and tipped my head back, relishing the warm sun on my face. A pungent, floral scent prickled my nose in a pleasant way. I breathed it in, hoping that one good inhale would soothe my frayed nerves and stop the erratic pounding in my chest. I held the air inside my lungs for as long as it took Darcy to unlatch the gate and stroll onto the porch, where a large swing creaked back and forth in the breeze. Then I finally let it go.

My heart slammed against my rib cage. Nope. Still terrified. But at least the sun was out, the breeze was cool, and there were no serial killers in sight. For the moment.

"Door's locked," Darcy announced, rattling the handle.

My father strode over to join her as I brought up the rear.

"Here," I said, tossing the key from the packet to him.

He caught it easily. Darcy bounced up and down on her toes as my dad opened the door. Spotting some hot surfer boys had clearly buoyed her mood.

The door squealed loudly, as if it hadn't been moved in years. Inside, the house was bright and sunny, and everything was polished to a gleam. Darcy ran right up the stairs, no doubt intent on getting the best bedroom. My father and

I just stood there for a moment, taking in the faded antique rugs, the dark wood floors, the antique furniture. A pastel fifties-style kitchen loomed at the back of the house.

My mother would have loved it.

"I guess we should unpack," my father said, looking tired and sounding exhausted.

"Okay. I'll go check out the—"

But he was already moving away from me back to the car. I climbed the rickety wooden staircase, my limbs feeling suddenly heavy. Darcy barreled out of the first room on the right, nearly mowing me down.

"That's mine," she announced before running downstairs and out the front door. I stepped inside her new room, surveying the yellow-and-white striped wallpaper and queen-size bed. A huge bay window faced the street, and I could see Darcy as she yanked open the trunk of the car and pulled out her bag.

Her choice was fine by me. After everything that had happened, the last thing I wanted was to face the street.

Across the hall was a master suite done up in blues and grays, which my father would claim, and the next door opened onto a white tiled bathroom. At the end of the hallway, a third door stood ajar, revealing a winding staircase. I peeked inside and tilted my head, but all I could see was a wood-paneled ceiling.

The stairway was so narrow that I was able to trail my fingers along the opposite walls as I made my way up, the stairs creaking beneath my every step. At the top, I paused. The room was wide, almost as wide as the house, with a sloped ceiling and white-washed walls. A double bed stood in the center under the highest part of the ceiling, with a six-paneled floor-to-ceiling window behind it facing the water. The only other window overlooked the beach to the north. The furniture was sparse—a wardrobe, a desk, a bookshelf filled with haphazardly shelved cloth-covered volumes.

In any other circumstance, I would have loved it. But right then, I wanted nothing more than to go home. I missed my room. I missed my desk and all my things. And being away from home, away from my mom's wallpaper, her kitchen utensils, the artwork she'd arranged so carefully in the living room, was making me miss her even more.

It's only temporary, I reminded myself with a deep, fortifying breath. But I knew the first thing I'd be unpacking was the framed picture of the two of us.

Turning around, I headed downstairs to get my stuff. As I passed by the open door to Darcy's room, she tugged her hood from her hair. In the back of her head was a huge blotch of blood, all dried into her tangled hair.

"Darcy! Your head! It's still bleeding!" I gasped.

She whirled on me, her green eyes flashing as she attempted to cover it up again. "It's fine."

"It's not fine," I said, a chill running through me.

Out of nowhere, a flash overtook my vision. A pale hand in the silvery moonlight. A distant hoot of an owl. A tumble of bloody black hair over a smashed-in skull. But when I blinked, the vision was gone. It was just a nightmare, I reminded myself. I pressed my hand onto the nearest wall and tried to breathe.

"Rory? What is it? What's wrong?" Darcy asked, alarmed.

"Nothing," I said, looking away, avoiding her eyes.

"That didn't look like nothing. It looked like . . . you got the exact same look on your face as when you had—"

"The flashes," we both said at the same time.

I swallowed hard and sat down next to her. My heart pounded with panic, and I tried to do what my psychiatrist had told me to do all those years ago—focus on what was real, focus on what was here. There was a gray smudge on my sneaker. A big black knot in the wood plank under my foot. A cuticle torn on my right ring finger. These things were real. This room, this seat, and Darcy. They were here.

"I knew it!" Darcy exclaimed, her face lined with concern. "It's happening again? Since when?"

"I don't know. Just . . . that was the first time," I said. "I'm sure it's nothing. Don't worry about it."

But even as I said it, my stomach was tied in knots. After my mother had died, I went through months where I'd get flashes every day. Vivid visions of her coughing up blood or moaning in pain or crying out for my dad. But they weren't just memories. It was as if I was transported back to the moment I'd seen these things happen and I was there all over again, reliving them in pure 3-D. My father had taken me to a psychiatrist, who had diagnosed me with post-traumatic stress disorder, and after a few months of therapy, the flashes had slowed, then finally stopped. But now, apparently, they were back. And I was flashing on the worst nightmare I'd ever had.

"You sure?" Darcy asked me.

"Yeah. I'm all right," I said, standing up again. The room spun for one split second, but I forced myself to focus and breathe. "I'll be right back. We have to clean you up."

"No. I can handle it. You should sit," Darcy said.

But I ignored her and headed for the bathroom. I was too glad to have something to do—something to distract myself from that flash. I found a washcloth in a linen closet behind the bathroom door and ran the water in the ceramic sink until it turned warm. Then I splashed some water on my face and gave myself a bolstering look in the mirror for good measure. When I returned to Darcy's room, she was sitting on the window seat, waiting for me.

"Do you want me to do it?" I asked.

She didn't say yes, but she also didn't throw me out of her room, which I took as a positive sign. Instead, she brought her feet up on the plaid bench cushion and turned to look out at the street. Tentatively, I touched the wet cloth to the wound. She winced.

"Does it hurt a lot?" I asked.

"Just get it over with," she answered tersely.

I cleaned up the blood and was relieved to find that underneath it all it was simply a superficial scrape. When I was done, I brought her leather hobo bag over to the bench, knowing she would want to work on her hair. She rummaged through it until she found her brush and started to detangle the ends.

"We should walk into town and find those guys," Darcy mused, pulling the ends of her hair around to study a stubborn knot. "If we're going to be here for a while, we might as well make friends."

I turned my profile to Darcy and stared at the hardwood floor. Three dark knots in the wood grain formed a wobbly smiley face.

"How long do you think we'll be here?" I asked quietly.

Darcy shrugged, working on her tangles. "I'd say it's a bad sign that they've been chasing him for ten years."

"Yeah," I said, my heart folding in on itself. "I guess he's pretty smart."

Darcy was silent for a moment. She was staring out the window, as though lost in thought, the brush limp in her hand.

"Do you want to hear something really sick?" she finally said in a disgusted voice. "I actually *liked* Mr. Nell. He always explained math in ways that I might actually use it in real life, which made it way more interesting. And I liked how he did speed-math contests for the last five minutes of every class because he knew that otherwise everyone would be watching the clock tick." She shuddered.

"I know. I liked him, too," I admitted. And I had. I liked how he carried his coffee in a Beatles travel mug, how he always had a dog-eared copy of *Auto Repair for Dummies* tucked under his arm, and how he never had bad breath when he leaned in to check my work, unlike every other teacher at Princeton Hills High. I used to smile when I saw him strolling the halls, holding the strap of his gray messenger bag with both hands, whistling like he hadn't a care.

"I guess you can never really know what's going on in someone's head," Darcy mused, beginning to brush her hair again.

I glanced over at her bright green eyes, which were so much like our mother's. We hadn't been the best of friends in a long time, not since before our mom died. But after Christopher dumped Darcy, she'd completely changed.

Every other sentence out of her mouth was a snap or an insult. The only thing that had stayed the same was her standing up to Dad. She was always the one to talk back to him while I cowered in the corner. I was grateful to her for that—for getting in his face a little so I didn't have to. But I didn't know how to tell her.

My mother would have told me to just say it. That it was important to let people know how I felt. My heart pounded nervous energy through my veins at the very thought, but I decided to try anyway. I could have been dead right now, after all. Then she never would have known. Apparently, "Life is short" was going to be my new mantra.

"Darcy, I—"

She stood up abruptly. "I'm gonna go check out the rest of the house," she said, turning away, avoiding looking me in the eye. It was as if she'd heard the emotion in my voice and it had scared her.

"Um, okay."

I tucked my hands under my butt, embarrassed, but she was already out the door. Sighing, I turned toward the window and glanced out at my new neighborhood. It was quaint, with brightly colored houses in lemon yellow and mint green. Each garden contained a riot of flowers and neatly trimmed trees. Only the house across the street seemed out of place. It was light gray with painted black shutters. It had no trees, no garden, no shrubs. The only interesting thing about it was the square grate in the center of the front door—one of those old-fashioned peepholes that opened like a mini door from the inside.

As I watched, a curtain fell over the window directly opposite Darcy's and I saw a hand disappear from view. My heart hit my throat. Was someone watching us? I leaned forward, squinting as the curtain fluttered.

Something crashed downstairs, and my hand flew to my heart. My father cursed at the top of his lungs. I got up and made my way to my new bedroom. Shaking off the quick scare I'd had in Darcy's room, I closed the door quietly behind me. We were safe here. No one was watching me anymore. People were allowed to look out their windows.

I climbed the stairs, sank down on the bed, and stared up at the wood-beamed ceiling with a sigh. So this was it. This was my new life. With my family but entirely alone. At least something about this place was familiar.

THE NEW GIRL

"*Rory . . .*"

I sat up straight in bed. My eyes darted around the unfamiliar room, the dark corners, the distorted shadows. Someone had just whispered my name.

"Rory Miller!" the voice sang again. "Can Rory Miller come out and play?"

I flung the covers aside, my bare feet hitting the cool wood floor. A quick turn of the room convinced me that no one was there, but the voice came again.

"Come on, Rory. Come out and play with me."

Goose bumps popped up all over my bare arms as I

shakily stepped toward the stairs and peeked over the guardrail. No one was there. Just the bare steps winding down into the dark.

"Rory?" It was Darcy this time. "Rory!" she screamed. "Rory, help!"

Heart in my throat, I stumbled down the stairs. When I opened the door, it stopped with a thud. I looked down, and there was Darcy, curled up in a fetal position on the floor. Her eyes were open and staring, dead. Her head was so crushed it seemed impossible it was ever whole.

"No!" I screamed, covering my eyes. "No! No! No!"

I whirled around on the stairs, right into Steven Nell's waiting arms.

"No!"

I startled awake on Sunday morning, my hands over my stomach, the bright sun assaulting my eyes. Sweat covered every inch of my body and my skin felt like it was on fire. My belly ached like I'd eaten too many bags of cotton candy and chased them with an entire bottle of Coke. I covered my face and told myself it was just a dream. It was just a dream. It was just a dream.

Breathe, Rory. Breathe.

As my breath started to calm, I heard the sound of my father slamming pots and pans around in the kitchen. I shoved my feet into my slippers and yanked on my $E=mc^2$

sweatshirt before padding down the two flights of stairs. I tiptoed through the foyer and paused by the table near the door. My father had placed the family photo there—the one that used to hang on our upstairs wall. I hadn't even seen him take it from the house. When another crash sounded, I slid over to the kitchen door and peeked inside. My dad was bent over in jeans and a T-shirt, rummaging through a low cabinet, every so often tossing a Teflon pan or a copper pot behind him onto the floor.

"Tell us we have to leave our house and then send us to some backward island with no phone service and no Wi-Fi," he muttered into the hollow of the cupboard. I'd noticed the Wi-Fi problem last night when I'd tried to log on to the Internet from my iPad, but I'd hoped it was a temporary glitch. "What the hell kind of way is this to run a government agency?" He started to pull himself up and slammed his head on the edge of the opening. "Motherf—"

I jumped back to hide before he could spot me and start yelling at me, too. Outside I heard a bicycle bell trill, and I made my way to the front door. I slipped onto the porch, closing the door quietly behind me. The warm summer air enveloped me from head to toe. I tiptoed over to the porch swing and sat, wrapping my arms around myself. Even from the front of the house, I could hear the waves rushing against the beach out back, and the air was filled with the tangy salty scent of the sea, plus that sweet floral infusion I couldn't quite place.

Someone nearby was humming. The tune sounded vaguely familiar as it floated on the breeze. Familiar enough that I started to hum along. Until I realized exactly why I knew the melody. I jumped up from the swing, whirling around.

It was "The Long and Winding Road."

I was flashing again. I had to be flashing again. But then a little yellow bird flew over and perched on the porch railing. I heard the distant sound of a bell. The magnolia tree across the street rustled in the breeze. I was here. In Juniper Landing. In the now. And the humming was real.

Trembling, I walked to the end of the porch and peeked over the railing toward the back of the house. Sandy, patchy crabgrass stretched out to a boardwalk that separated our house from the beach. But other than a blackbird perched in a flowering tree and a few bees buzzing around a coneflower, there was nothing there. I walked to the other side and looked back at the garage. Our new car sat in the driveway, its black hood glinting in the morning sun. I held my breath, closed my eyes, and listened. Nothing other than the crashing of the surf and the cawing of the blackbird.

But when I opened my eyes again, the very same curtain in the very same window of the house across the street fluttered closed. This time, I caught a glimpse of blond hair as someone turned away from the window.

"What the hell?" Before I could lose my nerve, I jogged down the steps of the porch, opened the latch, and stepped out onto the sidewalk for a better look.

"Whoa!"

I nearly jumped out of my skin as two girls about my age skidded to a stop on their bikes just outside our gate—and inches from me. One was pretty, dark-skinned, and round-cheeked, with curls sticking out in all directions and an eyebrow ring that glinted in the sun. She wore an army jacket, even though it was warm out, along with a black dress, a striped scarf, and tall black boots. The other was the petite girl I'd seen with Darcy's new conquest yesterday at the general store. She had straight black hair that fell to her chin, dark eyes, and sported a JUNIPER LANDING T-shirt over denim shorts. A weathered, woven leather bracelet clung to her right wrist.

"Close call," the girl with the eyebrow ring said, backing up her bike.

"Um, yeah," I said, my eyes darting back to the window. The curtain was still.

"You're new," the petite girl said coolly. She looked at me with pointed curiosity, like she was studying my face.

"That obvious?" I asked.

"To a native, yeah," she said with a short laugh that felt almost mocking. Like there was some private joke I was missing.

"Less obvious to me, but I'm just visiting." The other girl kicked down the stand on her bike and offered me her hand. "I'm Olive Walden. This is Lauren Caldwell."

I shook her hand, still staring across the street at the gray house.

"And you are . . . ?" Olive prompted, clearly amused.

"Oh, sorry," I said, blinking myself back into the moment. "Rory. Rory . . . Thayer." The new name felt odd on my tongue.

Lauren looked up at my home away from home. "Nice digs."

"Thanks. Do you have any idea who lives across the street?" I asked, lifting my chin at the gray house.

Lauren and Olive exchanged a look, then glanced back at the house.

"Already trying to get the dirt on your neighbors, huh?" Lauren said, a mischievous glint in her eyes.

I blushed. "No. I just thought I saw . . . I mean . . ." I trailed off, unsure how to finish the sentence. I couldn't exactly explain that a serial killer was stalking me, so mysteriously moving curtains were sending me over the edge.

"Don't sweat it. She's just giving you a hard time." Olive laughed, elbowing Lauren in the side in a *be nice* kind of way.

"Want to go for a ride with us? We can take you for a tour of the town."

I glanced back at the house. I didn't relish the idea of hanging out inside with sulking Darcy and pissed-off Dad, but the eerie humming was still echoing in my head.

"Thanks, but I don't have a bike," I said, happy for the excuse. "Besides, I'm more of a runner."

"Running? Really?" Olive shaded her eyes against the sun. "I never got the appeal."

"No? It's great. I love it," I told her.

"Yeah?"

I lifted my shoulders and took a breath. "It's . . . I just like being alone and not having to think about anything but the rhythm of my steps and the rate of my pulse," I said. "It's very . . ."

"Zen," she supplied.

"Okay, Zen," I said with a laugh. I looked her in the eye. She looked back with an intrigued expression.

Lauren, on the other hand, was starting to look bored. "Let's get going, Olive," she said impatiently, rolling forward on her bike. "I'm starved."

Olive hopped back on her seat, lifted her kickstand with her heel, then turned to me once more. "Oh!" she said, her eyes lighting up. "You should come to the party tonight."

"Party?" I asked warily. I detested parties. Avoided them

as much as possible. I'd always been okay with friends one-on-one, but crowds were not my thing. In fact, one of the ways I comforted myself over never having gotten together with Christopher was by telling myself that he would have dragged me to at least one party a weekend.

Of course, now that seemed like a silly rationalization. My heart squeezed just thinking about it. I should have said yes to him. I would have gladly gone to ten million parties if it meant being with him.

"We're having a bonfire on the beach," Lauren explained, fiddling with her woven bracelet. "We always invite all the vacationers," she added, as if wanting to make sure I didn't think I was special somehow.

"It starts around nine and we'll be out there till whenever," Olive said. "Just look out your window. You'll see us."

"Um . . . okay. Maybe," I said, even though I had no intention of going. Of course, it was totally Darcy's kind of thing, but if I told her, she would want to go, my father would say no, she would sneak out, and World War III would erupt inside our temporary home.

"Cool. See you later, then. *Maybe*," Olive said with a wry smile. Then the two of them rode off.

As soon as they were gone, the front door opened and my dad stormed out wearing Adidas shorts and an ancient Harvard T-shirt. He bounced on the balls of his feet a few times, his stomach moving up and down like a heavy ball.

"I'm going for a run," he said tensely. "You want to come?"

I blinked. My dad hadn't invited me on a run since before my mom died. He hadn't invited me to do anything since before my mom died. The very thought of going with him made my shoulders curl, like he expected me to forget five years of his ignoring my existence.

"Um . . . I still need to eat breakfast," I said awkwardly.

"Okay. I'll be back in an hour."

Then he opened the gate and jogged away. I was still standing there, gaping after him, when from the corner of my eye, I saw another flutter in one of the windows of the gray house. Heart in my throat, I turned and sprinted inside, locking both locks behind me. Then I moved over to the parlor window and hid behind the heavy, flowered curtain, angling myself so that I could just see outside.

All of a sudden the front door of the gray house opened with a creak. A guy with blond hair, a killer tan, and piercing blue eyes jogged down the steps, glanced over at our house almost furtively, and then speed-walked up the block with his head down. I recognized him instantly. It was the guy from outside the general store. The one who had looked at me like he knew me.

My breath caught in my throat. Blond hair. Piercing eyes.

Had he been the one watching me from the window? And if he lived there, wouldn't Lauren have said so? They'd been hanging out yesterday. It seemed as if they were friends.

I watched until he made it to the end of the street and disappeared around the corner that led to the town. Then I double-checked the locks, retreated to my room, and locked that door behind me as well. If there was one thing Steven Nell had taught me, it was to trust no one—especially people who seemed to have a thing for watching me.

BONFIRE

I was just finishing a chapter in a biography of Marie Curie when I heard the door at the bottom of the stairs creak open. My heart all but stopped, and my eyes darted to the plain gray-and-white clock hanging on the opposite wall. It was past midnight.

"Hello?" I said, my voice breaking as I sat up straight.

Rapid footsteps sounded up the stairs, and I curled against the headboard, clutching my iPad to my chest. I was just wondering how badly I would damage it if I had to use it as a weapon when Darcy appeared. She was fully dressed in skinny jeans and a sparkly tank top, and was wearing complete makeup.

"You scared the crap out of me!" I said.

"Check it out!" she said, ignoring me as she gestured at the north-facing window. "Bonfire on the beach!"

Damn. I should've known she could smell a party in the air. I sighed, put my iPad/potential ninja star down, and padded to the window. Sure enough, there was a raging bonfire maybe three houses up the beach, with at least twenty kids milling around it. From this distance, all I could make out was their shadows. It looked vaguely like the cover of that *Lord of the Flies* novel I'd been forced to read in English class last year. Fiction had never really been my thing.

"I bet that guy from the general store is there," Darcy whispered excitedly, raising her eyebrows. She turned and started rummaging through the armoire across from the foot of the bed, sliding the hangers aside one by one.

"What're you doing?" I asked warily.

"Finding you something to wear," she replied in her favorite condescending voice. "Go do something with your hair. It looks like birds are nesting in there."

"Darcy, I don't want to go to a party," I protested, running my hands over my braid nonetheless.

"Well, I do, and I don't want to show up by myself." Her hands flopped to her sides and she groaned. "Don't you own anything that's not a zip sweatshirt?"

"Oh, well. I have nothing to wear, so I guess we'd better

stay home," I tried, dreading the idea of standing around, trying to make small talk with strangers.

Darcy looked me up and down, taking in my white tank top and gray, wide-leg sweats with the side stripe. "You can borrow something of mine," she said reaching for my hand and pulling me toward the stairs.

"Dad will kill us if we sneak out," I said, grasping at straws.

"So? What else is new?"

"Darcy—"

"Oh, come on, Rory!" she whined, tipping her head back as she now took both my hands in hers. "Please? Please, please, please? I'm dying of boredom here. We've been locked up in this house for two whole days after being locked up in *our* house for a week. Please come with me? I'm begging you here. Please? You owe me."

I looked into my sister's eyes and felt a thump of foreboding mixed with overwhelming guilt.

"Why do I owe you?" I asked slowly. She didn't know, right? How could she possibly know?

She glanced away and lifted her shoulders. "I don't know. For defending you to Dad the other day? For defending you to Dad *every* day? For leaving behind all my friends and ditching Becky's party and missing my graduation to come here?"

"Like that was my fault," I pointed out. But still. I could breathe a small sigh of relief, because at least she hadn't been talking about Christopher. At least she hadn't somehow found out. But the damage was done, and the guilt was now pressing down on my chest.

Besides, Darcy was right. She had given up a lot to come here. When Steven Nell had attacked me, she'd been looking forward not only to her graduation and Becky's bash, but also to about a half dozen other parties and a trip down the shore. Not to mention another summer working at her friend Liam's family restaurant. This year she would be old enough to bartend and bring home "mad tips." I'd never liked or understood her friends, but she lived for them, and all of that had been taken from her.

"All right, fine. We'll go," I said, shoving my feet into the sneakers I had kicked off next to my bed earlier. "But I'm wearing my own clothes."

"Yay!" Darcy actually hugged me for half a second, and a smile flickered on my lips. I moved to the wardrobe, yanked out my favorite navy-blue Adidas zip sweatshirt and zipped it on over my tank. Then I followed my sister down the stairs and out the back door.

The air outside was cool, and even from down the beach, I could smell the ash on the breeze. Long, thin lines combed into the sand beneath our feet, as if it had recently been evened out and spruced up by a maintenance crew. I stuffed my hands in my pockets and matched Darcy's casual pace as we approached the bonfire. My pulse raced with nerves when the first revelers on the outskirts of the crowd started to notice us. I felt conspicuous, like I didn't belong here. But Darcy was in her element. She paused a few feet from the fire and pushed one hand into the back pocket of her jeans, shaking her hair away from her face.

"There he is," she said through her teeth, sliding her eyes to the right.

Darcy's dark-haired hottie stood with Lauren and Olive near a blue cooler. They were with the two boys and the pretty blond girl from the general store, along with two more surfer-type guys and the redhead who had stared at us from the sidewalk. All of them were beautiful and completely at ease, their hair wind-tossed, their smiles carefree, their clothes loose and beachy and casual.

"The key is to let the guy come to you," Darcy informed me, leaning slightly toward my ear. "Never, ever go to—"

"Hi, there."

We both jumped. Darcy's crush stood just to her right, holding a red cup and wearing a perfect, smooth grin. He had one dimple in his left cheek. His brown hair fell over his right eye, and the sleeves of his red T-shirt clung to his biceps. His jeans were frayed at the bottom, and he was barefoot, as was the rest of his group. Even Darcy had gone shoeless. Suddenly, I felt out of place in my laced-up running sneakers.

Then the blond guy from across the street fixed his eyes on mine. A split second later, he looked away and sipped his drink. I licked my dry lips and clutched my hands together behind my back. My pulse began to race as I wondered if he would talk to me—what I would say to him if he did.

"Hi. I'm Darcy Thayer," my sister was saying. She tilted her head with a smile. Her long brown hair tumbled over her bare shoulder.

"Joaquin Marquez," the guy said. He gestured at the blond guy, and I noticed that Joaquin was wearing the same woven leather bracelet Lauren had on. "This is Tristan Parrish."

Tristan simply nodded. My eyes darted to his arms. Sure enough, a leather bracelet was tied around his wrist.

"And that's his sister, Krista," Joaquin said, lifting his cup toward the blond girl, who wore a gauzy white dress; a long, delicate gold necklace; and the bracelet, although hers looked newer than the others.

"Hello," she said, her eyes trailing over me from head to toe as if she were a fashion designer scrutinizing her work. There was a sophisticated confidence about her, which wasn't all that surprising considering how beautiful she was. She had the same sharp cheekbones as her brother and the same stunning blue eyes. "I love your hair," she mused, touching the end of my braid.

"Um, thanks." I squirmed under her touch.

"How about we get through introductions first before you grope her, Krista?" Joaquin suggested lightly.

"Sorry," Krista apologized, dropping my hair.

"Don't mind her. She's cute but socially awkward," Joaquin said under his breath, leaning slightly toward us.

"Shut up!" Krista said, shoving his arm but smiling in a self-deprecating way as everyone else laughed. So he was that guy. Didn't matter if what he said was rude or obnoxious, everyone just let him say it. Darcy had one of those in her crowd—her friend Liam—and I couldn't stand him.

"Those guys back there are Bea, Fisher, and Kevin," Krista told me, slipping one arm around mine and gesturing at the redhead and her two guys. They silently lifted their drinks in greeting. Fisher was tall and linebacker-broad with dark skin and hair shaved so close to his head it was almost nonexistent. Kevin was lanky and pale, with black hair and an intricate fire tattoo cut across his right forearm. "And you know Lauren and Olive."

Darcy shot me a confused glance.

I cleared my throat, extricating my arm from Krista's. "Um, I met Lauren and Olive earlier," I explained to Darcy. "They were riding their bikes past the house."

Lauren was in the same T-shirt and shorts she'd had on that morning, but Olive had changed into a long-sleeved black sweater over baggy cargo pants. Her dark curls bounced crazily in the ocean breeze. She was the only one without a leather band on her arm, unless it was hidden under her sleeve.

"Hi, Rory," Olive said.

"Hey," I said. "This is my sister, Darcy."

The girls smiled politely at Darcy but said nothing. Darcy cleared her throat and shifted her weight.

"So, Rory, how do you like Juniper Landing so far?" Joaquin asked me, stepping past Darcy and over to my side.

While the rest of the group watched me, I glanced sideways at Darcy, whose smile faltered. She wasn't used to being ignored, especially not in favor of me. My face grew warm, and suddenly my heart seemed to be pulsating directly against my skin.

"Um, it's . . . nice," I said.

"Have you been into town yet?" Krista asked, toying with her necklace.

"The ice cream at the general store is to die for," Olive put in.

"And you have to check out the library," Krista added. "They have an amazing science section."

My heart thumped. How would Krista know I was into science?

"Because you were wearing that $E=mc^2$ sweatshirt this morning," Krista explained, clearly reading my startled look. "At least that's what Lauren told me."

"Oh," I said warily, shooting a look at Lauren, who stared straight back at me, as if it wasn't weird that she'd reported back on my outfit. "Right."

"She was? God," Darcy said in an apologetic way, touching my arm. "Forgive my sister. She's still learning how to dress herself."

I cocked an annoyed eyebrow at my sister.

"I think she looks fine," Tristan put in, speaking for the first time. The gravelly timbre of his voice sent a shiver down my spine.

"To each her own," Darcy sang, tossing her hair back. But I could see the red forming on her cheeks from being contradicted. The beautiful people were supposed to be her people, not mine.

"So, Rory, let's find someplace to sit," Joaquin said, reaching his arm around me and giving my shoulder a familiar squeeze. "I like to get to know all our new visitors."

I'll bet, I thought, wondering how many girls that line had worked on in the past.

Tristan looked me dead in the eye at this, his expression pained.

"Actually, I'm kind of thirsty," I said, dodging Joaquin's touch.

"Fisher'll get you something," Joaquin said, tilting his head toward the others. "Right, Fish?"

Instantly, Fisher was by Joaquin's side, as if ready to do his bidding. I glanced at Darcy, freaked, but she simply glared back at me.

"Um, thanks, but I can get it myself," I said, angling so I could slide past them.

"You sure?" Joaquin asked.

"Yep! Very sure. I'll be back," I told Darcy.

But by the way she was looking at me, it was pretty clear she wouldn't have minded if she never saw me again.

DEAD ZONE

I made my way to the other side of the bonfire, snagged a bottle of water from the cooler, and tried to look perfectly content sipping from it while I watched the surf. Surreptitiously, I kept an eye on Darcy and the others. She was getting her flirt on with Joaquin now, but every so often he'd look over in my direction. Olive and Tristan were chatting alone, their heads bent close together, while Fisher, Kevin, and Bea had found a pair of coolers to sit on, facing the fire. Lauren and Krista stood alongside them, whispering and glancing in my direction.

Just breathe. Just breathe and recite.

Hydrogen, helium, lithium, beryllium, boron, carbon, nitrogen, oxygen, fluorine . . .

A round of girlish laughter caught my attention. A few feet away, closer to the edge of the water, a guy about my age was talking to two younger girls. He had brown hair and brown eyes, a nice face, and was the only other person wearing sneakers. He was listening to what the girls were saying, but every once in a while, when they weren't looking, he would glance around, like he was bored.

As he surveyed the party, his eye caught mine. A moment later, he excused himself from his conversation and walked over to me.

"Care to save me from the most ridiculous conversation ever?" he asked in a lilting British accent. Clearly, he wasn't from the island, which meant he was not part of the Juniper Landing Super-Popular Crowd. I glanced at his wrist, testing a theory. No leather bracelet. It seemed like it was some kind of local trend, or maybe a cliquey-club-type thing. Maybe there was some secret society of locals, letting everyone else know how excluded they were by wearing the same piece of jewelry. Very mature.

"What was the conversation?" I asked.

He blew out his lips. "Would you believe they were going on and on about the royal couple, asking me if I knew them? Like all British people know one another."

"You don't?" I joked.

He laughed, and the warm sound of it put me at ease.

"I'm Rory."

"Aaron," he said with a slight nod. He moved next to me, surveying the party. On the far side of the fire, two guys were mock-wrestling while a group of girls squealed. Over to my right, a "chug" chant started up as a shirtless dude attempted to do a keg stand. Something I wouldn't have even recognized if not for a recent exposé about frat hazing on the nightly news. Joaquin and Darcy were among the chanters.

Aaron clucked his tongue. "Don't you hate these things?"

"So, so much," I replied. Then I tossed him a teasing grin. "Do your friends Lady Kate and Prince Will do keg stands?"

Aaron let out an exaggerated groan. "At my last party, I had to call the royal guard to come take them away," he said, his brown eyes dancing. "But I did see you talking to the beautiful people. What's the deal with the tall, dark drink of water?" he asked, looking Joaquin up and down appreciatively.

I shook my head. "No idea. Not my type."

"But *so* mine," he said, taking a sip of his drink. "They don't make 'em like that across the pond. Unfortunately, he seems to play for your team, not mine," he said, flicking a

look at my sister, who gripped Joaquin's arm as she laughed.
"If it makes you feel any better, he kind of seems like a
jerk," I said.

He smirked. "Thanks for that."

I smiled. "So what part of England are you from?"

"I'm a Birmingham boy, but I'm going to Oxford in
the fall."

"Oxford, wow. So you're ridiculously smart," I said.

He shrugged, shaking his head. "Nah. I'm ninth
generation so they had to let me in. I've decided to study
archaeology, much to the chagrin of my literary-minded
parents."

"Archaeology doesn't sound too shabby to me," I said.

"What about you? What do you want to study?" He
sipped his drink, turned slightly to face me, and planted his
feet, as if deciding this was where he wanted to stay, at least
for the time being.

"Me?" I put my water bottle down on the cooler, then
pulled my braid over my shoulder and started to fiddle with
the end. "Science. Medicine, specifically. I want to be an
oncologist."

I wanted to save people like my mom. People who didn't
deserve to die. People whose families didn't deserve to be left
behind. But I figured that was too morbid for party banter.

"Wow. You've got your life mapped out. Impressive," he

said. There was a long moment of silence between us, but it wasn't uncomfortable. We both sipped our drinks. "So, are you on holiday, or—"

I bit the inside of my cheek. "Yeah. We just got here yesterday."

"We?" he asked.

"Me, my dad, my sister." My heart skipped a beat. Talking about my family might mean I'd have to start recounting our cover story. I'd memorized the facts of our new life on the car ride down, but being able to pull off the lies was an entirely different story. "What about you?"

"Just arrived this morning," he said. He finished his drink, took my empy bottle of water, and launched them at a nearby garbage bag, which was already overflowing with cups and cans. "I actually came over here to visit my uncle, who lives up in Boston, but there was a fire while I was there and the whole family was displaced."

"Oh my gosh," I gasped. "I hope everyone's all right."

"Yeah, we all managed to get out unscathed, miraculously," he said, fiddling with a silver ring on his right hand.

"Good," I replied, thinking of my own narrow escape back home. Not that I could tell him about that.

"Anyway, they decided to fly back to the UK until the repairs on the house were done, but I wasn't ready to go back, so I figured I'd see a bit of the country first," he explained.

"Oh. Cool." This time the pause was awkward. I felt like I was supposed to elaborate on our vacation, but my tongue was tied. "We just . . . go away every year right after school lets out," I improvised.

Our school year didn't actually end for another week, but he had no way of knowing that.

"My family always goes to the beach on holiday," Aaron said with a wistful smile. "Being here is making me miss my sister, I must confess. I don't have anyone to go wind-surfing with." He looked me over curiously. "I don't suppose you . . . ?"

"Windsurf? No," I scoffed.

"Then I'd love to teach you. What do you say?" he asked, his eyes brightening with excitement.

My heart thumped with nerves. I'd never been really big on diving into new things. With strangers. In strange places.

"I promise I'll be gentle," he joked, raising one hand. "Please? I really want to go, but I'd rather go with a friend. And you definitely seem like friend material."

I blushed, flattered, then found myself imagining how Darcy would react if I told her I was going to go windsurfing. She'd probably laugh in my face with a "Yeah, right," and the very thought made my skin burn. I didn't want to be pre-dictable anymore. I didn't want to be the lame, boring, weak girl Steven Nell chose out of the crowd. I wanted to embrace this whole "Life is short" mantra, and if I was going to do that, it was time to start facing my fears and trying new things.

"All right," I said. "Why not?"

"Fantastic!" he crowed. "Meet me at the bay beach tomorrow afternoon at two. There's a rental place there. You can't miss it."

"I'll be there," I promised.

I heard my sister's flirtatious laugh carry across the party and sighed as she practically fell into Joaquin laughing. A couple of girls nearby shot her annoyed looks. I wished she didn't have to be so overt.

"Well, someone's having fun," Aaron said, following my gaze.

"You said you have a sister?" I asked, hoping to change the subject.

"And a brother," he said. He stooped to pick up a rock and tossed it toward the water. "I tried to call them today for the first time in a while, but I couldn't get any service." He squinted as he looked at me. "I don't suppose your cell works here, does it?"

I wouldn't know, not having one in my possession. But the GPS had gone dead when we got here, my iPad still wasn't working, and my father had said that even the landlines were

screwed up. Maybe this is why the FBI had sent us here—
there was no possible way for us to contact people from our
old life and blow our cover. "Nope. Apparently the island is
a dead zone."

He sighed. "I was afraid of that."

"Why was it the first time you'd called in a while?" I
asked.

Aaron kicked at the sand. "That's kind of a long story,
but basically, I had this huge row with my father before I
left, so I've been avoiding calling home."

"Ah," I said. "That makes sense."

"Of course, the great irony of ironies, I finally feel ready
to apologize and hash it out, and I can't get through to him."
He shrugged.

Before I could respond, the girls he'd been talking to
earlier rushed up to him with a loud squeal.

"There you are!" the brown-haired girl said, looping her
arm through his.

"We thought we lost you!" her blond friend breathed,
wobbling slightly in the sand. The red Solo cup in her hand
was nearly empty.

"Here I am," he said weakly, looking at me apologeti-
cally. "I'll see you tomorrow!" he mouthed as they pulled
him away.

"Okay!" I gave him a wave and an encouraging smile,

which he replied to with a grimace, but I was sure he could take care of himself. At least, I hoped so.

Left alone again, I knocked my fists together, wondering what to do next. I checked on Darcy, hoping she might be getting bored, but she was staring up at Joaquin, rapt, as he gestured his way through a story. I let out a sigh and was about to turn away when I noticed Lauren, Krista, Kevin, Fisher, and Bea sitting facing the fire, drinks in hand. The flames cast dark shadows on their faces, and the tongues of flame made their eyes glow red. Not one of them was talking. Instead, they were all staring at me, unreadable expressions on their faces.

His face. Nell's face. Spattered with blood. Glaring down at me. The flash of a knife. The twisted branch of a tree overhead. Someone screamed.

I sat down hard on the nearest cooler, gasping for air. Another flash. The scream had just been some random girl, running away from a couple of boys in the surf. I pressed my hand to my forehead and told myself it wasn't real.

I focused on the hard cooler top beneath my thighs. The surf crashing in my ears. The warmth of the fire against my skin. It brought me back down to earth, but all I wanted was to be back at the house, reading my book in the safety of my third-floor room.

I pushed myself up, walked shakily over to Darcy, and touched her shoulder.

"Can we go now?" I asked quietly. "Please?"

"Rory, we just got here," she said. Joaquin sipped his drink, studying me.

"Come on, Darcy. I came with you, now I need you to come home with me," I whispered.

"Everything okay?" Joaquin asked, stepping closer to us.

"Rory," Darcy said through her teeth, wide-eyed.

"But I—"

"If you want to go home, go. I'll be fine," she said a bit more loudly.

I stared at her. Right. Sure. She'd be fine. But what about me? I didn't exactly relish the idea of walking back alone.

"We're five steps from the house," she said quietly, her tone placating. "Don't worry. I won't stay too late."

I turned and looked up the beach at our house. It wasn't really that far, and all the homes between here and there had lights on their back decks. Besides, if something happened to me, someone at the party would hear me scream. Hopefully.

"All right, fine. I'll go. But be careful," I said, leaning in toward her ear.

"God. Chill out," she replied. Then she turned back to Joaquin. "So how exactly did you get into lifeguarding?"

I glanced back at the fire, and my eye fell on Tristan. Olive was talking to him, but he was looking right at me again, studying me, as if trying to read my thoughts. My heart started to pound in a shallow, fluttery way, and part of me wanted to just go over there and talk to him. Ask him what was with all the staring. But I couldn't bring myself to do it. Maybe he wasn't really staring at me. Maybe he just liked to stare. And all I'd do by confronting him was bring more attention to myself and come off like an egotistical idiot in the process.

So, instead, I turned my back on him and headed up the beach alone, my chin tucked into the high neck of my sweatshirt.

I'd gone about fifty steps when a gray mist started to swirl around my ankles. My heart skipped a startled beat, and then my feet entirely disappeared from view. The air around me seemed to be moving, curling in and out, undulating. Heart in my throat, I whirled to look back at the fire, but it was nothing more than a dull, glowing ball in the grayness. I couldn't make out a single face, a single figure. The fog had rolled in and distorted everything.

I turned around again, feeling utterly disoriented, and quickened my pace. I couldn't see more than two feet ahead, so I veered right, looking for a landmark. A set of stairs came into view, leading up to one of the houses, but it wasn't ours.

The laughter came out of nowhere.

I froze in my tracks, and a chill sliced down my spine.

The sound prickled my ears. It was exactly like the laugh from my nightmares. Exactly like Steven Nell's.

"No," I said under my breath. "No."

It came again, closer this time. Cackling. As quietly as I possibly could, I started to run. The sand beneath my feet made me stumble and I reached out, ready to fall, but my hand hit something hard. A scream rose in my throat until I realized it was just a railing. A railing to another set of stairs. I had no clue whether it was our house or a neighbor's, but at that moment I didn't care. I tore up the steps, taking them two, three at a time. All that mattered was getting inside. Getting away from him.

As I reached the top of the stairs, I heard the laugh again. It hovered in the mist, nearly on top of me. I scrambled across the wood planks and found that I was on the deck to our house. After fumbling for the key in my pocket, I managed to slip inside and close the door behind me, turning the lock as fast as I could. The gray fog swirled against the windowpane as I backed away, leaving a wet trail of condensation. Just on the other side of the glass, the mist moved in tiny, bursting pulses. As if someone was out there, standing just inches away from me, breathing slowly in and out. In and out.

I turned and raced up the stairs to the second floor, my heart pounding in my skull. At the top of the steps I heard a noise and paused, clinging to the wallpapered corner. But this time, it wasn't laughter. It was something else entirely.

Taking a breath, I tiptoed across the hall and stood outside the closed door of my father's bedroom. He let out a sob so pained I felt it inside my heart. My father was in there, alone, crying. Yet another thing I hadn't heard him do since the day we'd buried my mom.

I stood there, my hand on the door, and listened. Listened until the fear faded away. Until I started to realize how irrational I'd been. How I must have imagined it all. How I'd let a natural weather phenomenon freak me out to the point of panic. None of that was real. *This* was real. My father's pain. His finally breaking down.

This was real. And as much as it hurt, standing there in the hallway, listening in on his grief, it gave me hope.

AN INVITATION

After breakfast the next morning, I decided to walk into town and see if I could find a newspaper. There wasn't a single TV in the house, and I needed to know what was going on with the hunt for Steven Nell. Maybe the cops had found him. Maybe everything was fine and we could go home.

Just as I put my hand on the knob of the front door, I saw something move in one of the windows across the way.

"What're you doing?"

My hand flew up to cover my heart. "Darcy! You scared me!"

"Well, why are you standing there frozen?" she asked,

looking me up and down from the bottom step like she couldn't believe she was related to someone so weird. She reached back to tie her hair into a high ponytail with a sparkly black and gold band. "You looked catatonic for a second. Did you have another flash?"

"No." I couldn't believe she knew what *catatonic* meant. "I was just about to go for a walk—check out the town." I yanked the door open and paused. "Want to come?"

She narrowed her eyes. I was sure she was thinking the same thing I was thinking. The two of us hanging out together twice in less than twenty-four hours? Looked like hell had finally frozen over.

"Sure," she said finally, grabbing her purse from the table by the door and almost knocking over the family photo in the process.

"Should we tell Dad we're going out?" I asked.

"He went for a run, like, an hour ago," she said as she slipped on her dark sunglasses.

"Really?" I asked, following her out the door and across the porch. "Again?"

"What? Like that's so bizarre?" she asked. She opened the gate and strode through, not bothering to hold it for me.

"Dad hasn't gone out for a run in about five years," I told her. Leave it to Darcy not to notice. "Now he's gone twice since we've been here."

She lifted a shoulder, walking backward up the sunlit sidewalk. "Well, good for him. Maybe it'll chill him out."

Then she turned, flinging her hair, and walked ahead of me. As we reached the corner, I glanced back at the gray house, half expecting to see Tristan's face in one of the windows, but it was still. The place looked deserted. Even so, I quickened my steps, trying to make it look like I just wanted to catch up with Darcy, not like I was scared. A middle-aged man on a bike rode by with a surfboard tucked under his arm, and he rang his bell as he passed. On the other side of the street, a guy in his early twenties was watering his small lawn. I took a deep breath of the uniquely scented air and tried to relax.

"What is that smell?" I mused. "Is it honeysuckle? Lavender? I can't place it."

Darcy inhaled. "I don't know, but it's nice." She trailed her hand along the top of a neatly clipped rosebush growing along the sidewalk. "It's kind of . . ."

"Soothing," I supplied.

She tilted her head, considering. "Yeah. Like aromatherapy."

We walked a couple of blocks, past colorful Colonial homes with flower gardens and porch swings and peach trees, each one more stunning than the last. It was all very pretty, but almost too perfect. Like someone had come in and told everyone to get their houses ready for the postcard photographer.

"So you never asked me how it went with Joaquin last night," Darcy said.

"How did it go with Joaquin last night?" I asked.

"Amazing!" she answered, bending slightly at the knee. "He's a lifeguard. How hot is that? And he works at this bar down by the bay, so we have that in common."

"That's cool," I said.

"He is *so* beautiful, and he totally ate up the whole story about us being from Manhattan. He was fascinated," Darcy said, clasping her hands under her chin and then swinging her arms wide. "Thank god they made us from someplace cool and not, like, Kansas City or something. I can't wait to see him again."

Well, at least she'd gotten our cover story out there. Maybe now everyone would know and I wouldn't have to answer questions about our supposed past.

"That's great, Darcy, really." I was glad that she seemed to have forgotten all the attention Joaquin had showered on me when we'd first gotten there. And her anger toward me for it. Apparently, her Darcy charm had worked its magic.

As we turned up a side street and headed for the center of town, a cold breeze sent a skitter down my spine and I had an overwhelming feeling that I was being watched. I turned around slowly, checking each of the windows, but most of the curtains were drawn. There was nothing.

While I stood, Darcy had walked ahead and was almost at the top of the hill. I hugged myself as I passed an old, overgrown playground. It had two swings, one slide, and a set of rusty monkey bars. The fence was broken, and weeds had overtaken the one bench meant for watchful parents. It was the first ugly thing I'd seen on the island, and my steps automatically slowed again. One of the swings creaked back and forth in the ocean breeze, its tempo even, like a ticking clock.

Up ahead, Darcy turned left and disappeared from view. Out of the corner of my eye, I noticed a scrap of tan corduroy fabric stuck to one of the rusty fence links. The exact same color as the jacket Steven Nell was wearing when he'd attacked me.

My throat constricted with dread. I whirled around, but there was no one there. Pressing my lips together, I tugged the scrap of fabric free. Sewn into the wide wale were two small, square patches. One was checkered white and blue. The other was blue around the edge, with a white square inside of the outline and a solid red square at the center. They looked like flags sailors used to signal to passing boats. Nell hadn't had anything like that on his jacket.

I took a deep breath and blew it out. I had to chill. Steven Nell didn't own the only piece of tan corduroy on the planet. I pocketed the scrap and took off at a jog after my sister.

Ten seconds later, I skidded onto Main Street, where I could see the general store at the end of the block. In the park at the center of town, two men played boccie while the minstrel boy sang a reggae version of "The Remedy" under the banner advertising that Friday's fireworks display.

The boy bopped his head as he sang and played his guitar. He'd drawn a crowd, and one guy was playing air drums to the beat. I saw Tristan and Fisher approach the group from the opposite direction, and my heart skipped. Every time I saw Tristan, it was like I was surprised all over again by how gorgeous he was—his blond hair grazing those insane cheekbones, his deep tan, his strong-looking arms. He glanced over at me, then quickly trained his attention on the singer. I blushed at being caught staring.

Fisher was eating an ice-cream bar, and I saw him crinkle up the wrapper and start to throw it over his shoulder, but Tristan stopped him with a hand to his arm. He said something, and Fisher shrugged, tucking the wrapper into his pocket. Guess Tristan was green as well as beautiful.

"You know, he's actually not that bad," Darcy mused, nodding along to the minstrel's song.

I rolled my eyes. That was Darcy for you. Mocking something one day, loving it the next.

"Come on," I said. "Let's check out the general store."

We walked to the end of the street, and Darcy put her hand on the door, then froze, staring at something over her shoulder. Hovering over the ocean on a bluff at the southernmost point of the island was a huge house with a wraparound porch. It was painted blue with intricate, carved details around the many windows and dozens of flowerpots hanging from the porch. It had two turrets, almost like a castle, and gable windows facing the town, plus a huge patio with vine-covered trellises surrounding it. Atop one of the turrets was a golden weathervane with a swan motif, which I noticed was pointing due north, even though the wind was definitely blowing in from the west.

"Is that a hotel?" I asked.

"It has to be," Darcy said. "Either that or someone stinking rich lives there."

We turned to walk into the general store, but the door opened and we both jumped back as Joaquin exited.

"Hey, Rory," he said in his deep voice, giving me an *aren't you glad you bumped into me* kind of smile.

"Um, hi," I said, glancing over at Darcy.

"And Darcy!" he added quickly. He was wearing a black polo shirt with an embroidered swan on the left breast pocket, the words THIRSTY SWAN sewn in cursive over its head. I noticed Darcy admiring his biceps as he twisted the lid off a bottle of iced tea.

"Hi!" she said. "I thought you were working a double shift today."

"I am." He took a swig, then recapped the bottle and moved away from the door to let a pair of girls pass by into the store. I recognized them as the girls who had been talking to Aaron last night, but they didn't bother to say hi. "I just came over here for lunch."

"Oh. Us, too," Darcy said.

Neither of us had said a word about lunch, but it was like she had to agree with everything he said.

"Too bad I missed you," he said, looking her up and down. "I wouldn't have minded having the Thayer girls as my arm candy."

She blushed a deep red. I tried not to vomit. He stepped toward us, forcing us to part so that he could get through.

"You guys should come by the Swan tonight," he said, pausing near the edge of the sidewalk and looking directly at me.

"Why?" I said.

Darcy smacked my arm with the back of her hand.

"Because I'll be there," he replied. The glint in his eye was half teasing, half cocky.

"Ha-ha," I said flatly.

"I'm really not getting any love from you, am I?" he asked, still smiling.

My sister's obvious worship wasn't enough for him?

"No, really," he added when I didn't bother answering. "Everyone hangs out there. It's kind of our thing."

"Cool. We're in," Darcy said, pushing her hands into the back pockets of her jeans, which forced her chest up and out.

I shot her a look. There were only so many times we could get away with sneaking out.

"Cool," Joaquin said. "Just head down to the docks and look for the carving of the drunk swan. You can't miss it."

Then he flipped open a pair of aviator sunglasses, slid them up his nose with one finger, and strode away. I couldn't help noticing that every female he passed on the street, from the twelve-year-old with the ice-cream cone to the geriatric with the blue hair, turned to check him out.

"Why do you like that guy?" I asked Darcy as soon as he was out of earshot.

"How can you *not* like that guy?" she asked.

Because he was cocky. Because he was too sure of himself and obviously a player. Plus even after their supposed bonding session last night, he kept talking to me like she wasn't even there.

"We're not going out tonight," I told her, thinking back to the fog that enveloped me on the beach. Imagined laugh or no, staying in seemed like a much safer option.

"Yes, we are," she replied, yanking open the door to the general store.

"No. We're not," I shot back.

Darcy groaned loudly and stormed inside ahead of me. She was already trying on sunglasses at a wire rack as I closed the door behind us. Slowly, I made my way around the store and up and down the three short aisles. The place stocked everything from cereal to gardening gloves to underwear, but there was no magazine section. That was odd. I thought people in vacation towns were always clamoring for the latest issues of *Us Weekly* or whatever to read on the beach.

I approached the counter, where a woman with white hair was drying off tall soda-fountain glasses. She had on a blue-and-white gingham dress and a white, lace-trimmed apron.

"Excuse me," I said.

Her smile was brighter than the sun outside. "What can I do ya for, hon?"

"Do you have any newspapers?" I asked.

She chucked her chin toward the register. "Have at 'em. They're free." Next to the old-fashioned change return was a stack of folded paper that looked something like my school newspaper, which only printed four times a year. I walked over and lifted the top copy.

THE DAILY REGISTER:

JUNIPER LANDING'S ONE AND ONLY NEWS SOURCE

The first article was titled A DAY IN THE LIFE OF A JL LIFE-GUARD. Under the headline was a huge photograph of a smiling Joaquin Marquez.

"That's it?" I blurted.

"People come here to get away from it all," the woman said with a shrug. Then she shoved through the swinging door behind the counter and disappeared into the kitchen.

Unbelievable. "I'm going outside!" I shouted to Darcy.

"Whatever," she replied.

The bell tinkled again as I shoved through the door and dropped into the first wire chair. I quickly flipped through the thin rag, my hopes falling with each turn of the page. There were stories on the upcoming Founder's Day parade, a piece on a local jeweler, and a notice about a round-table the mayor was hosting, but there was no national news page. Not even a column. Not one single mention of Roger Krauss/Steven Nell or the "unnamed teenage girl" he'd attacked in the woods outside Princeton. Back home, our story had been front-page news every morning and splashed across all the local stations. It had been on CNN and *Dateline*.

But here in Juniper Landing, it was as if neither one of us even existed.

NEW THINGS

The wet suit was surprisingly comfortable, once all the neoprene had been stretched and adjusted and smoothed out. But thank god I had never been all that self-conscious about my body, because this thing showed every last curve of it. I stepped into the cool bay water and walked over to where Aaron was standing in a similar suit, though his was two shades of blue and modern, while mine was plain black and looked like something out of a 1950s spy movie.

"So. What do you think?" he asked, clapping his hands and rubbing them together.

I looked down at the red-and-white flowered windsurfing

board, its sail waterlogged on the opposite side. It wasn't until that moment that I felt the sheer force of the wind and heard it trying to rip a tunnel through my ear. Just a few yards out, the water was choppy and peppered with white-caps. Off in the distance, I saw the top points of the bridge sticking out above the ever-present fog, which clung to the water just north of us even though the sky was bright blue over our heads. I felt a chill at the mere sight of the swirling mist.

"I think I might be insane," I said.

A definite possibility after last night's panicked fog episode and the humming I may or may not have heard on our porch. Not that I'd be telling him about any of that.

Aaron laughed and stepped onto the board like it was nothing. "You're going to love it." He grabbed a rope attached to the sail with one hand and held the other out to me. "We'll go out together the first time, and once you see how simple it is, we'll come back in and get you your own board."

That idea was slightly less terrifying.

"Now get up here," he said with a grin.

My heart pounding, I took his hand. He pulled me up and slid me in front of him. He bent down to the side and tugged on the rope until the sail slowly rose up out of the water. My feet slipped and I almost went down, but Aaron somehow steadied me against his chest while continuing to hoist the sail with both hands.

"Hold on to the sail and lean back into me," he said, once it was up all the way. There was a bar in front of us, and I clung to it for dear life. He quickly grabbed a nylon rope and swung it around our waists, lashing us to each other and the mast. He was so self-assured and so quick I felt my pulse start to race.

"The three most important things are that you hold on to the sail, you keep leaning back, and you keep your feet as close to the mast as you possibly can," he said in my ear. "I'm going to turn the board to get us going."

"Okay." I nodded, looking down at my feet. My toes were curled, gripping the slippery surface for dear life, and the muscles in my arches were already starting to ache. "Where did you learn to do all this?"

His arms and feet were both working, moving the board around beneath our feet. I stepped up and down, too, feeling every second like I was going to lose my balance and splat face-first into the water. But then, I supposed that would be another first.

"My father taught me," he said. "We vacation every Christmas in St. Croix. My whole family windsurfs."

"That's cool," I said.

I couldn't imagine my whole family doing anything

together. Well, anything other than running away from a serial killer. My heart thumped at the thought of Steven Nell, but as fast as I could, I shoved it aside. I didn't want to be afraid. Not now. Right now I wanted to try something new. I wanted to be free.

The wind had just caught the sail, and all of a sudden we lurched ahead, headed out into the open bay. I pitched forward, but Aaron quickly locked his arms close to my sides, squeezing my shoulders to steady me, and I was able to right myself.

"Lean back!" he shouted to be heard over the wind. "Lean into me."

I did as I was told, letting my body graze his.

"Not enough!" he shouted. "You have to trust me, Rory. Lean into me."

I gulped down my fear, let my elbows relax, and leaned back. Instantly I could feel the difference. The board was more balanced and I felt ten times safer with my body against his.

"There you are," he said. "Keep your knees bent so if the board jumps you can absorb the impact."

I relaxed my knees. The board jumped and hopped, but it wasn't long before I found the rhythm and we were moving together like pros. Or at least like we'd done this before.

"In a little bit, I'll teach you how to tack, but for now, just sit back and enjoy the ride."

I took a deep breath and let it out slowly. The sun was warm on my face even as the wind whipped my wet hair back from my eyes. Aaron had complete control of the board, and I relaxed just a bit on the sail. I gazed off at the horizon, taking in the blue sky, the diving seagulls, the salty tanginess of the water. We jumped a particularly big wave, and I let out a shout of joy, giving myself over to the ride.

An hour later, I staggered up the bay beach and dropped on my side into the warm sand. Every muscle in my body was jelly. My shoulders ached. My feet were on fire. My face was so windburned I was going to need a galloon of aloe. But I couldn't wipe the smile off my face.

Aaron dropped, sprawled out next to me, and rolled over onto his back, letting out a satisfied groan.

"You can't tell me that wasn't the most fun you've ever had in your life," he said, squinting one eye as he looked over at me.

I pushed myself up onto my quivering elbows and looked at our two windsurfing boards, which were being hauled out of the water at the shoreline by the rental crew.

"You're right. I can't tell you that," I said.

I sat all the way up and tipped my head back to watch the clouds chase each other across the sky. Sand clung to every inch of my wet suit, and my face prickled with windburn, but I'd never felt better in all my life. I felt accomplished. I felt free. I felt alive.

"Thanks for bringing me out here," I said. "I needed this."

There were green and gold flecks in his brown eyes and a streak of sand stuck to his cheek. "Any time, Rory Thayer."

My pulse stopped. Aaron was my new friend, and yet he didn't even know my real name or anything about where I came from. But that was a good thing, I reminded myself. That meant I was safe. That he was safe. And as I lay there, the sun warming my body and the soothing honeysuckle-scented air enveloping my senses, I thought maybe, just maybe, everything would turn out okay.

THE THIRSTY SWAN

As soon as my sneakered foot stepped through the door of the Thirsty Swan on Monday night, I wanted to turn around and go home. Every last one of the wooden tables was jam-packed with people and every person in the place looked to be twenty-five or younger. The music was loud, conversations were held at a shout, and every so often a raucous round of laughter would burst forth from some corner of the room. Three walls were completely made up of screen windows overlooking the bay, and the cool breeze circulated throughout the room, mixing the salty sea air with the scents of frying foods and spilled beer.

"This is awesome!" Darcy cried, watching as two guys at the bar raced through a set of shot glasses, each filled with a dark brown liquid.

"Actually, I think it's kind of illegal," I replied, as one of the guys woozily slammed his last shot glass down. Everyone around him cheered, including Fisher and Kevin. The kid looked to be about fourteen years old. I scanned the crowd for Aaron, but he was nowhere to be found. I'd mentioned it to him this afternoon, but apparently he was smart enough to avoid this particular scene.

"Rory!" Joaquin shouted from behind the bar. He leaned into the counter as we approached, and smirked. "I knew you couldn't stay away."

I felt Darcy stiffen next to me.

"Actually, I'm only here to be Darcy's wingman," I said. "You remember Darcy, right?" I added pointedly, gesturing at my sister.

"Loyalty. I like it," he said, ignoring my dig. "Hey, Darce," he said, lifting his chin at her. "Why don't you guys have a seat?" He gestured toward three free stools at the end of the bar. Krista waved at us from the fourth, next to the wall.

"Hey, guys," she said, patting the stool to her left. "Saved you a seat, Ror."

Darce? Ror? Really? Hadn't we just met these people?

I sat down next to Krista while Darcy took the stool at the far end, leaving one open between us. It made me feel conspicuous and awkward, which was probably what she was hoping for. Tristan was busy cutting limes at the back counter. In front of him was a huge mirrored wall, lined with long shelves full of liquor bottles. He didn't say hello or even look up from his task. Joaquin turned sideways and slipped by him, then leaned one hand into the bar in front of me. His leather bracelet clung to his skin so tightly it looked uncomfortable.

"What can I get you?" he asked.

"Water, please," I said.

"Whatever you have on tap," Darcy responded, slipping off her leather jacket.

"You got it," he said with a smile.

"You're going to serve her?" I asked, surprised.

"Rory!" Darcy said, glaring at me.

Tristan looked over briefly, caught my eye, then went back to his limes.

"He serves everybody," Krista said with a shrug. She looked like a supermodel in a colorful maxi dress, tasteful jewelry, and, of course, her leather bracelet. As if noticing my stare, she placed her hand over the leather band. "That's our Joaquin."

"Not my job to tell people what they can and can't do,"

Joaquin replied, filling a beer stein to the brim. "But I like that you have a healthy sense of morality, Rory."

Krista smiled at this, and I couldn't help but wonder if they were making fun of me somehow. With a sigh, she withdrew a coin from her pocket and held it upright on the counter with the tip of her finger. As she flicked it to make it spin, I noticed it wasn't any regular American coin. It was about the size of a quarter, but light bronze in color, and I wondered what country it came from. Were the Parrishes world travelers? I didn't have time to see the etching, though, before it was rotating across the counter. Tristan glanced over and his eyes widened slightly. He slapped his hand down over the coin and slid it back to her.

"Don't play with that," he said through his teeth.

She rolled her eyes and pocketed the coin. "Was that the hundredth time you've told me what to do today, or just the ninety-ninth?" she quipped. Tristan ignored her and went back to his work.

I glanced at Darcy to see if she'd noticed the odd exchange, but she was too busy staring at Joaquin as he placed both our glasses down in front of us, then moved off to help someone else. Darcy sipped her beer, and I saw her trying not to wince. I forced myself not to roll my eyes and took a gulp of water.

"So have you guys been to the general store yet?" Krista

asked, turning to lean back against the counter now. It was as if she was working herself through a series of preset poses.

"We went this afternoon," Darcy replied, taking another sip.

"Oh! Too bad I missed you," Krista said with a small pout. "I would have hooked you up with free ice cream."

"You work there?" I asked.

"Yep," she said, rolling her eyes again. "Mom insisted I get a job. Gotta keep up ap—"

Tristan tossed a towel at her face, where it clung to her hair and covered everything down to her mouth. She pulled it off slowly, turning bright red.

"Thanks a lot, *bro*," she said sarcastically, whipping it back at him. He snatched it out of the air and gave her a warning look. "He thinks family matters should stay in the family," she explained.

I glanced over at Tristan, whose face looked a bit pink, too. "What's up, guys?"

Olive slid onto the stool next to mine, filling the void between me and Darcy. "Can you believe this place?" Olive asked, smirking as a guy at the other end of the bar did a spit-take with his drink and everyone laughed. "It's like spring break on steroids."

As if on cue, a group of girls near the windows let out a resounding "Wooo-wooo!"

Olive and I locked eyes and cracked up.

"Hey, Olive."

My heart warmed at the sound of Tristan's voice.

"Hey, T," she replied in a familiar way, adjusting the sleeve of her flowy black top.

"Hello," I said pointedly, trying to highlight the fact that he hadn't greeted me or Darcy yet.

He turned to gaze at me but said nothing. The blue of his eyes was a deep, almost Caribbean Ocean color, solid and flat, unmarked by variation or flecks. He wore a light blue Thirsty Swan T-shirt that showed off his chest muscles and brought out his dark tan.

"Can I get you anything, Olive?" he asked, still looking at me.

"You know me, T," she replied, fiddling with a cocktail napkin. "Diet Coke, straight up."

He gave her a small smile, the first I'd seen on him, and it changed his face completely. If possible, it made him even handsomer.

"On it."

He turned away and grabbed a clean glass.

Olive nudged me. "So I've been thinking about this whole running thing, and I've decided to give it a try," she said, standing up on the rung of her stool and reaching over the bar for a swizzle stick. She placed it between her lips and chewed on the end. "You wanna go with me tomorrow?"

"I'd love to go for a run!" Krista enthused.

"You don't run," Tristan said, placing Olive's Diet Coke in front of her.

"But I—"

"Aren't you working tomorrow anyway?" he asked.

Krista's face fell, and she pouted again. "Fine," she said through her teeth as Tristan moved away to fill a glass for another customer.

I gnawed at my bottom lip, considering. I hadn't been out for a run since we'd gotten here, and I knew I'd never go by myself, not with the specter of Steven Nell hovering over me.

Still, beneath my stool, my feet bounced crazily, itching at the idea of a good workout. "Why not?" I said finally. "There's safety in numbers, right?"

"Safety?" Joaquin asked, rejoining us. "What're you worried about?"

My face flushed. Dammit. Why had I said that out loud? I shot Darcy a *save me* glance, but she was frozen, her lips on the rim of her glass. Tristan came over and slapped Joaquin on the back, but he paused when he noticed the tableau of me and Darcy in suspended *oops* mode and Olive, Krista, and Joaquin waiting for my response.

"Okay. What did I just walk in on?" Tristan asked.

"We were just going to find out why Rory's worried about her safety," Krista said as Joaquin leaned his elbows on the counter.

Darcy placed her glass down and cleared her throat.

"Oh," Tristan said, a shadow passing through his eyes. "That sounds ominous."

My heart pounded horribly.

And when you get where you're going, you can't tell anyone who you really are or where you're from or why you're there, Agent Messenger's voice said in my ear. *For your safety and theirs.*

"It's not. I just . . . I don't like to run by myself," I improvised, taking another gulp of water. "It's always better to go out with a buddy."

"But you said you liked to be Zen," Olive told me. "You said that was what you loved about it."

"I did say that, didn't I?" I said. I returned the glass to the counter with a clatter. "I just—I don't know." My whole body burned as everyone around me stared. God, I hated this. "Um, running around a strange place . . . not knowing where you're going . . . it just seems smarter to have someone with you, right? I just . . . I . . . I just—"

"Rory, there's nothing to worry about." Out of nowhere, Tristan reached for my hand, placing his fingers on top of mine. I instantly went rigid. Darcy, Olive, Krista, and Joaquin all stared down at our hands, but Tristan didn't seem to notice. His skin was impossibly warm, his fingertips comfortingly calloused, and his touch sent goose bumps up my arm. "Juniper Landing is practically the safest place in the universe. Honestly. Nothing bad ever happens here."

I gazed into his eyes, breathless, and believed every word he said. Or at least, I believed that he believed it. My heart rate began to slow. When Tristan broke contact and swiped some lime rinds and napkins into a small garbage can, my fingers tingled where his hand had been. I had a sudden mental image of melting into him and was so startled by it I actually had to shake my head to clear it away.

Tristan grabbed up the garbage can and shoved it back under the counter. I got a clear look inside as he did so and felt a snap in my brain, like whiplash. Even though he'd just tossed debris in there, the garbage can was empty.

Olive narrowed her eyes at me. "Are you okay? Your face is bright red."

Tristan wiped his hands on his half apron, like nothing was amiss.

"Oh, um. I'm fine. I'm just going to . . . run to the bathroom," I fumbled, pushing off my stool. What I needed was a minute to collect myself. Not only was I the worst liar on the planet, but now, it seemed, I couldn't even trust my own eyes.

I sidestepped a drunken staggerer and was weaving my way through the tables toward the screen wall, when abruptly the music on the jukebox changed. The dance tune that had been playing cut off abruptly, and suddenly a familiar, reedy tune filled the bar. "The Long and Winding Road." I stopped moving. Stopped breathing.

"*Rory Miller*," someone whispered.

My heart turned to stone. I turned around. And around. And around.

"*Rory Miller*," the same voice whispered again.

Someone was saying my name. Except no one in Juniper Landing knew that name. To them I was Rory Thayer.

Suddenly, I was running through the woods, my neck wet with sweat, my heart pounding in panic. Darkness everywhere. A snap of a twig. A laugh. A horrible, horrible laugh.

Someone slammed into my shoulder.

"Ow!" I said aloud, crashing back to the present.

"Sorry," some dude in a flannel shirt said sarcastically, looking me up and down like I was a freak.

My eyes darted across the room. Darcy still sat eyeing Joaquin longingly. Olive was making some kind of artwork on the bar with swizzle sticks and pretzels while Tristan stood with his back to me behind the counter, gazing intently at something I couldn't see. Fisher and Kevin were leaning into the counter, whispering something to Joaquin. All at once, the three of them turned to look over at me, their expressions blank, and I quickly glanced away. There

were kids in baseball caps, girls in tight skirts, a couple arguing near the bathroom. But nowhere, nowhere, nowhere was
Steven Nell.

I stood there for a moment longer, listening. There was
nothing. Nothing other than shouting, laughter, and that
awful music. But when I glanced one last time at the bar, I
saw Tristan watching me again as well, his eyes bluer than
ever, staring at me like he knew every detail of my life.

Even my real name.

RUN

"I think Joaquin is the hottest guy I've ever met," Darcy said as we stepped onto the boardwalk outside the Thirsty Swan. "Way hotter than Christopher, don't you think?"

I shot her a quick glance, but she was too busy tipping her head back to gaze at the stars. Christopher. I hadn't thought about him all day. I guess between Aaron and Tristan and Olive and Joaquin, plus all the potentially-losing-my-mind fun, I'd been kind of distracted.

"Sure. I guess," I said carefully, listening to the sound of the bay water gently lapping against the pylons as we walked. It was a relief to be out of the bar and away from the noise. Away from that crowd and the jukebox with its oddly disconcerting selections.

Every time I thought about that song coming on, about that whisper, about the humming I'd heard the other day, the laughter in the fog, and the scrap of fabric in the park, my heart seized up painfully and I felt like I wanted to scream. If I didn't talk it out with someone, I was going to go crazy.

"Darcy, I have something to tell you, but please don't freak out," I said.

She stopped walking and eyed me with interest. "What?"

"I thought I heard Steven Nell in the bar tonight," I said.

My sister's jaw dropped. It was almost like she'd expected me to say one thing, and I'd done a one-eighty on her. "*What?*"

"Someone whispered my name. And not Rory Thayer, Rory Miller," I said. "Didn't you hear 'The Long and Winding Road' on the jukebox?"

Darcy blinked. "Yeah, but the Beatles are the most popular band ever," she pointed out.

"And I heard someone humming it outside our house the other morning, too," I persisted. "Then this morning, I found this scrap of fabric in the park that looked just like that tan jacket he always wore."

For a long moment, she just stared at me, like she was waiting for more. "That's it?"

"What do you mean, that's it?" I squeaked. "That's not enough?"

"Rory," she said, clucking her tongue impatiently. "Did you ever stop to think that maybe you're just hearing things?"

"Hearing things?" I repeated.

She lifted her shoulders. "I don't know. Maybe it's like your flashes—a symptom of post-traumatic stress. It totally makes sense that it's happening again, right? I mean, you were almost killed."

I gritted my teeth. "This wasn't like the flashes, Darcy," I told her. "I can tell the difference between the flashes and reality. I know what I saw! I know what I heard!"

Darcy rolled her eyes and groaned. "Can we please just go? It's getting cold out here."

I should have known she'd never take me seriously. In Darcy's world, nothing bad ever happened. And if it did, she just ignored it or never talked about it. Like after my mom died. All Darcy did was make more friends, buy more clothes at the mall, go to more parties. She never got depressed or nostalgic; she never wanted to reminisce. She was too busy having fun. Too busy moving forward.

"Fine," I said tightly. "Let's go."

We were just about to turn off the boardwalk and head toward town when I saw something shift out on the water.

The air seemed to be moving. I grabbed Darcy's arm, my throat going dry. It was the fog again, and it was rolling in quickly.

"Darcy, look!" I whispered.

"What? Is Steven Nell hanging out on one of the boats?"

By the time she turned her head, the mist was already swirling around us. The odd hissing sound started my pulse pounding in my ears. Darcy was so tense I could practically feel it coming off of her in bursts.

"Come on. It's getting late." Darcy started up the hill and completely disappeared. The fog swallowed her whole. Heart in my throat, I lunged forward and sprinted a few steps until I caught sight of her calves—two white stripes flashing in the grayness as she speed-walked ahead of me.

"Darcy!" I whispered. "Slow down."

"Why don't *you* keep up, track star?" she shot back.

I tried, but the fog was too disorienting. At the top of the hill, my foot hit an uneven crack in the sidewalk, and my ankle twisted. By the time I'd righted myself, my sister had vanished again entirely.

"Darcy!" I hissed, turning around in the mist. "Darcy! Where are you?"

No answer. Nothing but the hiss of the undulating mist.

"Darcy?" I whimpered.

"I'm right here!" Her voice was practically in my ear.

"You scared the crap out of me," I whispered, flinging my arm out. My hand hit her shoulder. I'd had no clue she was standing that close.

"Ow!" she said.

I reached to take her hand so we wouldn't get separated again. "Is that really necessary?" she griped, trying to pull away.

"Yes. Yes, it is," I replied, crushing her fingers.

"God! Fine! Just loosen it up, would you?"

I did. But only slightly.

Matching our steps, we cut diagonally across the wet grass of the park and headed down the hill toward our house. I could hear the surf rolling into the shore up ahead and started to relax. We were almost there. Almost safe.

Then, somewhere deep inside the fog, someone laughed.

Darcy and I both froze. She squeezed my hand so hard I felt a pop.

"Did you hear that?" she said.

"Yes," I breathed.

It came again. Another laugh. A low, menacing sort of chuckle. "Darcy?" I whispered hoarsely.

"Run," she ordered.

We turned and tore off down the street, tripping off the unseen edge of the sidewalk and stumbling across the wide road. The fog tugged at my hair as I ran, pulling it from my cheeks and leaving its warm, moist trail along my skin. My toe hit the opposite curb, and I flew forward, going weightless, but Darcy stopped my fall with a stiff yank on my arm.

"The gate is up here!" she whispered.

We whirled around and screamed as we ran headfirst into someone's chest. A strong hand clamped around my upper arm. I was about to start begging for our lives when I recognized the evergreen scent of my dad's shower gel.

"Girls! Get inside! Now!" my father demanded.

I felt like my heart was going to burst. Darcy clung to my side, and we staggered through the open gate, up the steps, and into our house. The bright lights stung my eyes after the darkness of the street, and it took me a second to focus. My father slammed the door behind us, and I lunged to double lock it.

"What were you thinking?" my father fumed, whirling on us. "You leave the house without telling me? Stay out past midnight? What do you think this is, some kind of vacation?"

Darcy crossed her arms over her chest. "What do you expect us to do? Stay locked up in here all the time?"

"Yes!" he screamed, shaking as his face turned fuchsia. "That's exactly what I expect you to do! We don't know anyone in this town. You two could have been hurt! Or killed!"

"But we weren't!" Darcy pointed out angrily. "We're fine!"

But my dad didn't seem to hear her. "From now on, you two are grounded. No leaving the house at night. And during the day you're to tell me exactly where you're going and who you're going with. No discussions."

He turned and started to stomp up the stairs.

"But, Dad," Darcy whined.

"Don't talk back to me!" he roared. "It's for your own safety."

Darcy's eyes flashed. "When was the last time you asked me where I was going at night? When I was coming home after school? Who my friends were? Who my boyfriend was?" she ranted, tears spilling over onto her dark red cheeks. "You never ask me anything! You never listen to anything I say! And now all of a sudden you want to tell me what to do, who I can see, where I can go? No! No way! You can't just suddenly decide to be a father again after five years of complete silence!"

She shoved past him and barreled up the stairs.

"Darcy!" he shouted after her.

"No!" she screamed back. And then her door slammed.

I stood against the wall, staring at our family photo on the table with blurry eyes, trying to catch my breath. Darcy had talked back to my father before, but never like that.

She'd never screamed at him. Never laid out all his faults. And now here we were, the two of us, standing amid the destruction of her nuclear bomb.

After a long moment, I heard my dad sigh. I looked up, one tear spilling free, and he gazed back at me. His eyes were heavy and sad. His posture curled. For the first time in a long time, he looked sorry.

"I'm just gonna go to bed," I said quietly.

He sank down on the stairs, as if the air had been let out of him. By the time I slipped past him, he had his face buried in his hands. I thought of what I'd heard last night, him sobbing alone in his room, and my heart went out to him.

"G'night, Dad," I said, realizing I hadn't said it in an impossibly long time.

He didn't reply at first, but when I got to the top of the stairs, he turned and looked up at me, tears shining in his eyes.

"Good night, Rory."

GIFTS

This island was not stingy with its gifts. The fog. The fantastic fog. Its blinding quality was so complete. So utterly encompassing. It was like nothing he'd ever seen or heard of or read about, but it was lovely. It was empowering.

He'd been so close to her tonight. So very, very close. He'd tasted her fear again, so sweet and salty. It was all he could do to keep from reaching out and plucking a strand of that hair for himself. To taste it again. To own it. The possibility was almost too much to bear.

But now was not the time. He had already set his plot in motion and could not risk it now. This time, everything was going to happen as planned. This time, nothing and no one would stop him. This time, she would be his.

PERFECT

My thigh muscles were on fire, and my calves were cramping. There was a blister forming on the side of my big toe, and sweat soaked the back of my gray T-shirt. My lungs burned, my eyes watered, and my neck itched whenever my hair brushed against it.

I was in heaven. Why had I waited so long to do this?

As I came around a bend in the trail, the top of the bluff loomed into view. For the first mile, Olive had kept pace with me, panting at my side. After that, she'd dropped back, and now there was nothing but the crashing surf and whipping wind. I hoped she was okay, because I was *not* about to stop. This was way too much fun. Imagining the finish line up ahead, I turned on the heat and pushed myself into a sprint for the last incline. As soon as I reached the top, I let out a triumphant, euphoric laugh. I slowed my steps to a walk and held my fingers to my neck to check my pulse.

Perfect. Everything, at this moment, was perfect. I decided to relish it. Relish the sun on my face, the clean air whooshing in and out of my lungs, that lovely floral scent all around me. I wasn't going to think about the weird gray house or the scrap of fabric or the whispers, the laughing, or the humming. I wasn't even going to ponder the fact that Darcy had refused to take me seriously last night, or that my dad hadn't come out of his room this morning. I was just going to stand here and breathe.

Just beneath me on the hill was a small outcropping with a pretty white gazebo at its center, and farther below I could see the roof of our house on Magnolia Street. Beyond that, the ocean went on forever. I reached my arms over my head and stretched.

My mother would have loved this place. She lived for the beach, for quaint little shopping towns. The gardens here would have had her falling over with envy, and I could just imagine her peppering the locals with questions about how they got their tulips to bloom so late in the season and whether her roses needed more or less pruning. I felt a pang of sadness, wishing she were here in this place that seemed tailor-made for her, and did my best to brush it aside. Those pangs were part of my life now—they would be forever—and while I sometimes let myself wallow in them, this was not one of those times. Not when I was trying to appreciate the perfect.

To my left, a thin, paved walkway cut into the grass, which eventually broke off in two directions. One led right to the big blue house Darcy had noticed yesterday, the other toward the street where it turned into a wide sidewalk. I walked over to a bench situated right at the fork in the path and set myself up behind it for a calf stretch while I waited for Olive. As soon as I turned my back to the house, I felt a chill as if someone was watching me and glanced over my shoulder. The hanging plants swung in the breeze, and the weathervane atop the roof held a position of due south. Otherwise, the place was still.

"God, you weren't kidding when you said you were a runner!" Olive said between gasps when she finally joined me a good five minutes later. She dropped down onto the bench and put her head between her knees. Her long-sleeved gray-and-black striped T-shirt was saturated with sweat. "You're wicked fast."

"Eh, I'm a solid third-placer," I said, lifting one shoulder.

Her eyes went wide. "Third place? Do the people who come in first have wings on their feet?"

I laughed and reached back to grab my ankle to stretch my quads. "So I guess you've decided running's not your thing?"

"Not even a little bit," Olive said, holding her hand to her heart as she tried to regulate her breathing.

I gave her a wry smile. "Well, thanks, anyway, for getting me to come out with you. This was exactly what I needed. For the last half hour, I didn't have one serious thought."

"No problem," Olive replied. She tugged her headband out of her hair. "Do you usually have a lot of serious thoughts?"

My heart thumped at all the thoughts darkening my mind—thoughts that I couldn't share. I walked around and sat next to her, resting my forearms across my knees.

"Things have just been really . . . tough for my family lately," I hedged.

Olive pursed her lips. "I hear you." She stuffed her headband into the pocket of her shorts, bulky cargo things that were not made for running, and leaned back, crooking her arms behind her head. "Of course, I'm the one who made things tough, so . . ."

She trailed off, pulling her feet up onto the bench and looking past my shoulder to the west. In that direction were the docks of the boatyard and about half a dozen boats bobbing peacefully on the bay. Looming in the distance to the north was the bridge, surrounded, as always, by thick fog. There was something mesmerizing about all that slowly swirling gray mist. From a distance, it wasn't as terrifying.

"How so?" I asked.

She looked me in the eye, and the depth of the sadness and regret I saw there made something flip inside me.

"I mean, you don't have to tell me if you don't want to," I backtracked.

"Nah, it's just . . . for the last few years I wasn't exactly the best daughter. And then one day I up and left," Olive said, lifting her shoulders. "I'm better now . . . I mean, I got myself better, but I know I really hurt my mom. I did things . . ." She sighed ruefully and shook her head. "Well, anyway, I have to apologize to her, to find a way to make it up to her, I just . . . don't know how."

"I'm so sorry," I told her, not knowing what else to say.

I was no good at this kind of thing. I'd never really had any close friendships, unless Darcy counted, and even that felt like a million years ago. Olive looked around and up at the sky, and I saw that there were tears in her eyes. I swallowed hard, hating how stupid and useless I felt.

"What about you?" she asked. "Do you want to talk about what's going on with your family?"

I felt breathless and hot, wishing I could tell her, wishing I could just blurt out the whole insane story. I had a feeling it would make us both feel better, her knowing she wasn't the only one with a depressing past, me because venting it all would be so freeing. But I couldn't. I had to keep it all bottled up inside. Maybe that was why I was having nightmares. Because I had no one to talk to about things. No release.

That was just one more thing Steven Nell had taken from me.

"I can't," I said finally. "It's too . . . complicated."

"I get it," Olive said. "No one knows all the gory details of my life, either. Well, except Tristan." She blushed and looked down at her feet. So Olive liked Tristan. Of course she did. I thought back to that first night on the beach when they'd been so wrapped up in conversation. The familiar way they'd talked with each other at the bar and how she'd kept glancing up at him when he wasn't looking. I felt a flash of jealousy before I remembered that I didn't want Tristan. I wanted Christopher. I just wished he wasn't hundreds of miles away. And my sister's ex.

"But if you ever do want to talk, I'm a fantastic listener," Olive added, nudging me with her shoulder.

I nudged her back. "I believe that." I stood up. "Want to head back to town?"

"Sure. But we're walking, FYI, because I think my legs might revolt if I try for anything faster."

"No problem," I replied with a laugh.

Before we headed toward the street, I turned around to look at the blue house once more. There was something almost foreboding about it, even in its cheerful beauty. It sat up there like some kind of fortress or castle, lording its immense presence over the rest of the quaint town.

"Gorgeous, isn't it?" Olive said, glancing over her shoulder as we strolled downhill. "You should see the inside."

"You've been inside?" I said. "Who lives there?"

Her eyebrows came together, and she looked at me as if I'd just asked her how to spell *the*. "That's Tristan and Krista's house. Their mom's the mayor."

I stopped in my tracks and stared at her, feeling like someone had just yanked the asphalt out from under me.

"Wait. Tristan lives *there*? I thought he lived in the house across the street from me," I said.

"Um, no," she said. "The prince of Juniper Landing lives up here in the castle with the princess and the queen, just as it should be," she said, lifting her nose in the air comically. "Not that they act like a prince and princess. They're just sort of treated that way."

"I would have thought that Joaquin was the prince of this place," I said vaguely.

"Really? I see him as more of a rogue knight," Olive replied.

I supposed everything was perception, and if she liked Tristan, maybe she perceived him as the leader of the pack. But I had yet to see him order anyone around like Joaquin had with Fisher. Tristan seemed more refined. More modest. More comfortable in the shadows.

More like me.

"Interesting," I said, mostly to say something.

I turned and narrowed my eyes at the house, and my heart caught in my throat. Someone was standing on the porch, shaded by the wide overhang, staring down at me.

"Oh my god," I said, angling myself away from the lurker and talking through clenched teeth. I grabbed Olive's arm. "Someone up there is watching us."

Olive followed my gaze. "Where?" she said, her brows furrowing in confusion.

"Right there." Emboldened by her blatant move, I turned back around as well, but then froze. The porch was deserted. Whoever had been there, watching us, had vanished.

CONFRONTATION

My feet pounded against the pavement as I sprinted down-hill toward town. If Tristan lived all the way up here, why the hell was he lurking in the house across the street from mine? Was he there just to watch me? Was he some kind of bizarre stalker keeping an eye on the new girl? And who the hell had been watching me from his *actual* house? I wanted answers, and I wanted them now.

I crossed through town, zipping past our favorite local musician in the park, who was jamming on his guitar with his eyes closed and a smile on. Near the far corner, I caught a couple of disturbed stares from an older couple chilling on a bench. Not that I was surprised. I must have looked like a crazed lunatic, sprinting for all I was worth and completely ignoring the sidewalk. I just hoped Olive hadn't thought I was nuts when I'd blurted that I had to go and taken off, leaving her behind to stare after me.

I ran down the diagonal cut-through street, purposely averting my eyes from the rundown park, and took the corner onto our block, skidding so hard I almost hit the dirt. I was about to beeline it for the gray house, when I saw something hanging off the gate in front of our place across the way.

I stopped short and gasped for breath. It was a gray canvas messenger bag with a frayed strap. Exactly the same bag Steven Nell carried to school every day.

The air was cold and the ground wet against my back. Pine needles pierced my arms. The clouds parted overhead. A perfect half moon and Steven Nell's sadistic smile, his watery eyes, his thin, dry, lips.

A bell trilled and sucked me back into the now. The warm sun tickled my flesh. I blinked as the middle-aged man with his surfboard rode by me with a smile. Aside from him, the street was deserted, but that bag was still there. This couldn't be happening. It couldn't be real.

Part of me wanted to turn around and run straight to the police, but what was I going to tell them? That someone had left a bag on our gate? I was just going to have to deal with this myself. Maybe it was nothing.

Defiantly, I stormed across the road and over to the bag. The flap hung open, practically daring me to look inside. But what was I going to find if I did? A threatening note? A severed hand? What?

Holding my breath, I yanked the bag open. I blinked, surprised. It was filled to the brim with model lighthouses of various sizes. The smallest one was about two inches high, carved of stone and meticulously painted. The largest was about six inches tall, made of crappy plastic and topped by a tiny light that illuminated with the press of a button. There were dozens of them, each with a Juniper Landing swan stamped on its walls.

"Hey."

I whirled around, dropping the bag back where it hung, letting it slam against the fence. Tristan stood right in front of me, looking perfect in a white T-shirt and tan cargo shorts, his blond hair falling forward on his cheeks.

"What the hell?" I shouted, shoving him with both hands as hard as I could. He didn't move an inch, but he did look down at me, surprised. "You scared the crap out of me!"

"I'm sorry," he said, his expression sincere.

Over his shoulder, I saw the door of the gray house

swinging slowly closed. Suddenly, I remembered why I'd sprinted home.

"Why are you always here?" I demanded, crossing my arms over my chest. My face was on fire, and I felt my throat trying to close—my body's way of rejecting confrontation—but I pressed on. "Olive told me you live up on the bluff, so why are you spending so much time in that house?" I said, gesturing across the street. "Why are you always watching me?"

Tristan glanced over his shoulder. "I just . . . I know the person who lives there," he said. Then he shoved his hands under his arms and looked at me squarely, as if that explained everything.

"Oh, yeah? Who? Who lives there?" I demanded.

He frowned slightly. "My nanna," he said. "My grandmother. On my father's side. She's confined to a wheelchair so I . . . we . . . me and Krista try to come visit her whenever we can."

"Oh." Color me guilt-ridden. Here I was, jumping all over his case, and all he was doing was being the perfect grandson.

"She likes to sit and look out the window a lot, so if you see the curtains moving or whatever, it's probably her," he added with a shrug.

"So that was her I saw watching me that first morning?" I asked.

"Probably," he replied. "Actually, I remember her mentioning it. The pretty blond girl moving in across the street."

He stopped and cleared his throat, looking away. Like maybe he'd said too much. Like maybe he agreed with Nanna.

"Oh," I said again, blushing. "Well, that's nice of her."

"Yeah."

Tristan knocked his hands together, and I saw his Adam's apple bob as he pressed his lips into a line. For a long moment, we just stood there, until just standing there felt completely awkward. I was about to make an excuse to go inside when Joaquin came around the corner and strode purposefully over to me, a line creased into his forehead.

"Rory. There you are," he said, his breath slightly ragged. He walked right over to me and enveloped me in a big, warm hug, forcing Tristan to sidestep away from me.

I squirmed and ducked out of the circle of his arms, almost losing my balance. Tristan reached out and quickly steadied me. "Um, what was that for?"

"I just saw Olive in town. Are you okay?" Joaquin asked, holding my wrist. "She said you guys were hanging out when you all of a sudden bolted like you'd seen a ghost."

I glanced at Tristan and blushed. "Oh, that. I'm fine," I said, pulling my arm out of his grip. "I told her I had to get home. Is she mad?"

"Not at all," Joaquin said. "Just worried."

"Well, I'm fine," I repeated, looking from Tristan to Joaquin and back again. Two pieces of perfection—physically, anyway—and all I could think about was getting away from them. The cross-country girls back home would probably have me checked for brain damage. "Anyway, I'd better—"

"So did you invite her yet?" Joaquin asked Tristan.

"I was just about to," Tristan replied.

"Invite me to what?" I asked.

"Tristan and Krista are having a party tomorrow night," Joaquin said, crossing his arms over his chest. "I think you should come."

I felt my blush deepen. "*You* think I should come," I repeated. I glanced at Tristan. "What do you think?"

He blinked, startled. "What? Oh, sure. Yes. You should definitely come. If you want to."

Wow. So one of them expected me to come just because *he* thought I should and the other clearly couldn't care less whether I showed or not.

"That's some invitation, you guys. Thanks," I said sarcastically. "I'll be sure to give it a nice, long consideration."

"Rory," Joaquin said in a condescending tone as I turned to go.

But I didn't stop. I jogged up the steps to the house,

slamming the door behind me and leaning back against it. What was with these guys? Why couldn't they stalk Darcy instead of me? She would have loved every minute of it.

I glanced out the window and saw Joaquin say a few words to Tristan before sauntering off. Once he was gone, Tristan looked down at the gray bag, and I felt my heart skip a beat. I'd momentarily forgotten it was there. He lifted the flap and peeked inside, his brows creasing in confusion. At least I wasn't the only one who thought a bag full of lighthouses was odd. He looked up at my house, and I ducked back behind the wall again.

When I glanced back out the window again, I half expected Tristan to still be standing there, but he was gone. The gray bag, however, remained hanging from the gate, taunting me. I double-checked that the door was locked and then retreated to my room. I hoped whoever had left it there would come back for it soon, but I also didn't want to be here when they did.

SURRENDER

The moment was nearing. The moment when he would finally have what was rightfully his. He had been so close so many times, but now, nothing would stand in his way. Once the last step in his plan was complete, there was no way she would say no to him. There was no way she would resist.

Yes. She would come to him, willingly. And perhaps, perhaps, perhaps . . .

Perhaps that would be the most satisfying end to this pursuit. Knowing that he had broken her, finally. That she wouldn't fight. That her surrender would be complete.

MIRACLE

Wednesday morning I sat at the Formica table in the kitchen, eating cornflakes out of a chipped bowl, watching the old-school phone that hung on the far wall. We'd been in Juniper Landing for four days. It hadn't rung once.

"Okay, what is your deal?" Darcy demanded, striding into the room in her black silk pajamas and pulling out a chair diagonal from mine. She had her hair back in a sleek ponytail and had already washed her face. "Did you cast a spell on this island or something?"

"What're you talking about?" I asked, picking up my bowl to drink the last of the milk.

Darcy watched me with a look of utter disgust and waited for me to put the bowl down again.

"Last night, Joaquin finally asked me out to some party at Tristan's house tonight, and I was all excited until he basically hinted that I had to bring you or I couldn't come," she said, slouching back in her chair with her arms crossed over her spaghetti-strap top.

"Oh, that," I said.

"You know about it already?" Darcy asked, her eyes incredulous.

"They invited me yesterday, too," I told her.

"Unbelievable," she said, shoving the chair back and crossing to the cabinet. "The wallflower is officially off the wall." She grabbed a box of Froot Loops and brought it back to the table. "So would that have been when Joaquin walked up to you outside and gave you that totally intimate hug?"

I felt my skin warm. "You saw that?"

"Everyone on the block saw that," Darcy replied, tossing a Froot Loop into her mouth. "I bet someone out there was inspired to write a blog about it. I don't think there was one inch of your bodies that wasn't touching."

I shuddered. The very thought gave me the skeeves. "Darcy—"

"Are you and Joaquin, like, having a thing behind my back?" she interrupted.

I snorted a laugh. "What?"

Darcy walked around to the far end of the table so she could look me dead in the eye. The expression on her face, the pointed, knowing set of her chin, the slight apprehension in her eyes, made my heart stop. Did she know about Christopher and me? Was that why she was imagining some tryst between me and Joaquin?

"He keeps asking me about you, first of all. And then there's all the hugging and smiling and complimenting . . . Tell me the truth, Rory. I'm a big girl. I can handle it," she said. The tips of her fingers turned white as she gripped the cereal box.

"Darcy, I can one hundred percent guarantee you that I have no interest in Joaquin," I told her firmly. "I promise."

She eyed me for one moment longer before walking back to her chair and digging into the cereal bag with her hand. "Good."

I watched as she came out with a handful of the colorful loops. There was no way she could know about me and Christopher. I hadn't told her, I was sure he hadn't told her, and no one else on Earth knew. I was just being paranoid. As usual.

"What, exactly, did Joaquin say to you?" I asked, leaning my chest into the table. "Why do you think you have to bring me?"

"He fed me some weird thing about there having to be an even number of guys and girls . . ." She trailed off, popping cereal bits in her mouth as she narrowed her eyes. "It made sense at the time, but he *did* have his arm around me, so I was a little distracted . . ."

"What a jerk," I mused, reaching for my orange juice.

"Whatever," Darcy said, placing the box down on the table. "But this is good! You're already going, so no big deal."

This was insane. How could she still want to go? How could she still like this guy after he was feeding her such obvious crap? I was never going to understand Darcy's brain. Never in a million years.

"Except that I'm not going," I said, shoving away from the table.

"Uh, yes, you are," Darcy said.

"No. I'm not," I said as I dumped my bowl and glass into the ceramic sink. God, I wished we were back home. If we were home, I'd be in calculus right now, solving problems I could solve. Not dealing with the quandary of whether I should help keep Darcy's social life alive—a quandary I never thought I'd have to deal with in a million years and had no clue how to handle. "And you're not, either. We're grounded, remember?"

At that moment, my dad stopped inside the open door-way between the kitchen and the entry hall. He was fully dressed in jeans and a T-shirt, his face cleanly shaven and his hair slicked back. He'd started to get a tan, probably from all the running, and he looked different. Healthy.

"Actually, I wanted to talk to you girls about that." He did a double take and his face fell slightly. "Oh. Did you eat already?"

"Not really," Darcy said warily, her cheek still full of cereal.

"I just had cornflakes," I said. "Why?"

"Let's go out to breakfast," he said. "I heard the general store has excellent pancakes."

Darcy and I exchanged a look. Who was this person and what had he done with our real father?

"Um . . . I'd have to get dressed," Darcy said, swallowing.

"Me, too," I added, looking down at the T-shirt and sweatpants I'd slept in. "I can wait," he said with a semblance of a smile.

Neither one of us moved.

"Come on, girls," my father wheedled. "It's just breakfast."

"Okay," I said finally.

"Sure," Darcy added.

Then we both padded out of the room past him.

"What's with him?" Darcy whispered as we climbed the creaky steps.

"I have no idea," I replied, following her into her room.

"Maybe you yelling at him the other night got through to him."

"You think?" she asked, surprised.

"You never know. But I'd be nice to him at breakfast," I said as she slipped inside her closet. I leaned against one of her bedposts and stared across the street at the windows of the gray house. My heart skipped a beat at the very sight of it, but the place was still. "Maybe you can get ungrounded."

"And then you'll go to the party with me?" Darcy asked hopefully, gripping a white sweater to her chest as she came to the closet doorway.

I rolled my eyes but smiled. It was nice, sharing this sisterly moment with her. Feeling hopeful about my dad.

"Fine," I told her. "If, by some miracle, we get ungrounded, I promise I'll go to the party with you."

"Yay!" She jumped up onto her toes, then dove back into the closet to get dressed.

I laughed and started to turn away so I could go get dressed myself, but at that moment, the curtain across the way moved. And this time, I could have sworn I saw a leather bracelet disappear behind it.

AN APOLOGY

Tristan was definitely watching me. Unless good old grandma had a leather bracelet, too. But what about me was so freaking interesting that it had him squatting in a house a tenth the size of his own? And was it possible that it was something innocent? That maybe he just . . . had a crush on me?

"Everything okay, Rory?" my father asked, looking down at me. My skin was burning over my last thought, and I quickly looked away from him. We were just passing the eerily silent park, where the swings hung still and heavy over the scraggly weeds. The gate was pushed all the way open so that it was flush with the fence on the inside, and as usual, there were no kids in sight.

"Fine," I said distractedly. "Why?"

"You just looked . . . serious," he said with a small smile.

Darcy shot me an alarmed look, and I knew she was wondering if I'd just had a flash. I gave her an almost imperceptible shake of the head, and her shoulders relaxed. I hadn't told my father about the flashes because I didn't need him worrying and scouring the Yellow Pages to find me a shrink on the island. Not that I'd seen any Yellow Pages since we'd gotten here, even though back home our mailman was leaving them on our front step, like, every other week. In fact, now that I thought about it, I hadn't seen a mail carrier here, either. Or a mailbox. I glanced around at the houses, and sure enough, not a single mailbox in sight. Huh. Maybe everyone here had their mail delivered directly to a PO box. It wouldn't be the first random, quaint, old-fashioned thing about this island.

"I was just . . . trying to remember the last time we all ate out together," I said in answer to my father.

"Oh. It wasn't that long ago," my dad said vaguely.

Darcy and I exchanged a look. It had to be at least four years ago. The only instance I could even remember was Darcy's thirteenth birthday and an ill-advised trip to Friendly's during which my dad had insisted she eat one of those clown sundae things, as if she were six years old. Since she'd just gotten her first period and started her first diet with no mom around to advise her on either, Darcy had burst into tears and run out of the restaurant. Which was maybe why we hadn't eaten out together since.

We came to the top of the hill and turned onto Main Street. My dad looked up at the sky and smiled.

Now *that* I was *certain* I'd not seen in years. At least not since my mother had died.

Across the street, the fountain at the center of the park burbled and splashed while two guys with shaggy hair and baggy plaid shorts jumped their skateboards off the pool's edge. The banner for the fireworks display flapped in the breeze.

"Hey, Darcy, your Rasta boyfriend's MIA," I joked, pushing my sunglasses up into my hair. The spot at the top of the path where he normally stood seemed oddly lonely without him.

Darcy looked at me blankly. "What?"

"Look," I said, lifting my chin toward the park. "Do you think he made enough money to take his act on the road or something?"

I couldn't see Darcy's eyes behind her dark sunglasses, but her expression was blank as she turned to look at the park. "Okay, I have no idea what you're talking about."

I gaped at her, my heart giving an unpleasant, nervous squeeze. My dad had walked ahead and was a few steps from the general store's outdoor tables.

"Darcy, come on. He's been there every morning since we got here?" I said, forcing a laugh in my voice. "The Bob Marley–type guy . . . ? You said he was embracing the cliché?"

Darcy looked at me like I was crazy.

"I think you need your head examined," she said, turning on her heel. Her floral miniskirt swished as she walked away. I felt like my brain had just been switched into hyperdrive. It wasn't like I imagined the guy. I'd seen him three or four times, I'd seen other people standing around enjoying his music, I could name every song I'd heard him sing, and Darcy and I had talked about him on more than one occasion. Had falling down the stairs and smacking her head somehow affected her short-term memory?

Taking a deep breath, I glanced back at the park one more time before walking into the general store. Dad and Darcy had already found a small booth, just across from the old-fashioned, chrome-rimmed counter. The couple I'd seen getting off the ferry on our first day here sat at the counter, their pinkies linked between them as they sipped their coffee. The taller guy's fedora hat sat on the counter next to him. He smiled when he caught me checking it out, and I smiled back as I slipped onto the bench next to Darcy. My father handed me a small plastic menu. I let my eyes slide over the classic diner selections, then trail back to Darcy. She had her sunglasses off and sat with her head casually resting on her hand as she scanned the menu.

"Hey, folks! What'll you have?" A waitress in a blue-and-white gingham dress appeared at our table, pen at the ready.

"Girls?" my dad asked.

"I'll have a short stack of blueberry pancakes," Darcy said, shoving the menu across the table. "And coffee."

"Toasted bagel and orange juice, please," I said.

"I'll try the whole wheat pancakes with a side of bacon and coffee as well," my dad put in. He stacked up the menus and handed them to her. "Thank you."

"Thank *you*," she said with a smile, then turned and sauntered away.

My father blew out a sigh and laced his hands together on top to the table. "Listen. I owe you guys an apology."

I gripped the edge of the vinyl seat on either side of my legs. Next to me, Darcy stopped breathing.

"It's been really hard on me . . . since your mother died, and I know that's no excuse, but I didn't realize until recently how . . . closed off I've been," he said, looking back and forth between the two of us. "How . . . angry."

I cleared my throat. Darcy shifted in her seat.

"Actually, that's not true," he said, rubbing his forehead. "I did realize how angry I was, but I didn't want to admit it, because I was angry at her and that just felt wrong."

My stomach hollowed out because I knew exactly what he meant. There were times when I felt mad at my mother for leaving me, for leaving us. Like she had any control over it. Last year I'd taken first place in the regional science fair with my study of cancer cells in field mice, beating out Samir Clark and his robotic arm, and while all the officials and teachers and students had been applauding my victory, I'd just stared at the crowd, wishing she was there. She'd been a biology major in college and had taught at Princeton like my dad, and I knew how proud she would have been, but it wasn't enough. I wanted her *there*. Somehow I'd gotten through the reception and all the photos, but as soon as I'd gotten home I'd dropped the trophy on the couch, run to my room, and started screaming into a pillow. I'd yelled and yelled and yelled until I'd started to feel stupid for yelling. Until I'd realized she would have been there if she could have been. And then I'd just felt stupid and sorry.

"I don't think I've truly accepted that I'm never going to see your mom again," my dad said, tears shining in his eyes. Darcy sniffled. Her eyes were full, too. Maybe she did think about our mother. Maybe she did miss her. "And you two girls have so much of her in you . . . I see her every time I look at you. And it makes me so proud, but at the same time, it makes me so sad. I've just never known how to deal with it. I've never known how to be the person you need me to be."

He swallowed hard, containing the tears. Darcy grabbed a napkin out of the dispenser and covered her eyes briefly.

"I get it, Dad," I said, my voice a croak. "I really get it. I just . . . I think she'd want us to do better. I think she'd want us to try harder to be . . ."

"A good family," Darcy finished, sniffling again. "She'd want us to be a family."

Dad nodded and looked away. "Do you think we could do that?" he asked after a moment. "Do you think we could try? For her?"

"I think we could," I said, my heart slamming against my rib cage.

Darcy nodded, still trying not to cry.

"Good," my father said. He took a deep breath, sitting up straight as he took it in, then blew it out and leaned his arms into the table. "Thank you," he said. "For hearing me out."

"Thank you," Darcy said softly, her voice watery.

There was still a ton of crap between us. All the yelling, all the confusion and anger. But right then, at that moment, my dad looked, sounded, felt like the old him. Like the dad I'd known before the word *cancer* had entered our lives. I'd loved that dad.

So I forced a smile. "Any time."

I looked over at Darcy, expecting her to jump at the chance to ask Dad about the party, but she was staring down at the table, her bottom lip trembling as she toyed with her quaking fingers in her lap. She looked broken, like if I touched her the wrong way she would crumble. I swallowed hard. I felt so guilty, all of a sudden, for thinking she didn't care that Mom was gone. Maybe she just dealt with it differently than I did. Maybe all the parties, the shopping, the cheerleading and hostessing—maybe it was her way of distracting herself. Because wasn't that all I was doing, studying my ass off all the time, running whenever I had too much time to think?

"Dad?" I said suddenly. "There's this party tonight, and Darcy and I were wondering if we could go."

Darcy lifted her chin and looked at me as if she'd never seen me before.

"A party?" he said hesitantly. "I don't know if—"

A plate of pancakes dropped onto our table with a clatter. "You guys are coming to the party?"

Krista stood next to our table in a blue gingham mini-dress that made her legs look like toothpicks, her hair back in a high ponytail, and an expectant grin on her face. She placed Darcy's food in front of her, then mine. I glanced past her and saw that our original waitress was busy making a new pot of coffee.

"This is so great! Tristan didn't think you were going to come!" Krista said, clasping her hands as she grinned down at me.

"And you are?" my father asked pleasantly.

"Dad, this is Krista," Darcy piped up. "The party's at her house."

"Oh," my father said, clearing his throat. "Nice to meet you, Krista. Will there be adults at this party?"

"Dad!" Darcy said through her teeth.

"Oh, of course!" Krista replied, giggling. "My mom's the mayor, so she always makes sure to let the police know when my brother and I hold a party. She's totally overprotective, so they usually send a couple of officers to sort of 'police the perimeter,'" she said, adding some air quotes. "They're, like, the tamest parties ever." Then she looked at me and Darcy and colored. "But still fun!"

"See?" I said, raising my eyebrows. "A party with police presence. Doesn't get any safer than that, right, Darcy?"

"Totally!" Darcy exclaimed.

"You have to let them come, Mr. Thayer," Krista said, touching my father's arm. I glanced at her leather bracelet, which looked stiff in comparison to her brother's soft, broken-in one. "I'm *dying* to get to know Rory better." She grinned at me.

I forced myself to smile back even though the last thing

I wanted was for Krista to fire questions at me all night. I couldn't help but feel like she was looking for a reason to get close to me. For something to bind us together. She held my gaze, and a smattering of goose bumps popped out along my arms.

"All right. If it's at the mayor's house, I'm sure it'll be fine," my father said finally. "You girls can go."

"Yay! Thank you thank you thank you!" Darcy cheered.

I blew out a breath. "Thanks, Dad."

"Thank you, Mr. Thayer!" Krista said.

My father smiled. Maybe he was realizing it had been a long time since he'd done anything to make so many people happy at once.

"You guys let me know if you need anything, okay?" Krista said. "I'll be right behind the counter!"

She practically skipped away, her skirt flouncing, and grabbed the old-school phone behind the counter. After dialing quickly, she turned her back to us to whisper to whoever was on the opposite end. When I heard her squeal, I knew she was telling someone that we'd decided to come to the party. I wondered if it was Tristan. I wondered if he was smiling.

And I wondered why I cared.

A LIFER

I jogged down the street leading to the docks that afternoon, telling myself that I wasn't going this way because I wanted to bump into Tristan. I was going this way because I wanted to check out the island, I wanted to try different running routes—to be somewhere populated, to feel slightly safer on my first solo run since Nell.

But as I took the corner and headed toward the Thirsty Swan, my heart fluttered with nerves and I found myself wondering if I was overly sweaty, if my face was too red, if—oh god—what if I smelled?

What the hell was I thinking, coming down here?

I upped my pace as I passed by the bar, a round of laughter wafting out to engulf me. A glimpse inside told me nothing. All I saw was a blur of faces, the lights of the jukebox, and someone in shadow keeping bar. I jogged past the alleyway between the bar and a restaurant next door called the Crab Shack and paused, bracing my hands above my knees and trying to catch my breath. I couldn't believe I'd run all the way down here for nothing. Maybe I should just turn around and walk to the general store right now, where I could promptly nurse my inner humiliation with a nice, big bowl of ice cream.

I stood up straight and was about to put my plan into action, when a door nearby squealed open and I heard Tristan's voice.

"All I'm saying is you have to back off her a little."

My heart skipped about two thousand beats. Whoever he was talking to, they were in the alleyway just around the corner from where I was standing. I leaned back against the wall of the Crab Shack and, as carefully as I could, glimpsed around the corner. Krista stood in front of Tristan in the empty, clean-swept alley, still in her general store uniform. She said something in reply that I couldn't make out.

Tristan sighed heavily. "I understand why you're so—"

The door to the Crab Shack opened and slammed, drowning out his next few words. I cursed under my breath and tried to look natural as a group of young guys strolled out the door and loped past me.

" . . . want to get to know her. That's all," Krista was saying when I was able to tune in again.

"I get it, but you're starting to freak her out," Tristan replied. "I can tell."

"How do you know you're not the one freaking her out?" Krista demanded.

"Maybe I am, too. I don't know," Tristan said. "She's different."

"Well, duh!" Krista exclaimed. "Even I know that!"

The Crab Shack door opened again and a couple of older men walked out, talking loudly about some fishing trip. It seemed to take them forever to move away from the door and walk by. As soon as they'd disappeared around the corner, I held my breath and listened.

"—even sure that she's a lifer," Tristan was saying.

"Whatever," Krista said. "If you want me to back off, fine. I'll back off. You've made it perfectly clear who's in charge around here."

She was about to storm away. If she came out of the alley onto the boardwalk I was screwed. Glancing around, I quickly ducked behind a tall potted evergreen shrub outside the Crab Shack and held my breath. After a few seconds, I hazarded a glance around the side of the topiary and saw

Krista storming along the wood planks in the direction from which I'd come, headed back toward town.

I stayed there, hidden, and waited for Tristan to go back inside. And waited. And waited. Every second I expected him to pop around the corner and snag me. But then, after what seemed like forever, I finally heard the door squeal open and slam shut again. I let out the breath I'd been holding and walked slowly toward the water. A few empty benches sat facing the bay, hovering over a small beach where two seagulls roosted in the freshly combed sand.

I sat down on the warm sand and watched as a huge fishing boat moved toward the docks to my right, its bell clanging. I sighed and went over Tristan and Krista's conversation in my mind.

First of all, there was no reason to believe that Tristan and Krista had been talking about me. They could have been talking about anyone. There was that. But then, Krista *had* been really eager, and after yesterday, Tristan knew I had a lot of questions about him, too. So they *could* have been talking about me. I supposed I should have felt grateful toward Tristan for trying to help me out with Krista.

But what was a lifer, and why would I be one?

I finished up my stretching and strolled toward home, not even daring to give the Thirsty Swan or its back alley another glance.

PARTY TIME

"So, wait. You've never played a musical instrument? Not even, like, 'Chopsticks' on the piano?" Olive asked, her eyes wide.

We were sitting on a brocade couch against one of the light yellow walls in Tristan's living room as dozens of kids talked and laughed and flirted around us. The air was cool, thanks to the breeze moving through the wide windows, and the steady hum of conversation filled me from the inside out. Olive had been right about the interior of the house being just as impressive as the outside. The whole place smelled of wood polish and coconut sunscreen, like some kind of upscale beach resort. All the furniture was antique and perfectly maintained, with colorful cushions and whimsically mismatched pillows. Across the room stood a massive fireplace with a single, mosaic tile vase at the center of its mantel. There were no other knickknacks, no stacks of magazines, no family pictures. Clearly Tristan's parents kept it simple.

I hadn't see Tristan or Krista yet. Darcy stood near the sliding doors to the patio, flirting with Joaquin, which was good. Tonight was important to her. Thank god Joaquin wasn't screwing it up.

"Well, back in grade school we had required music class, so I guess I've used a tambourine and some bongo drums, but not since I was eight or nine." I shifted in my seat, moving my bag to my side. "I've never really been into it."

"Wow." Olive sat back, looking out at the party in shock. "Do you want to learn? I could teach you how to play guitar."

I hesitated. I liked Olive and I didn't want to let her down, but learning to play an instrument had never crossed my mind in my life.

"Come on!" she wheedled, pinching my arm. "I went running with you! Who knows, maybe you'll like it."

Be unpredictable, Rory, I told myself. Life is short.

"You know what? Sure. I'd love to learn," I said.

"Cool." Olive's face completely lit up. "Why don't we

meet up for breakfast tomorrow at the general store? Then we can go back to my room at the boardinghouse, and I'll show you the basics."

"Sounds good."

She dug around in her bag and came out with a small pad and a pencil. "I'll write down the address and room number for you," she said. "It's Mrs. Chen's boardinghouse on Freesia. The landlady's totally nosy, but her place has killer acoustics."

She tore off the scrap of paper, and I tucked it into my pocket. "How long have you played guitar?"

"Ever since I was little," she replied, reaching for her cup of water. The sleeve of her sweater started to ride up, and she tugged it back down again. She tucked her free hand under her arm like she was cold.

"Then you probably noticed that guy in the park," I said. "The one who was playing for money every day?"

Olive's eyes narrowed over the edge of her red cup as she considered. "No. When was this?"

At that moment, Tristan and Krista appeared at the bottom of the wide stairway. He wore a white T-shirt under an open, blue plaid button-down and cargo shorts. She had on a flowy, light pink dress that swished around her knees when she moved. They really did make a stunning pair, and for the first time I saw what Olive meant about how they were treated like the prince and princess of Juniper Landing. As they moved through the living room, everyone stopped what they were doing to greet them. I could almost imagine some of them wanting to dip into curtsies and bows.

Just as I had the thought, Tristan looked over at us, and our eyes locked. I felt warm all over, like he somehow knew what I was thinking. Then Kevin and Fisher commandeered him by the keg, and the moment passed. I half expected Krista to come over and demand a hair makeover, but instead she found Lauren and Bea by the fireplace and started to chat. Maybe she and Tristan *had* been talking about me this afternoon. It definitely looked as if she was heeding his warning to back off.

My heart raced at the thought, but I returned my attention to Olive and cleared my throat. "What were we talking about?"

"Some guitar player in the park?" Olive reminded me.

"Right! He was there for a few mornings and then today he just . . . wasn't."

"Maybe he made enough money and hopped a plane to New York," Olive joked.

"Maybe, but the really weird thing is, Darcy didn't remember him," I said, toying with the zipper pull on my sweatshirt as I watched Krista. She hadn't looked over at me once.

"What do you mean?" Olive asked.

"She was the first one to point him out the day we got here," I explained, keeping one eye on Krista and her friends. "And then a couple days later, we watched him play for a few minutes together and she said he was growing on her. But when I pointed out he was gone, she had no idea who I was talking about."

"That *is* weird," Olive said, fully alert. She put her cup down and sat forward, like a talk-show host with a particularly interesting guest. The possibility of minstrel boy disappearing hadn't bothered her, but clearly the idea of Darcy spacing on his existence did. "She just didn't remember him?"

"No," I said, glad someone thought this whole thing was as odd as I did. "It was like he was erased from her memory."

"That used to happen to one of my friends back home," Olive told me, lowering her voice. "Every once in a while, he would black out whole hours of his life. Sometimes even days."

"Really?" I asked, intrigued. "Did he see a doctor?"

Olive laughed sarcastically. "I kind of think a doctor would have just told him to lay off the heroin."

My jaw dropped, and I felt my neck grow warm. "You think my sister's a *drug addict*?" I whispered, surprised and kind of offended. "Darcy's never done drugs in her life."

Olive looked at me like she'd just been slapped.

"What? Are you okay?" I asked.

"I'm fine," Olive said. "I just—something just flew into my eye." She got up and grabbed her purse, holding her fingers over her right eyelid. "I'm just going to run to the bathroom. I'll be back in a sec."

"Olive, wait." As she ducked around a corner, I got up as well, but when I picked up my bag, it overturned and everything spilled out—my wallet, my hair bands, my lip balm. I quickly shoved it all back in the bag and followed Olive, but as I rounded the corner, I found myself at the end of a long hallway with at least half a dozen closed doors.

Sighing, I knocked on the first one. "Olive?"

Nothing. I moved on to the second. "Olive? Are you in there?"

No answer. Moving slowly down the hallway, the noise from the party started to fade. I knocked on the third door and heard a muffled response. Slowly, I tried the ancient, brass door handle and the door creaked open, but it wasn't a bathroom. It was a massive bedroom and it was filled from floor to ceiling, with junk.

"Whoa," I said under my breath.

My curiosity getting the better of me, I took a step inside. Shelves lined every wall, each one overflowing with all kinds of stuff, and even more items were piled up into teetering towers in the center of the floor. There were books and magazines, tangled masses of jewelry, purses and backpacks and suitcases in all shapes and sizes, some of them stuffed to the gills. There were laptop computers piled up on the floor, wires curling everywhere, and a wide shelf nailed to the wall jammed with iPads and other tablets. As I moved farther inside, my hip bumped a huge cardboard box that was filled to the brim with cell phones.

"What the hell . . . ?"

Maybe this was why Tristan's house was so decluttered. His family was made up of closet hoarders who kept their belongings behind closed doors. Slowly I turned around to leave, and I froze. Along the wall next to the door was a rack of hanging clothes stuffed to bursting, and next to that was a hat rack full of cabbies and baseball caps, sun hats and visors. Slung over the uppermost hook was a well-worn guitar strap in yellow and green and red.

ANSWERS

"Rory."

I blinked. Tristan was standing in front of me, framed by the doorway, his posture ramrod straight.

"What're you doing in here?" he asked flatly.

"I—I'm sorry, I just—" I cleared my throat, heat creeping up my neck. My eyes darted back to the guitar strap. It was there. It was definitely there. This was no flash. "I was looking for Olive."

"Well, she doesn't seem to be in here, so . . ."

He held the door open for me. I took the hint and slid by him. He closed the door firmly behind me and pushed his hands into the front pockets of his shorts. "Sorry. My mom just doesn't like anyone coming in here."

He turned and led me back down the hallway, toward the party.

"Oh. Sorry. Olive said she was going to the bathroom, so—"

"That's on the other side of the kitchen," he said, tipping his face down so his hair fell across his cheekbone. "If you need it."

"Oh, well . . . thanks," I said.

We had come to the end of the hallway. To my right, Darcy and Joaquin chatted with Bea and Kevin. To my left was the living room and the brocade couch I'd vacated. Olive wasn't back yet. I turned to Tristan, dying to ask him about that room, about the guitar strap. It belonged to the missing minstrel boy. I was certain of it. But how had it ended up here? Did Tristan know the guy? Had he given it to him? Or had someone in Tristan's family taken it from him?

"So," Tristan said. "You came."

A blush swirled up on my cheeks. "Darcy wanted to come, so . . ."

"Do you always do stuff you don't want to do for your sister?" he asked.

He crossed over to the brocade couch and sat. Still trying to figure out how to broach my questions, I sat next to him.

The skin on my legs tingled just from the proximity of his knee to mine. I turned in my seat slightly, angling myself away from him.

"No," I said. "This was really important to her."

"Why?" he asked, looking across the room, where Darcy was laughing with her hand on Joaquin's arm.

Because she's massively crushing on your annoying friend was the first answer that came to mind.

"She likes parties," I said simply.

"And you don't?" he asked, turning back to me again.

He was gazing at me, like he was staring into my soul. No guy ever looked at me that way. Maybe not even Christopher. They were always too busy fidgeting, or looking past me for something better. They had the attention span of flies. But not Tristan. Tristan knew how to focus. I just didn't know how to be the object of that focus.

"Why do you care?" I asked, my body temperature off the charts under his scrutiny.

"I just do," he stated simply. "I imagine you avoid stuff like this because it's beneath you."

"Wow. So you think I'm stuck-up," I challenged.

"Not at all," he said matter-of-factly. "I think you know who you are and don't give in to peer pressure. But with your sister it's different, so here you are. That doesn't make you stuck-up. It makes you special."

I swallowed hard, feeling flattered, but also thrown.

"Do you like to people-watch?" he asked.

"What do you mean?"

"Sometimes when I'm at a party, I just sit back and observe," he said, glancing around the room. "Like that guy over there." He nodded at an adorable but nerdy redheaded boy leaning against the far wall. "He's clearly nervous as hell."

The boy was wrapping the string on his sweatshirt around his finger so tightly the tip was turning white. Meanwhile, the girl he was talking to lifted her arm to smooth her hair and surreptitiously checked her watch.

"And that girl couldn't care less," I pointed out.

"Exactly," Tristan said, smiling back at me over his shoulder. "So I was right. You *are* a natural observer."

I shifted under his gaze, finding it slightly unsettling that he kept acting like he knew so much about me.

"Maybe," I shot back. "But at least I've never openly spied on anyone."

Tristan blinked, then finally looked away. He rested his forearms across his knees and laced his fingers together. The braided leather bracelet clung tight to his wrist. It looked like it was melded to his skin. Like it had been there forever. He started to absently toy with the weave.

"Is there something you want to ask me, Rory?" he said finally, looking across the room at Krista, who was still standing by the fireplace.

"Yeah, there is," I said, sitting up straight and facing him completely. Somehow, his direct question made me brave. "What happened to the kid in the park?"

He looked me in the eye. "The kid in the park."

"The guitar player. The one with the dreads. I saw you watching him play the other day with Fisher, so I know you know who I'm talking about," I said, warming to my inquiry. "Where is he, and why doesn't my sister remember him? Oh, and why is his guitar strap hanging in your storage room back there?"

"Rory . . ." he began, his voice low.

The way he said my name, like he really knew me—like he'd always known me—sent a warm rush through my chest. I looked up at him, right in the eye, and found I couldn't look away.

"Rory!" a familiar voice called out.

"Oh, hey, Aaron!" I said, standing up to give him a hug and trying not to groan at his timing. Tristan had just been about to tell me something about the minstrel. I could feel it. "Have you met Tristan? This is his house."

"Oh, yes. Of course." Aaron offered his hand, and

Tristan pushed himself up to shake with him. "Killer party, man."

"Thanks." Then he glanced over at his sister, who was giving him some kind of eye. Unspoken words between siblings, I guessed. "I've gotta go . . . do a thing." Tristan said. He looked from me to Aaron and back to me again. I could tell there was something he wanted to say, but he thought better of it. "You two have fun."

Then he made his way through the crowd, over to his sister.

"He seems like a good guy," Aaron said.

I took a deep breath. "That's still to be determined."

"So, you sore from the other day?" Aaron asked, taking a sip from his drink.

I frowned in thought. "No, actually. That's weird."

I had been exhausted after windsurfing—in a good way—and sure that the muscles I almost never tapped into would be hurting for days to come.

Aaron laughed. "Guess you're a better athlete than you thought."

"Apparently," I said.

"So let's go out again? Say, Friday morning? I'll pick you up at your place?" Aaron suggested.

"I'm in," I said with a smile.

It might be good for me to spend more time with Aaron

and less with the locals. So far, he was the least enigmatic person I'd met on this crazy island.

"Hey, check it out," he said, glancing over my shoulder. "The fog's coming in again."

Sure enough, the air outside was swirling, the lights along the bluff winking out one by one. All the partygoers began to gather at the windows to watch, and Aaron tugged me over to join them.

"This is so cool," someone in the crowd breathed.

"Creepy, you mean," someone else replied.

"I read this book once where there were monsters living in the mist," a guy said, putting on an eerie voice. A few of his friends laughed, and we all fell silent, watching the fog envelop the house.

Out of nowhere, I felt a niggling at the back of my neck and I turned around. Krista was slipping out a side door near me, while at the other end of the hallway, Tristan was sliding open the glass door to the patio, holding it for Olive. She smiled up at him as they stepped outside, the gray mist swirling around them. I felt a sudden thump of fear, and opened my mouth to call out to them, but no words came. What would I say? Be careful? Don't go out there? Tristan lived here. He knew this place and he knew about the fog. He wouldn't be taking Olive outside if it was dangerous. I hoped.

As everyone else at the party gaped out the front windows, I watched Tristan and Olive walk down the steps, his hand on the small of her back, until they both disappeared into the fog.

BROKEN

The moment he saw a girl, he knew whether or not she was his type. It was not physical. No. Physically, the variety of his conquests was great. So great that all the profilers in Washington and California, in Virginia and D.C., had a difficult time figuring him out. He was certain that, at first, they believed he didn't have a type. Lacey Turner was, after all, short and fat and blond, while Gigi Abassian was tall and lithe, with dark skin, dark eyes, dark hair. Jenna Moskowitz had acne and eczema and braces, while Felicia Renee had modeled for magazines. And then there was Rory Miller. Rory Miller, the plainest of the plain.

Except for the hair. That lovely, delicious hair . . .

So, no. It was not a physical thing at all. It was internal. Every girl he'd ever chosen was broken. No matter how brave she was or how tall she carried herself or how defiantly she looked at the world. He could spot a broken girl a mile away. It was all in the eyes.

And this one, this friend of Rory Miller's, she was the most shattered of them all.

DITCHED

As I crested the hill onto Main Street on Thursday morning, I crossed my fingers, hoping the singing boy would be back in his spot, belting out a reggae version of "Sweet Dreams" or something. Hoping I'd imagined what I'd seen at Tristan's. But he wasn't. Instead, a young woman in gray yoga pants struck a twisted pose beneath the fireworks banner, lifting her face toward the sun.

My shoulders slumped, and I turned my steps toward the general store. Maybe I'd try the blueberry pancakes Darcy had ordered yesterday. They'd looked amazing. Maybe that would cheer me up and get me ready for this conversation. I wanted to ask Olive what I'd said that had sent her running to the bathroom last night, but I was nervous about bringing it up. Hopefully it was nothing. Hopefully I'd just imagined that, too. As I yanked open the door, I told myself that was the case, just to take the edge off my nerves.

Glancing at the counter, I was relieved to find two unfamiliar waitresses bustling around the coffeemaker. I didn't want Krista there busting in on our breakfast. I took a seat facing the door so I could see Olive when she came in.

"What can I get you, miss?" an elderly woman in the general store uniform asked, approaching the table.

"Just orange juice for now, please. I'm waiting for a friend," I told her.

She popped the tip of her pencil against her pad. "You got it!"

I settled into the cushy seat and read over the menu, item by item, just in case there was something better than blueberry pancakes to tempt me. The door opened and I looked up, but it was just one half of the couple we'd seen eating here yesterday, the preppier, blonder half. I watched the door, waiting for his boyfriend to join him, but no one else appeared. The guy moved to the counter and greeted the waitress with a smile, then ordered a cup of coffee and a bagel.

I read over the menu again, word for word. Still no Olive. I checked my watch. She was only seven minutes late. My juice arrived, and I gulped it down, my stomach growling. I read the menu over again. The door opened, and I looked up once more. This time, it was Tristan. He was wearing a damp bathing suit, and his white T-shirt clung to him in wet splotches. His hair was slicked back from his face, accentuating his sharp cheekbones and the startling blue of his eyes.

My heart did this odd sort of hopeful-yet-dread-filled somersault as I remembered our conversation last night. I started to open my mouth to say hello, but he took one look at me, turned beet red, and backed out.

That was new. I glanced around, embarrassed, until I realized that no one had even noticed him or his retreat. They'd have no way of knowing I'd been the one to scare him off anyway.

The guy at the counter got his bagel and started to eat. I sipped my juice and tried not to think about how hungry I was. The waitress approached my table and cleared her throat.

"Can I get you anything else, hon?" she asked.

I smiled up at her. "I think I'll just wait for my friend." We both looked at my now empty glass. "Can I get a refill, please?" I asked.

"Sure."

She took my glass and returned with it brimming. "Enjoy!"

I waited another fifteen minutes, wishing I had a cell phone so I could text Olive. Had she forgotten about our breakfast date? Or had I possibly offended her so much last night that she'd simply decided to ditch me? I drained my OJ again. Checked my watch. She was over half an hour late. Clearly she wasn't coming. Finally, I pushed myself up, fishing a couple of dollars out of my wallet.

"Giving up?" the waitress asked, hovering over me.

"She probably just slept in," I told her with an awkward smile. "I'm going to go check on her, and hopefully we'll be back."

"All right, then," the waitress said with a pitying smile, like she didn't believe I'd be back. As I pushed open the door, the bell overhead tinkled and the waitress lifted a hand. "Have a good day!"

I tugged the scrap of paper with the address of Olive's boardinghouse out of my bag pocket. Twenty-two Freesia Lane, Room 2A. I glanced around, realizing I had no clue where I was going. Then I saw the redheaded guy from Tristan's party hook a right down the side street with the park. I started after him, figuring I'd ask if he knew the street, and stopped in my tracks. The sign directly over my head read FREESIA LANE. I just hadn't noticed it before.

"Great. She has to live on the spooky park street," I said under my breath, shoving the scrap of paper in my pocket.

Swallowing back my nervousness, I turned down the street. Luckily number twenty-two was only a few houses in, a block away from the park. It was a tall, skinny white house that cast a long shadow over the street. Its wrought-iron flower boxes burst with red impatiens. I paused on the sidewalk for a second to gather the courage to go inside, hoping she wasn't trying to avoid me.

I strode up the front walk, the floorboards of the porch creaking beneath my feet. When I tried the door, it swung open easily, the old hinges letting out a high-pitched wail. There was no one in sight, all the lights were off, and there was a distinct chill in the air despite the heat of the day.

My skin tingled and my chest felt tight. I checked over my shoulder, half expecting to see Steven Nell lunging toward me. But all that was there were the silent, lifeless row houses across the street.

I swallowed hard and stepped inside.

"Hello?" I called out. A tall, narrow staircase led up to the second floor, and faded tan-and-green flowered paper lined the walls. "Hello? Is anyone here?"

There was no answer. Somewhere from the depths of the house I heard a humming. The tune was familiar, but I couldn't place it. I licked my lips and swallowed hard. Olive came and went from this house every day. There was nothing to be afraid of. I grasped the chipped handrail and crept slowly up the stairs. After a few steps, I started feeling like I was in the middle of some horror movie and jogged the rest of the way casually, refusing to play the part of the nervous schoolgirl.

The first door on the left had a gold-plated 2A nailed into its center. I held my breath and knocked. The door creaked open half an inch at my touch.

Heart pounding, I peered through the opening. Inside, I could just make out the sleeve of one of Olive's sweaters, thrown across the bed. Then, I noticed the incessant beeping and pushed the door wide.

Next to her neatly made bed, Olive's alarm was going off.

"She's not here."

I whirled around, my hands flying out to brace against the open doorway. A tiny Chinese woman with white hair and huge eyeglasses stood behind me.

"Who're you?" I asked.

"Mrs. Chen. I run this place," she said, gesturing with a huge ring full of keys. "She never came home last night."

"Oh . . . okay," I said.

Then she shook her head and started down the stairs very slowly, her slippers making shushing sounds against the aging wood.

My heartbeat racing wildly, I turned back to Olive's room. I knew going in was a huge invasion of her privacy, but

I rationalized it with the thought that someone should really turn off her alarm before it started to annoy her neighbors. I walked inside and flipped the switch on the clock. Merciful silence.

Olive's closet door was open and only a few pieces of clothing hung inside. Her guitar leaned against the chair on the other side of the room, and some sheet music was spread out on a low table. Fresh-cut flowers stood on the far windowsill.

A bike bell trilled out on the street, and I turned toward the window closest to me, above the desk. The second I did, a big blackbird took flight from the windowsill, its wings making a racket that sent my heart into my throat.

I leaned both hands into the desk, struggling to get a hold of myself. Clearly, I was on edge if an old lady and a bird could take this much out of me. I breathed in and out, telling myself to chill, but I just couldn't.

When I lifted my hand, a piece of paper stuck to my palm. It was a pickup ticket for a bike repair, which was supposed to be done today. Beneath it was a piece of old-fashioned pink stationery. At the top, Olive had written the words DEAR MOM. The letter was only half finished.

I paused. I knew what it was, and I wasn't about to read it.

I turned around and took in the room one more time. The made bed. The strewn clothes. The empty cup on the bedside table. It was eerie. Like someone had frozen Olive's life in time. Suddenly, a horrible, unsettling feeling took root inside my chest. Something had happened to Olive. Something awful.

And I knew who'd done it.

CRAZY

I ran home so fast anyone who saw me would have thought I was being chased. I *felt* like I was being chased. Every time I took a turn, I was sure I was about to run headfirst into Steven Nell. Every time I thought about stopping to take a breath, I saw him jumping out from behind a hedge. I couldn't believe I'd just ignored the warning signs, that I'd chosen to turn a blind eye and pretend to be safe when everything was pointing to the opposite. Steven Nell was here. He was stalking me, taunting me, and now he had Olive. I had to warn Darcy. I had to warn my dad.

I skidded around the corner onto our block and sprinted

across the street to our house, my hair sticking to the back of my neck. When I barreled through the front door, my dad and Darcy were both sitting at the kitchen table, eating from ceramic bowls.

"Rory? What's wrong?" my dad asked, standing. He was wearing his running gear and a baseball cap. Laid out in front of him on the table were stacks of typed pages. I recognized them with a start. Those pages had been laid out on our dining room table my entire childhood, but had disappeared when my mom got sick. It was his novel. He'd stopped working on it years ago. I would have been excited that he was taking it up again, if I wasn't about to burst with terror.

"He's here!" I gasped, staggering toward them. "Steven Nell is here."

"Rory—" Darcy began.

"You saw him? Where?" my father asked, going pale.

"No. I didn't . . . I didn't see him." I leaned into the back of Darcy's chair, my hand to my chest, trying to catch my breath. "But he's here. Darcy, tell him! Remember the other night, when we heard the laughter in the fog? That was him!"

Darcy sighed. "Come on, Rory. I'm sure that was just someone messing with us."

"Yeah, and Steven Nell's the someone!" I shouted. I

turned to face my father, desperate. "Dad, listen. Our first morning here, I heard someone outside the house humming 'The Long and Winding Road,' which Mr. Nell always used to hum in the halls. And then someone put it on the jukebox at the Thirsty Swan the night we snuck out. I've heard him laughing, I've heard him whisper my name. And there was this scrap of tan fabric exactly like the fabric of his jacket, and a messenger bag hanging from our fence a couple of days ago just like the one he used to carry to class."

"Wait a minute, wait a minute," my father said, reaching out to hold both my arms. "You're basing all this on a series of random coincidences?"

My heart sank. He didn't believe me. I felt like I was about to explode.

"No! I'm basing it on the fact that all these things happened, and now Olive's disappeared!" I blurted.

"Who's Olive?" he and Darcy both asked at the same time.

My blood turned to ice in my veins. I felt like someone had just slammed me upside the head with a two-by-four. Slowly, I turned to face Darcy. My vision blurred around the edges.

"What do you mean, who's Olive?" I asked.

She lifted her shoulders and got up from the table, picking up her bowl and spoon. "I *mean*, who's Olive?"

Casually, she strode past me and my dad to dump her dishes in the sink. She ran the water for a second, then shook her hands dry and turned to face me, jutting out one hip as she leaned against the counter. I searched her eyes. She looked back at me curiously, waiting. Waiting for me to answer her. To explain to her who this person was—a person she'd hung out with on several occasions.

"Darcy, come on," I said. "Now I know you're screwing with me."

"How am I screwing with you?" she asked.

"You know who Olive is!" I shouted. "We hung out with her at the bonfire and again at the Thirsty Swan! I went out for a run with her two days ago and you talked to her at the party last night before going off with Joaquin." My voice got progressively louder as she continued to stare back at me like I was speaking in some foreign tongue.

"Wait a minute, who's Joaquin?" my dad asked Darcy, completely oblivious to my growing panic.

She turned pleasantly pink. "He's just this guy I—"

"Darcy!" I interrupted. "You *know* who Olive is!"

"God, Rory! Give it up!" Darcy blurted, clearly frustrated. "I know Krista, I know Lauren and Bea, but I don't remember Olive. And I think I'd remember, because that name? Ew."

My knees gave out, and I dropped into her vacated chair.

This wasn't happening. This was *not* happening. First minstrel boy and now Olive? I didn't fabricate these people. They were real. Darcy knew them. It was like she'd developed some kind of freaky selective amnesia that made her delete entire people. I gaped at her as she walked out of the room and headed for the stairs.

"I'm gonna go take a shower and then hit the beach," she said. "Let me know if you want to come."

"We're going to need to talk about this Joaquin person!" my dad called after her.

"Yeah, yeah," she said lightly. "Later."

I waited until I heard the door slam and the water turn on before turning to my father, half expecting him to lay into me for scaring him. That would have been his normal reaction. But today he just stood there, looking at me with a concerned frown.

"Dad, there's something seriously strange going on around here," I said. "Darcy *knows* Olive. I swear to you. I met her our first morning here, and we've hung out with her all week. She's the friend you let me go running with. And I was supposed to meet her for breakfast, but she never showed, and when I went to her boardinghouse, she hadn't been home all night, and all her stuff was still there."

"Maybe she slept over at a friend's," my father said. "Or maybe she went out this morning for coffee or a run. She could have forgotten about your plans. It happens."

"Yeah, or maybe when she was walking home from the party last night, some psycho serial killer grabbed her and murdered her and buried her body on the beach somewhere!" I said, my fingers curling into fists. Why didn't he believe me? Why was my sister losing her mind?

Or was it me? Was I the one who was going crazy? But it wasn't like I had made Olive up. She was a real person with real stuff in her room and real feelings about her past and her mom and her future. And now she was gone.

My dad sat down diagonally from me and took one of my hands in both of his. His hands were warm and enveloped mine.

"Rory, listen, I understand why you're upset," he said patiently, looking me in the eye. I blinked and stared down at our hands, unaccustomed to this kind of contact, this kind of gentle treatment. "You've just been through a horrifying experience. Remember after your mom died? Those flashes you used to have? Maybe this is something like that. Maybe it's just another manifestation of post-traumatic stress."

He reached out and tucked my hair behind my ear, just like he used to do when I was little and I'd skinned my knee or fallen out of bed. I clenched my hands until my fingernails cut into the flesh of my palm. Little did he know I *was* having flashes and that these other things I was seeing, hearing, feeling, experiencing had nothing in common with those. But now didn't seem like the time to bring up my little disconnects from reality. It would only prove his point—that I was losing it.

"Why don't you go down to the beach with Darcy and try to relax?" he suggested.

My mouth was completely dry, my heart working overtime. As I sat there, my hand inside my father's hands, I'd never felt so alone, so utterly baffled, so scared.

He didn't believe me. He was never going to believe me.

But I knew Steven Nell was out there, and it was only a matter of time before he struck.

THE REAL THREAT

I woke up with a start in the middle of the night, certain the sound of breaking glass had interrupted my sleep. Heart in my throat, I whipped the sheets aside and crept downstairs. The fog was thick outside every window, and all I could hear was that incessant hissing as the wet mist crept along the shingles, the rooftop, the windowpanes.

I paused outside the door to Darcy's room, my pulse pounding in my ears, and pushed it open. Her bed was empty.

"Dad?" I called. I crossed the hall and shoved his door open. There was no one there.

Another crash, this one closer. I whirled around and raced downstairs.

"Dad? Darcy?"

That was when I heard the laugh.

I screamed at the top of my lungs and lunged for the front door. My hands trembled as I worked the locks and flung myself outside onto the deck. The fog was so thick I could have balled it up in my hand. All I could hear was the hissing. The hissing and the sound of ragged breath.

"Please, no," I whimpered quietly. "Daddy? Help me."

The fog swirled dead ahead, and that was when I saw their bodies, all lined up in a neat little row. Darcy with the back of her head bashed in. My father's leg broken, his throat slit. And Olive. Olive was . . . barely recognizable.

"No!" I screamed, backing away from them. "Nonononono."

I bumped into someone, and a dry hand came down over my mouth.

"Miss me?"

I sat up straight in my bed to a deafening crack of thunder accompanied by a flash of lightning. Struggling for breath, I placed my hand over my stomach, which was clenched in pain. I grasped the sheets with my other hand and held my breath until it dulled into a mere ache.

"It was just a dream," I said out loud. "Just a dream."

Slowly, I lay back on my sweat-drenched pillows. This was the drawback of being on the third floor. There definitely wasn't as much insulation up here, and I was sure I was hearing every raindrop, every rumble, much clearer than Darcy or my dad.

I got up, grabbed my iPad off the desk, and took it back to the bed. I'd tried several times today and still hadn't been able to get any service, but it couldn't hurt to try again. I had to at least check the news sites and find out if there was any new information about Steven Nell. Maybe I *was* being paranoid. Maybe they'd caught him. Maybe tomorrow we'd be able to go home.

But when I clicked open the browser, there was nothing but a blank white screen and that colorful spinning wheel. I sighed and powered down the iPad.

Rolling over onto my stomach, I stared out the huge window, watching the lightning strikes over the ocean. Each jagged bolt lit up pockets of waves, pockmarked by the rain as the water raged and roiled. As I breathed in and out, in and out, slowly the nightmare faded.

Suddenly, I heard a whoop, and when the sky lit up its brightest yet, I could just make out four silhouettes out on the water, straddling surfboards. I scrambled up to my knees and leaned forward. People were surfing in this mess? Were they insane?

Two of the figures turned the tips of their boards toward the shore and started to paddle furiously. They jumped to their feet and rode a massive wave in, side by side, until one of them tumbled forward, careening face-first into the water. My hands flew up to cover my mouth and stayed there until he surfaced once more. He half swam, half staggered his way to the shore, where his friend greeted him with a high five. Soon after, another of the four rode a wave in and joined them near a red cooler in the sand. Rain pelted their shoulders, but they didn't seem to care—like they thought they were invincible. I envied them. I used to feel that way, and I wished I could go back.

Lightning flashed again, and in that split second I recognized them. Kevin, Fisher, and Bea. The three of them talked for a couple of minutes before they all turned to look out at the water. I turned to look, too. The fourth surfer was still out there. He'd paddled out past the breakers and now sat, his legs dangling casually on either side of his board as he bobbed up and down on the rough sea like a buoy. He was turned out toward the horizon, just staring, his hands lying flat on his thighs.

My heart gave an extra beat. A sad beat. There was something about that lonely figure, something about the way he stared, that spoke of loneliness, of mourning, maybe even regret. Then the guys on the beach shouted something, and he turned his head just as the sky illuminated again. My breath caught. The angular face and wet, haphazard blond hair. It was Tristan.

For some reason I dove backward on my bed, landing on my butt with my knees akimbo. The second I did, I felt foolish. It wasn't like he was going to look up and spot me. And even if he did, who cared? I lived here. I was allowed to look out my window. Besides, he'd spied on me enough. He was fair game.

I crept forward on my hands and knees and peeked out the window again. He paddled in front of a wave and popped up onto his board. I marveled at how graceful he was, how effortless he made it look, balancing barefoot on a soaking wet slab of waxed wood while rain battered his face.

Finally, he arrived safely onshore, tucked his board under his arm, and jogged up the beach. He laughed it up with his friends, slapping hands and shaking his wet hair back from his face.

I pressed my lips together as I watched, and suddenly a realization hit me so hard I gasped. Last night, Olive had left the party with Tristan. I'd seen them walking out together into the fog. It hadn't meant anything to me at the time, because they were friends. Because she liked him. But then I remembered how eager he'd been to get away from me this morning at the general store. Did he know something about

Olive? Maybe all this time, he hadn't been watching me but watching Olive. Maybe he really was some kind of obsessed stalker, just not *my* creepy, obsessed stalker. I got a chill now, thinking about how I'd let him touch me. How I'd let him comfort me.

Arms and legs trembling, I crawled closer to the window, watching as the four friends popped open beers and clinked bottles. Tristan took a long drink, then tipped his head back and shook his hair away from his face, letting the rain pour down over him like he was being cleansed.

I curled my hand over the windowsill, gripping tight. Maybe Mr. Nell wasn't the only threat out there. Maybe there was an even bigger menace much, much closer to home.

THE JLPD

The sun was just hovering over the ocean on Friday morning when I zipped up my hoodie and slipped out the front door. There was a chill in the air, and I shivered as I gazed at the gray house across the street. The curtains were still. I looked left and right. There was no sign of anyone lurking, but for good measure, I flipped the hood up to cover my hair and hurried down the front steps.

Out on the ocean, a sailboat sliced through the water toward the horizon. Seagulls cawed, diving toward the whitecaps. Somewhere, a set of wind chimes pinged happily. There was no humming. No laughter. Just the sound of my breath and the nervous but determined beat of my heart.

I speed-walked around the corner and almost ran over Aaron.

"Hey!" he said happily. He had a duffel bag slung over one shoulder. "I thought I was meeting you at your house."

I blinked up at him. His face was already falling when I finally remembered. "We were supposed to go windsurfing!" I exclaimed.

"You forgot," he said, biting his bottom lip.

"I'm so sorry." I brought both hands to my forehead. "There's just a lot going on. I'm on my way to the police station."

His eyes widened. "Whatever for?"

"It's a long story, but . . . my friend Olive is kind of missing," I told him.

"Olive?" he asked. "Have I met her?"

A cool breeze chilled my nose as my heart gave an extra-hard thump. I wanted to reach out and shake him. Why didn't anyone remember Olive? But then I realized that even though they'd been at the same parties, they hadn't actually met. There was no reason for him to remember her.

"I don't think so. I met her when I first got here, and we were supposed to go out for breakfast yesterday, but she never showed," I said, starting to walk again. He fell in step beside me. I couldn't tell him about my Steven Nell suspicions, and I didn't know how to put into words what I felt about Tristan. Instead, I twisted my hands together and forced myself to keep it simple. "She hasn't called, she hasn't stopped by. I'm just really worried. I'm on my way to the police station right now."

"Isn't going to the police a bit extreme?" he said, his bag bumping against his leg as he walked. "Maybe she simply forgot about your plans."

I bit my tongue, wishing like hell I could just tell him the truth. "I know. I guess I'm a better-safe-than-sorry person."

We arrived at the top of the hill. Across the street to our right was the brick facade of the Juniper Landing Police Department.

"You don't have to come in with me if you don't want to," I told him.

He reached for my hand and squeezed it. "No. I want to."

My heart warmed, and we exchanged a brief smile. We took the stone steps at a jog and walked inside. The air was frigid, thanks to some pumped-up air-conditioning, and I couldn't help noticing how squeaky clean everything was. The marble floor gleamed, the wooden bench under the announcement board looked freshly waxed, and the announcement board itself was practically empty. The only notice inside the glass case was an advertisement for Movie

Night in the library's activity room. No pictures of wanted criminals, no warnings about night safety, no reminders to get your dog license renewed or keep your property hazard-free.

Aaron shoved open the swinging glass door to the main room and held it for me. I felt this overwhelming wave of gratitude to him for not leaving me alone, even though he clearly thought I was overreacting.

Leaning against the long, wooden counter was none other than my favorite local, Joaquin, wearing a red JUNIPER LANDING hoodie and talking with four uniformed police officers, who stood in a close-knit circle behind the counter. There was a box of doughnuts and a large, leather-bound ledger open between them. It almost looked like Joaquin was explaining something to them. One tall officer nodded while he listened, and another was taking notes. Then Joaquin must have said something funny because they all laughed, their eyes shining as they watched him, like he was the second coming.

Of course. Of course Joaquin was friends with the cops. He probably brought them doughnuts every morning so that they would ignore little infractions like bonfires on the beaches and underage chug lines at the Thirsty Swan. My heart fell as we slowly approached. How was I supposed to tell the police that I suspected Tristan had something to do with Olive's disappearance with his best friend standing right there?

The door finally closed behind us, and everyone looked up. Joaquin smiled, pushing the book toward one of the officers, who quickly closed it and tucked it under the counter. The cops, meanwhile, shot us semi-annoyed looks, as if whatever Joaquin was telling them was too important to be interrupted.

"Rory!" Joaquin said, flicking his eyes over Aaron dismissively. "What're you doing here?"

I screwed up my courage and faced the men behind the counter.

"I need to talk to someone about a missing person," I said, ignoring Joaquin.

They all fell silent. One of them exchanged a glance with Joaquin, who swallowed the last of his doughnut with a gulp. The officer was tall and broad and looked as solid as a rock. He looked like an ex-Marine—and not someone a person would want to mess with. I might have felt comforted by that fact if he wasn't giving me a look like I was something rancid he'd scraped off the bottom of his boot.

"Welcome to the Juniper Landing Police Department. I'm Officer Dorn," he said, as if he hadn't heard a word I'd said. He laid his hands flat atop the desk. "Now what's this about a missing person?"

"My friend is missing," I said. "We went to a party together two nights ago, and no one's seen her since."

Dorn's lips twitched ever so slightly. Joaquin cleared his throat and closed the top of the doughnut box, pushing it away.

"Was this girl a local or one of our vacationers?" Dorn asked.

Something inside me shifted. Why would he use the word *was*? "She *is* a vacationer," I said. "She's staying at the boardinghouse on Freesia."

"Ah, Mrs. Chen's place," Dorn said with a big smile. His teeth were very straight and very white. "Nice lady. She makes a fine lemon poppy loaf."

The other officers laughed and made sounds of general agreement. Aaron and I exchanged a look. Okay, good. He was as irked by this behavior as I was.

"Wait a minute," Joaquin said, dusting off his hands. "Are you talking about Olive?"

My spirits instantly brightened, and I felt a rush of gratitude toward him that was totally incongruous with everything else I felt about the guy. At least someone recalled Olive's existence. At least I wasn't going totally insane.

"Yes!" I exclaimed.

"Do you know her?" Aaron asked.

"Yeah, I know her. Of course I know her," Joaquin said

in a "duh" tone. He leaned sideways into the counter, propping one elbow up and crossing his flip-flopped feet. "Don't worry about Olive. She's fine."

"You know where she is?" I asked.

"No, but I'm sure she's fine," Joaquin said, flipping open the doughnut box and casually surveying the contents. "She's Olive."

What the hell did that mean?

"She's not fine," I said. "She's missing."

"Listen, miss," Dorn said, clearly losing patience. "What you've told us is you two went to a party and then she didn't come back to Mrs. Chen's," he said, looking down his nose at me. He reached back to straighten his waistband and sighed. "What that says to me is either she got lucky and stayed with some other . . . *friend*—" More chuckling from his cohorts. "Or she decided to cut her vacation short and went home."

"She didn't go home," I insisted.

"And you know this how?" he asked.

"I went to her room. All her stuff is still there," I said.

Dorn blinked, and Joaquin's smile froze on his face. The guys behind him whispered something to one another and then one of them crossed the room, went into another office, and closed the door. My fingers started to tremble.

"Besides, she can't go home," I pressed on. "She's in a fight with her mother, and she can't go back until she makes up with her." I glanced sideways at Joaquin, hating that I had to say this in front of him, that I was letting him hear Olive's secrets.

"You know what? I've gotta go," Joaquin said suddenly, glancing at a clock on the far wall. "You guys enjoy the doughnuts," he told the cops. Then he looked at me and Aaron. "See ya."

I let out a sigh of relief at his departure. At least now I could talk freely about Tristan.

As the door swung closed behind Joaquin, Officer Dorn exhaled loudly. "Listen, honey—"

My face turned tomato red. *Honey?* Really? Apparently they didn't have sexual harassment awareness programs in Juniper Landing.

"I want you to talk to Tristan Parrish," I said loudly. I wasn't usually one to order around authority figures, but my anger and terror were, ironically, making me brave. "He was the last person I saw her with."

There was a prolonged silence, and then Officer Dorn and the other two remaining cops burst into laughter.

"Tristan Parrish," Dorn said incredulously. "The mayor's son."

"Yes!" I exclaimed. "Maybe he knows where she is."

"We're not going to be interviewing the mayor's son," Dorn said. He picked up his coffee mug and took a casual sip. But from the corner of my eye, I saw just the tiniest hint of a tremble in his grip.

"Why not? Just because she's the mayor? What if he knows something?" I asked. "I'm not asking you to arrest him. I just want you to talk to him."

Finally, one of the other officers walked over to join us. He was older than Dorn and shorter, paunchier, and uglier. "Listen, miss. People come and go around here all the time. That's just the way it is in vacation towns. Now, why don't you and your friend here go out and enjoy this beautiful morning we're having?"

"I'm telling you this is different," I said shrilly. "Something's happened to her. I can feel it."

The paunchy guy crossed his arms over the top of his belly. He studied me for what felt like forever.

"Okay, fine. If it'll make you feel any better, we'll send out some officers to canvass the beach and the docks, see if anyone's seen her, okay?" he said. "Now, you two get out of here and have some fun. We'll worry about your friend."

Aaron put his hand on my back, and I reluctantly turned to go, but the moment we were outside, I realized something and sprinted back up the steps.

"I didn't even tell you her last name," I announced as I walked through the door. "Or what she looks like."

But there was no one behind the counter anymore. Paunchy, Dorn, the other officers . . . everyone was gone.

EMPTY

"Where are we going now?" Aaron asked as I breezed by him and jogged down the steps. My face was on fire. My heart pounded against my skull. I gritted my teeth as I speed-walked across the park, hugging myself against the cold breeze.

"They don't believe me? Fine. I'll get proof," I said, fuming.

Fisher and Lauren were sitting on the edge of the fountain talking, but they both stopped to stare when I raced by, their gaze hard and silent. I almost tripped when I got a glimpse of what Fisher was wearing. Sitting at a cocky angle on his head was a funky straw fedora, one I recognized all too well.

"What the hell?" I said, stopping dead.

Even though they were yards away, Fisher and Lauren got up, as if they'd heard what I said, and started off in the other direction. At the edge of the park, Fisher slipped the hat off his head and held it in front of him, out of my line of sight.

"What is it?" Aaron asked, watching after them.

"Nothing," I said, shaking my head.

I felt like a series of puzzle pieces were trying to fit themselves together inside my mind. First, the minstrel disappeared and then his guitar strap mysteriously shows up at Tristan's house. Then, the blond guy showed up at the general store solo, and now his absent boyfriend's hat was sitting on Fisher's head. Were the local kids on some kind of crime spree? Stealing random accessories from the visitors?

Unless, of course, the tall guy had given the hat to Fisher. Maybe that was why he wasn't with his boyfriend yesterday. They could have broken up. He could have dumped the other guy for Fisher.

Except they'd seemed so happy, their pinkies linked, their smiles true. Could they have really broken up just like that?

"Rory? You're starting to freak me out here," Aaron said.

"Sorry," I said, starting to walk again. "I'm fine." Aaron hustled to keep up with me as I crossed Main Street and hooked a left onto Freesia Lane.

"What kind of proof are you looking for?" he asked me.

That was a good question. What was I looking for? Evidence of the fact that she still wasn't there? From the corner of my eye I saw a shadow in one of the upper windows of a yellow house, and I walked even faster. In the park, the swings creaked in the increasing wind. Overhead, gray clouds began to gather.

"I don't know," I told him. Shaking my head, I shoved open the front gate. "But there's got to be something."

"I'll wait out here!" Aaron called after me. "Just in case she's there and you two need to talk!"

In case she's there. God, it would be so amazing if she was just *there*.

One fat drop of rain plopped onto the back of my hand as I reached for the porch's banister, and all of a sudden I was in the woods. Raindrops plopped from slick wet leaves. Mud like sludge under my fingernails. The pain in my gut was excruciating as I lifted the knife and swung.

The front door squealed open, and Joaquin slipped out. I blinked, forcing myself back into the present. Into reality. I bounded up the five steps to the porch.

"What the hell are you doing here?" I demanded.

He looked back over his shoulder and closed the door behind him, forcing me to stay on the porch.

"What're you, following me?" he asked with a casual smirk.

"No, I'm not following you," I snapped. "What're you *doing* here, Joaquin?"

"I just came to check on Olive," he said, turning up his palms, then crossing his arms over his chest. "You're right. She's not here."

My heart fell slightly. I glanced over at Aaron, who shrugged up at me from the street as if to ask "What's going on?"

"I'll be right back!" I shouted to him, reaching for the door handle.

"Whoa, wait. Where're you going?" Joaquin asked, gripping my wrist. "I just told you she's not there."

I'd never liked Joaquin, but this was the first time his touch felt threatening. My palms turned clammy as adrenaline rushed hot through my veins.

"I didn't think she was going to be here," I told him, trying unsuccessfully to wriggle myself from his grip. "I just want to see if I can get some proof that something happened to her."

"You're not gonna find anything," Joaquin said with a condescending laugh.

"Can you please take your hand off of me?" I asked, a hot rage simmering just under my skin.

"Hey, friend! I think she said get your hand off of her," Aaron yelled, starting up the walk.

Instantly, Joaquin raised his palms in surrender. "Sorry, man. Didn't realize you were her bodyguard."

The moment I was free, I shoved inside, tore up the stairs to the second floor, and threw open the door to Olive's room.

It was empty. The bed was made, all the corners neatly tucked and the pillows perfectly arranged. The furniture had been dusted and it gleamed in the sunlight pouring through the freshly wiped windows. There were no papers on the desk, no clothes on the chair. Even the fresh-cut flowers were gone. It was as if Olive had never been here.

I stepped tentatively into the room. The windows were closed and locked, and the air was still and stifling. I stared at the spot where her guitar had stood, as if I could will it to reappear. Slowly, I walked around the bed to the desk. I ran my fingers over the surface, pausing where the letter to her mother had been. The silence was so complete my ragged breath sounded like a freight train. Had she come back to pack up and then left? Why hadn't she come to see me? Why hadn't she said good-bye?

A squeak sounded nearby, and I whirled around. The

door to the closet was slightly ajar and I could have sworn I saw a shadow slip deeper inside, out of sight. I froze in place.

"Hello? Is someone in there?" I said, my voice cracking with fear.

Nothing. Fingers trembling, I reached for the brass knob. Another creak. I looked up and saw Mrs. Chen pause just outside the door. I let out a sigh of relief. It was only the landlady. Clearly, my mind was messing with me.

"Hi, Mrs. Chen," I said. "Do you know if—"

She was so stooped the hem of her faded flowered house-coat grazed the planks of the floor, but the moment I spoke, she started moving again, faster than I would have thought possible.

"Mrs. Chen?" I said.

She ignored me, darting up the stairs to the third floor.

"Wait! Mrs. Chen!" I said, going after her. "Where's all of Olive's stuff?" Mrs. Chen stopped at a door and fumbled with her huge set of keys, her fingers trembling.

"She sent for it," she said.

"She did?" I said, half-relieved, half-baffled. "When? Where did she have it sent?"

"I don't know." She shoved a key into the doorknob in front of her. "You need to go."

"What do you mean, you don't know?" I said as she opened the door and moved inside. I could see a sparsely decorated living room behind her and stacks of magazines piled up under a window, everything from *Popular Mechanics* to *InStyle* to *Cottage Home*. "Did you pack it up?" I asked. "Did someone come for it, or did you have to send it out?"

"It's not my business and you're trespassing," Mrs. Chen said, already closing the door on me. "Now go!"

"No, wait! Mrs. Chen! I just want to know where she is. I want to know if she's okay," I said.

The door stopped closing with inches to spare. Mrs. Chen peeked out, her eyes watery behind her thick glasses. "She's fine, miss," she whispered, glancing toward the stairs. A chill went through me. Why was she whispering? And what did she mean by fine? Then she reached out one craggy hand and clasped it around my wrist. Her skin was surprisingly warm, and I felt a pleasant, almost comforting flutter inside my chest. "She's . . . better off where she is. Now go."

And then she closed the door.

EXPLANATION

As I staggered down the steps toward Aaron, everything tilted. I grabbed for the banister and paused, bringing my hand to my forehead, trying to breathe.

"She's still not there?" Aaron asked me.

I shook my head, not trusting my voice or what I might blurt out, and started slowly past him. Joaquin was gone, thank goodness. I wasn't sure I could deal with him right now.

Why would she just send for her stuff? Why wouldn't she come by and explain?

"Rory? Where're you going?" Aaron asked.

"Home," I said, staring at the sidewalk as I turned right

and started down the hill. "I don't feel well." Major under-
statement. I felt nauseous. And tired. And nervous. And
confused.

He jogged to catch up with me, placing a comforting
hand on my shoulder. "Let me walk you."

I sidestepped away. "Thanks, but I'll be fine," I told him
tightly.

"Okay," he said, gripping the strap of his bag with both
hands. He stood in the center of the sidewalk as he watched
me walk away, a confused and slightly hurt look on his face.
"Hey! I was going to ask if you wanted to go to the fireworks
together later!"

"Sure!" I shouted back, mostly to get him off my case.

"I'll come by and get you at eight!"

"Okay!" I yelled, quickening my pace.

All I wanted was to get off the street. Get back to my
room. Sit down and think. Nothing made sense right now.
Not Darcy deleting Olive's existence from her memory. Not
Tristan and his friends' constant staring. Not the cops' complete disregard of my fears. Not Joaquin showing up at the
boardinghouse or Mrs. Chen's explanation that Olive was
better off wherever she was now. And what was with that
storage room in Tristan's house? Why did Fisher have that
guy's hat? And what did all those Steven Nell mementos
have to do with all this?

As I stepped up to the gate in front of our house, a curtain moved in a window across the street. Instantly, all my confusion and terror formed itself into one giant ball of anger, and all of it was directed at Tristan. He knew something. I was certain of it. And I was going to make him tell me.

I stormed across the street, up to the front door, and banged on it as hard as I could. Pain radiated up my arm and into my shoulder, but that only made me knock harder. I was starting to wonder if his nanna really lived there. If anyone really lived there. Or if he was just squatting in the house so he could keep an eye on me. Or on Olive. Or on everyone.

Suddenly, the door flew open, and there stood Tristan in all his tanned, blond, chiseled perfection. His white T-shirt brought out his bronze glow, and when he pushed his golden hair away from his face, it fell right back where it had been, grazing his incredible cheekbones. He looked me up and down with a sort of resigned sorrow on his face. It was clear that he was not at all surprised to see me.

"Hello, Rory," he said.

"Visiting Nanna?" I said sarcastically.

He simply stared, like such behavior was beneath me. And he was right. I gulped back my humiliation. I was here for a reason.

"What do you know?" I demanded.

"What do I know about what?" he asked calmly.

"Olive!" I said, irritated. "Where did she go after the party at your house? Where did you take her?"

His blue eyes darkened. "What makes you think I took her somewhere?" He started past me, but I stopped him with my hand to his chest.

"I saw you leave the party with her."

He paused and stared down at my fingers. I couldn't help but notice how solid his chest was. Slowly, shakily, I removed my hand.

He narrowed his eyes and blinked up at the sun. "We didn't leave. We went outside to hang out with some friends on the bluff."

"In that fog?" I demanded.

"Visitors always want to check out the fog," he said, sounding mildly amused, like we vacationers were some kind of lesser, ignorant subset of humanity.

"And then?" I asked.

Staring into my eyes, he shrugged. "I don't know," he said slowly. "It was a party. There were dozens of people there. I can't keep track of everyone."

"Yeah, well, she's missing." I said. "And as far as I know, you were the last person to see her."

Tristan shook his head, looking at some point over my shoulder. "I'm sorry. I can't help you."

"Great!" I said, tears suddenly springing to my eyes. He

looked down at me, alarmed. "Just like everyone else in this messed-up town. What is wrong with all of you? How come no one cares that people keep disappearing?"

I brought my hand to my head and turned away, kicking at an empty wooden-plank planter near the edge of the front step. I expected Tristan to walk away to avoid my meltdown, especially since it was so clear he'd wanted to escape even before I started crying, but instead he reached out and put his hand on my shoulder. His fingers were so warm I could feel their heat through the fabric of my thin hoodie. He tugged, forcing me to face him.

His eyes were bright. "Do you really want to know?"

"Yes," I said, pitching my voice low like his. "I really want to know."

"No," he said with a frustrated shake of his head. "No. You need to think about it for a second, Rory. Look at me. Look at me and tell me. Do you *really* want to know?"

I looked at him, stared into his eyes, and thought about it. Did I really want to know what had happened to Olive? Did I really want to know what was going on with my sister? Did I really want to know why the guy who'd been playing in the park every morning seemed to have vanished? Did I really want answers to my million-and-one other questions, like why was he spying on me? Why did Joaquin and Krista seemed obsessed with me? And was I going crazy thinking Steven Nell was leaving me random, taunting gifts?

I stared into his beautiful, Caribbean-blue eyes, and suddenly something opened up inside me. It started small, like a pinprick of doubt deep within my chest. But rapidly it grew. It grew into a great, wide, yawning, black hole of emptiness that froze my blood inside my veins. The world around me seemed to quiet and dim, all the colors muted, all the smells going sour. My heart pounded so hard I felt like I was going to black out. I had a sudden sensation that the sidewalk was tipping backward beneath me. It was as if the ground was opening up, threatening to swallow me whole. Stifling a cry, I grabbed for Tristan's hand to keep from sliding off into the abyss.

The second his fingers closed around mine, the world snapped back into focus. Sound, smell, sight, everything came rushing back. The birds tweeted in a nearby dogwood tree, someone somewhere was mowing their lawn, the scent of frying bacon wafted through the air through an open kitchen window. I could breathe again.

Tristan inched closer to me, almost as if he was pulling me in for a kiss, but stopped inches from my mouth. He looked sad. He looked sorry.

"Listen to me," he said softly. "Olive has some issues."

I blinked. "What kind of issues?"

"Issues with . . . addiction," he said.

"What?" I backed up a step. Still, he kept his grip on my shoulders. "What kind of addiction?"

Tristan swallowed hard. He looked down at the sidewalk for a second, then back into my eyes. Something was different now. He seemed less sure of himself.

"She's okay now—she got herself clean—but I know she really wanted to make amends with her mom," he said. "That's what she's gone to do. She's fine. In fact, she's better than fine. She's . . . moving forward."

The rhythmic, buzzing sound of the mower grew closer, humming inside my ears. Suddenly, I remembered what Olive had told me that day on our run. That she'd gotten herself better. She must have meant that she'd kicked her addiction. And then the other night at the party, when I'd been so offended that she thought Darcy was doing drugs . . . I *had* offended her. I'd offended her with my shock and disgust, because she herself had been an addict. She'd said her friend had blacked out thanks to heroin. That must have been why she always wore long sleeves, why she made sure to cover up her arms. She was covering up track marks.

"I'm so stupid." I breathed, closing my eyes as a wave of shame overtook me. When I opened them again, Tristan was still there, still holding on to me, still studying my face. "She told you this?" I asked, feeling almost jealous. Olive had clearly felt closer to Tristan than she'd ever felt to me.

"It's something we talked about," he replied.

"But why didn't she tell me she was leaving?" I asked, my voice cracking. "Why wouldn't she at least say good-bye?"

"I'm sure she had her reasons, but the point is, everything's going to be okay," he said firmly. "People come and go around here all the time. That's just the way it is in vacation towns. I've gotten used to it, and you will, too."

"You sound just like the cops," I said with a scoff. I turned, releasing myself from his grip, and sat down on the top step. Tristan sat next to me, our thighs touching.

"You went to the cops?" he asked, surprised.

"Well, what else do you do when your friend goes missing?" I asked.

Tristan looked across the street, off toward the ocean, with a small, amused smile. "That must've been interesting," he said under his breath.

"What?" I asked.

"Oh, nothing," he replied. "It's like we were saying the other day. Nothing bad ever happens around here. They probably didn't know what to do with you, right?"

I let out a quiet laugh. "Pretty much."

"It's gonna be okay," Tristan said confidently, placing a comforting hand on my back.

"Yeah?" I said.

"Yeah," he replied, turning to look at me. As I gazed into his steady eyes, the awful tightness around my heart began to ease.

Who was I to think that after three days of friendship I merited an explanation or even a good-bye? Olive wasn't from my world, and she clearly had problems I couldn't even begin to understand. It was perfectly reasonable to assume she was the type of person to just bail, and if she'd gone home to patch things up with her mother, good for her.

Just then, Joaquin appeared at the end of the walk. I hadn't even noticed him turn onto the street. "Everything okay?" he asked, leaning one hand casually on the fence post.

I pushed myself to my feet, still annoyed by the way he'd treated me at the boardinghouse and laughed me off earlier. "I was just leaving."

"What did I do?" Joaquin asked, raising his hands as I shoved the gate wider to get by him.

"Like you don't know," I shot back.

"Rory, wait," he said, taking my wrist, but much gentler this time. He glanced meaningfully up at Tristan, but I had no idea what he was trying to communicate. "We need to tell you something."

"I just told her, man," Tristan said, rising and pushing his hands into his pockets.

Joaquin blinked, annoyance flashing across his face. "You did?"

"Yeah. About Olive's drug problem," Tristan replied, his tone pointed.

Joaquin dropped my wrist and crossed his arms over his chest. "That's not what I'm talking about."

Tristan jogged down the steps and crossed the walk in two long strides. "Yes, it is."

"No. It's not," Joaquin said with a sardonic laugh.

My pulse raced with curiosity. For a second, they just stared each other down. Joaquin's nostrils flared. Tristan's breath grew quick.

"Would *one* of you just tell me what the hell is going on?" I demanded.

"We need to talk," Tristan told Joaquin through clenched teeth. "In private."

He turned and walked back toward the house. After a long moment's hesitation, Joaquin followed. They stood under the shade of an orange tree, their heads bent close together as they argued in low tones. I tried my best to hear, but the buzzing of the lawn mower was now annoyingly close and I could make out only a few words.

"But she saw me at the station with—"

"Doesn't matter! She's not—"

"And then Krista was in the middle of—"

"I'm telling you, I tried and she can't—"

"Fine!" Joaquin blurted suddenly. "Whatever you say, golden boy."

He turned and stormed toward me, his face contorted with anger, but he paused on the sidewalk and seemed to make a decision. He put both hands on my shoulders and leaned in close to my ear. I was so startled I almost recoiled, but his grip held me firmly in place.

"Rory, if you want to know anything . . . if you have any questions at all . . . you come see me, okay?" He leaned back to look me in the eye, and for the first time the superior glint was gone. He was all sincerity. My heart thumped in surprise. "Anything at all," he said. "Got it?"

I nodded slowly, baffled and intrigued. "Got it."

He released me and shot Tristan a sort of defiant, triumphant glare before slipping by and speed-walking up the street. I turned to ask Tristan what that was all about, but he was already gone. All I saw was the door of the gray house closing me out with a resounding thud.

THE FIGHT

"He probably forgot he said he was going to pick me up," Darcy theorized later that night, pulling the long sleeves of her white cardigan sweater over her hands as we walked up the steep path toward the bluff where we'd watch the fireworks. The sun was rapidly sinking in the west, and a cool breeze made us all shiver. "At one point we *were* talking about just meeting on the bluff. I bet he just got mixed up."

"I'm sure you're right," Aaron said. "He's going to feel like a stupid git when you tell him."

Or he really is a stupid git. But I decided to keep my mouth shut. I wanted to have fun tonight, and that meant not fighting with Darcy. Aaron looked so adorable in a white-and-blue striped rugby shirt and tan shorts, his floppy brown hair tossed by the wind. It made me wish Joaquin *was* gay so Aaron would have a shot and Darcy could move on.

"Hey, thanks. You look pretty, too," Aaron said suddenly, slinging his arm over my shoulders.

I blushed. "How did you know what I was thinking?"

"I never miss an admiring glance, especially when it's focused on me," he replied with a smile. "But I'm serious. The dress suits you. You should wear dresses more often."

I glanced down at the sundress I'd borrowed from Darcy, with its cap sleeves and a swishy skirt that tickled my thighs as we walked. I'd even ditched the braid, going with a low ponytail instead. The whole getup made me feel lighter somehow. More free.

"Maybe I will," I replied.

As we got to the top of the bluff, and the crowd of fresh-faced, tanned locals and visitors came into view, I took a deep breath of the floral air and sighed.

"Glad you came?" Aaron asked, giving me a squeeze.

"Definitely."

We walked toward the gazebo at the center of the out-cropping. Most people seemed to be gathered near its steps, and as we got closer I saw why. There was a big table offering trays of cupcakes, cookies, and fruit bars. A couple of standing coolers held lemonade and iced tea. Just beyond the gazebo, I saw Tristan's house, sitting at the highest point on the island, the American flag out front whipping in the breeze. I saw myself standing there that day Olive and I had gone for a run together—saw me looking down at this very gazebo, feeling, if only briefly, that all was right in the world as I waited for her to catch up. I wondered where Olive was tonight, and I hoped that wherever she was, she was feeling that way now.

"Why don't you guys find a place to sit and I'll get us some food?" Aaron suggested, handing me the plaid blanket he'd brought along.

"Sounds good. Darcy?" I asked.

She was standing on her toes, craning her neck, searching the crowd. I rolled my eyes and grabbed her hand.

"Come on," I said. "Let the guys come to you, remember?"

She sighed, bringing her heels back to earth. "Did I say that?"

We walked around the gazebo and saw that people had set up chairs and blankets facing the water. I unfolded our blanket, and Darcy helped me flatten it out on the grass. We settled in next to each other, and I leaned back on my hands.

"Too bad Dad decided to write tonight," I said with a sigh. "He used to love fireworks."

"I know, right? Running, writing, apologizing . . . it's like the last five years never happened," Darcy replied. She sat up on her knees, her butt leaned back on her feet, scanning the crowd.

"Weird, right?" I said, warming to the topic. Darcy and I almost never talked seriously about anything. "Do you think he'll—"

"I'm sorry. I can't just sit here," Darcy interrupted. "I bet he's looking for me."

I groaned. So much for that.

"Then let him find you," I suggested. "Didn't Mom always say that if you ever get lost, the best way to be found is to stay in one place?"

Darcy chewed on the inside of her cheek. "She did say that." She took a deep breath, and for a second I thought she was going to relax, but instead she jumped to her feet. The sky overhead had darkened to a deep purple, and people were starting to move from the gazebo, closing in around us. "I'll just do a quick loop of the crowd."

"Darcy," I said, pushing myself up. "Look at yourself. This isn't you. Why are you going out of your way for someone who's clearly blowing you off?"

Her green eyes flashed. "I can't believe you just said that to me," she said, crossing her arms over her stomach.

I tried to think of some way to take it back, but it was too late now. And besides, I was right and she needed to hear what I thought.

"I'm sorry, but I think Joaquin is a total player, and I just don't want you to get hurt," I told her.

"If you care so much about me not getting hurt, then maybe you should stop flirting with him in front of everyone," she spat out.

"What?" I said, my face screwing up in confusion.

"Oh, please! Drop the innocent act already, Rory!" she cried, throwing her arms up and letting them drop down at her sides. I saw a couple of passersby whisper about us but couldn't have cared less. "First I see you guys hugging, then this morning he's whispering in your ear in front of the house? You like him, Rory! Admit it!"

"What do you do, spend all your time in your window seat spying on me?" I shot back. "And for your information, I didn't ask him to do either of those things!"

"Oh, no? Well, what about Christopher? Did you ask him to break up with me, or was that all him, too?"

A single firework popped overhead, a bright, white, earthshaking blast to announce the start of the show. Everyone around us cheered and clapped. Darcy and I simply stood there, facing off.

She knew about Christopher. She *knew*. I felt like the bluff was slowly crumbling beneath my feet.

"How . . . how did you . . . how long have you known?" I stammered.

"Oh, only since the day I overheard him begging you to go to the winter formal with him," she shot back, leaning forward at the waist.

Another firework exploded, followed by a series of merry crackles. I shook my head, completely thrown. Christopher and I had that conversation at our house right after school. Darcy was at cheerleading practice, like she was every day. Or she was supposed to be.

"You were there?" I asked meekly.

"I told Coach Haskins I wasn't feeling well and went home. I'd been having a lot of trouble sleeping, in case you don't remember," she said bitterly.

She'd been having trouble sleeping because she'd been crying practically nonstop for the forty-eight hours since Christopher had broken up with her. I still remembered lying in bed, counting the star stickers I'd stuck to my ceiling in fourth grade, clutching my blanket to my chest as I listened to her sob.

"But if . . . if you were there, then you know that I turned him down," I stammered. "You . . . you *know* I told him I couldn't do that to you."

Darcy let out a strained laugh as everyone started oohing and aahing over a loud series of fireworks.

"Oh, yeah, I heard. And thanks so much for your pity," she said, tears streaming down her cheeks, cutting lines through her carefully applied makeup. "That's just what every girl wants. To hear the love of her life begging her younger, dorkier sister to be with him and hear her say no to spare her feelings. Thanks so much, Rory. And I believe all this happened *after* you spent an entire afternoon making out with him? I definitely remember him saying something about that."

A huge, wet ball was choking off my air supply. "You guys were . . . you were already broken up."

"Oh, we were already broken up!" She threw her hands up. "Wow! Thanks so much for giving our two-year relationship eight hours to grow cold."

I brought my hands to my forehead for a second, trying to catch my breath, trying to organize my thoughts. When I looked up at her again, there were tears in my eyes. "Darcy—"

"No. You're not allowed to look at me that way. I'm going to go find Joaquin, and if you don't like it, or if you don't like him, then good," she said. "At least that means you won't try to steal him, too."

Then she turned on her heel and cut through the crowd, practically shoving Aaron and his carefully balanced plate of treats out of her way.

"What's going on?" he asked, dipping down to place the food on our blanket. "Where's Darcy going?" He tilted his head in concern as he got a close look at my face. "Rory, why are you crying?"

"I have to go after her," I said.

"Now?" He gestured up as the sky turned blue, then purple, and then bright gold.

"I know, but . . . it's too much to explain. I just have to talk to her," I said. "Will you help me?"

"Of course," he said. "Follow me."

He took my hand and wedged through a small opening in the crowd. My back grazed a denim jacket, and I tripped over the metal leg of a lawn chair as I clung to his fingers. The sky seemed to darken by the second as more people pressed in and the fireworks popped, turning the unfamiliar faces around me blue, then purple, then red.

"Do you see her?" I asked Aaron.

"Not yet!" he shouted to be heard over the show. "Was she looking for Joaquin? Maybe we should find *him*, and then we'll find her."

I turned to walk backward, letting him carve a path for me. The redheaded boy from the party at Tristan's hung out near the gazebo, chatting up a girl with thick glasses. The blond boy from the general store stood with his back against the gazebo's lattice, still solo, as he watched the sky. A shower of white sparks illuminated the world, and I saw Bea, Lauren, Fisher, and Kevin leaning into the gazebo's railing a few steps up. My heart stopped. There were a hundred people in the crowd, yet every one of the four locals was watching me. I wrenched my hand out of Aaron's and shoved my way over to the gazebo. "Have you seen Darcy?" I demanded.

"Who?" Fisher asked.

"My sister! Darcy!" I shouted. They all stared at me blankly. I felt like hurling something at them. Something seriously, heavy. "Forget it. Where's Joaquin?"

"Dunno," Kevin replied. He shrugged, then turned his back on me and the fireworks, leaning his butt into the railing. "Haven't seen him."

"Well, if you see him, can you—"

Someone jostled me from behind, and I whirled around, hoping it was Darcy. Instead, I caught a glimpse of a tan corduroy jacket just before it was swallowed up by the crowd.

My blood turned cold in my veins.

"No," I said under my breath.

It was him. He was here.

I darted after the jacket. The crowd was thick and pressed in around me. A pigtailed girl glared at me as I stepped on her toes, and a beefy guy in a sweatshirt cursed as I elbowed him in the ribs to get through. The sky flashed pink. I whirled around, scanning the crowd for a glimpse of tan corduroy. A gap emerged in the crowd, and there it was, dead ahead. That ugly, puke color. That awful, wide wale. I swallowed hard as the man wearing it turned his head, and I saw his silhouette in profile.

He had on glasses. Wire-rimmed glasses.

He turned away from me, and his pace quickened.

"Steven Nell!" I shouted at the top of my lungs.

He froze. And then he really started to move.

Heart in my throat, I kept elbowing through the crowd and chased after Nell. My sleeve caught on someone's button and tore. I shoved a guy in a plaid shirt so hard he hit his knees in the dirt. My ankle caught on an outstretched leg, and I flew forward, only to catch myself on a skinny girl's knee.

"Sorry," I muttered, hurtling over her.

He was near the edge of the crowd now, heading back toward town. He was going to get away. But then a whole group of girls in miniskirts and tiny tops traipsed in front of him, arm in arm, gossiping and giggling and taking their sweet time, and he was forced to stop. He was feet away. Inches. I was closing in.

"Where is she!?" I shouted, my hand coming down on his shoulder.

He whirled around to face me, and I felt my heart explode. Angry red acne dotted his right cheek. A small scar cut the flesh over his lip. His wide forehead was dotted with sweat and his glasses didn't have wire frames, but thick, blue ones.

It wasn't Steven Nell at all.

"What?" the guy said, raising his meaty white palms. "What'd I do?"

I felt my stomach turn, and it was all I could do not to boot it all over his white Nikes.

"I'm sorry. I . . . I thought you were someone else," I told him.

"Whatever," he said, shaking his head.

Then he sniffed, muttered "Crazy person" under his breath, and headed back toward town. I pushed my hands into my hair and forced myself to breathe. Maybe I *was* crazy. Maybe Darcy was fine. She was probably off with Joaquin right now, kissing the night away. Maybe I should chill the hell out.

I turned back toward the crowd, intent on finding Aaron and getting on with my night. There was a brief moment of silence between firework explosions, and then I heard a scream. Darcy's scream. Her scream as the truck slammed into our car. As he bashed her head in. Her hair tangled over her face, her pale fingers splayed out on the dirt. Her wrist still warm but without a pulse.

Another firework popped, and my heart slammed inside my rib cage.

"Darcy!" I yelled toward the pack of people in front of me. "Darcy! Where are you? Answer me!"

A few people near the back edge of the crowd shot me annoyed looks. Slowly, I turned in a circle, trying to stifle the sound of my breath, the pounding of my pulse in my ears, hoping to hear a shout or another scream, something that would pinpoint her location for me. Everything flashed by quickly. Trees, lights, gazebo, ocean, fireworks, crowd, rocks, rooftops. Trees, lights, gazebo, ocean, fireworks, crowd, rocks, rooftops. Over and over and over again, the sights whirled, but there was no Darcy. I stopped turning and pressed my hands to my eyes, waiting for the world to stop spinning. Waiting for some sound, some clue. But there was nothing. Nothing but the earthshaking explosions overhead, the delighted cries of the spectators.

When I finally opened my eyes, I focused right in on a streak of white in the dirt a few feet in front of me. My pulse skipped a thousand beats. I raced over and stopped dead. It was Darcy's cardigan. It lay flat in the dirt next to a garbage can, a man's muddy boot print pressed into its otherwise pristine fabric. My vision blurred.

"Darcy?" I whimpered. "Darcy?"

My hands trembled as I bent to pick it up. Another firework exploded, showering the town of Juniper Landing in red sparks.

"Darcy!" I screamed as loud as I could. "Darcy, where are you!?"

Suddenly, the lights of the town dulled, then were extinguished altogether. I took a staggered step back as the air around me began to move, began to creep in toward me. Within seconds, the fog had whipped around my ankles and swirled up to my knees. I heard the crowd behind me groan as the thick, gray mist formed a seal between us and the sky, blanking out the fireworks.

"Darcy!" I screamed again. "Darcy, please answer me!"

Somewhere off in the distance, somewhere impossibly far away, I heard a shout. I heard Darcy cry out.

My hands reached up to cover my mouth. There was no way to know where the shout had come from. No way to tell which direction I was even facing. I stood there and listened, hoping for another shout, another sign, anything. But all I could hear was the pounding of my heart and the incessant hissing of the mist.

Darcy was gone. And Nell had her.

SISTERS

Over the years, he had learned that sisters were not the same. It didn't matter how alike they looked, how close in age they were, that they'd grown up in the same household under the same rules. In his experience there was almost nothing about them that was similar. Not their smell, not their taste, not their spirit. Often, one sister was far more successful, in colloquial terms, than the other. Prettier, more outgoing, more popular. Some theorized that this was a simple fluke of nature, but not him. He believed that it was all because of psychological warfare.

The sisters might not have even known this war was

being waged, but it always was, and it was often the second- or third-born who suffered. She slipped out of the womb fresh and full of hope and purpose, but was quickly taught that she was not special, she would never be the one-and-only, she would never be as good or as loved as the first. And so, she receded. She curled in on herself. She found a way to survive, but not to shine.

Rory Miller deserved to have a chance to shine, but alas, she was the second-born. Perhaps she would thank him when she saw what he'd done for her. Thank him for giving her the opportunity she never had, to be the one, the only, the star.

Of course, she would only have one, precious, fleeting moment to take her rightful place in her family, before he slaughtered her, too.

NOT YET

Someone slammed into my side, and I staggered to the left, my hand gripping the cold metal garbage can to keep me from going down.

"Sorry. Didn't see you," a guy's voice said.

The crowd was moving around me, headed back toward town in the disorienting fog. Someone stepped on my foot. A hand grazed my hip. Another person walked right into the garbage can, nearly knocking it over. I clung to Darcy's sweater and turned around and around, trying to find someone I recognized, desperate to do something.

A hand came down on my shoulder, and I screamed.

KATE BRIAN

"Rory! It's just me!" Tristan held both my arms. He took one look in my eyes and paled. "What's wrong?"

"My sister," I said. "I can't find my sister."

Joaquin and Krista materialized out of the mist, standing just behind Tristan. Joaquin was wearing a red-and-white striped polo shirt with the collar flipped up, and the whole preppy-superior look made me want to smack him.

"What?" Joaquin said, a shadow crossing his face.

"She went looking for you after you stood her up!" I snapped, venom spewing from my tongue. "And now he's—"

I stopped, biting down on my tongue. I couldn't tell them about Steven Nell. I wasn't allowed.

"And now she's just disappeared!" I finished.

"Disappeared?" Krista asked, alarmed.

"And don't tell me, 'She's Darcy, she's fine!'" I shouted at Joaquin sarcastically, mimicking his voice. "And don't you dare tell me people come and go around here all the time!" I added, whirling on Tristan. "This is my sister we're talking about."

"What's going on?" Kevin asked.

He, Fisher, Bea, and Lauren appeared as if from nowhere, gathering around Tristan, their expressions serious. Oh, so now that Joaquin was officially involved they were willing to help.

"Darcy Thayer is missing," Tristan said.

"Wait, like *missing* missing?" Fisher asked.

"What?" Lauren asked. "But it's not—"

"We know," Joaquin said, cutting her off. "Everyone, fan out. We have to find her. Fisher, you get the beach. Kevin, you're on the docks. Lauren and Bea, you guys go into town, and Krista—"

"I know," Krista said. "I'm on it."

She turned and took off into the fog as the others disappeared as well, moving off in all directions. The mist shifted and swirled before swallowing them whole, one by one. Somewhere in the distance, a boat's bell clanged, the sound muted by the thickness of the air.

"What's going on?" I asked. "What's Krista 'on'?"

Joaquin looked stonily away from me.

"Hello? You said I can ask you anything, right?" I said, grabbing his arm. "So what does she know? Where's she going?"

My chest was about to burst in frustration, but Joaquin remained silent. I turned to Tristan. "Will someone tell me what the hell is going on?"

"Rory—" Tristan started.

"Dude, now is not the time," Joaquin said warningly, grabbing Tristan's shoulder. "We have to go."

Tristan's face flushed with color. "You have to be kidding

me. *Now* you want to shut her out? This is her sister we're talking about!"

My pulse pounded in my very eyes. What were they talking about? What were they keeping from me?

"This is different, Tristan," Joaquin said through his teeth. "This is DEFCON One. Something's wrong. The girl wasn't ready yet. We have to get inside. We have to tell them what's going on. You know this." He turned to me, his jaw clenching and unclenching. "I'm sorry, Rory," he said, his tone all business.

Then he turned and started off in the direction of Tristan's house. At least, I thought his house was off that way. In the fog, it was almost impossible to know for sure. Tristan looked at me and pressed his lips together, clearly desperate to speak. I felt like I was being folded inside out.

"Come *on*, dude," Joaquin said, his voice coming from somewhere deep within the fog.

Tristan took one step back, one step away. "I'm sorry," he said.

"Tristan, no. Don't go," I pleaded. "Please, just tell me what's going on. I know you want to. Just tell me!"

He shook his head. "I can't," he said. "Not yet."

"What does that mean, not yet?" I cried, tears streaming down my face. With one last, regretful look, he turned and walked away from me, the mist swirling around him.

"Wait! What does that mean, not yet? Tristan! Tristan, come back! Don't just leave me here!"

But Tristan didn't come back, and I was left alone in the fog, holding my sister's sweater.

CANADA

I was right on my father's heels as he shoved open the doors of the Juniper Landing Police Department and barreled into the freezing cold lobby, slipping his Yankees baseball cap from his head.

"It's my daughter!" he shouted. "She's—"

We both stopped in our tracks in the center of the wide room. There were about fifty people gathered there in dark blue JUNIPER LANDING jackets, and they all fell silent and stared. Most of them were gathered around the counter, where it looked like the police had laid out a map of some kind. I heard a rustling, and suddenly the heavyset officer from that morning stepped out from behind the counter, hiking up his pants at the back.

"You must be Mr. Thayer," he said, holding out his hand. "I'm Police Chief Grantz. We already know about your daughter, sir. We're putting together a search party."

He gestured around the room, and a few of the people around us nodded. A man with white hair tucked a piece of paper behind his back, and I thought I saw a glimpse of Darcy's face on it. I glanced around quickly and saw a few other people shove photos into their pockets as well. Where had they gotten a picture of Darcy?

"Thank you, but we don't need a search party," my father said gruffly. "What we need is to call the FBI."

A murmur went through the crowd and quickly grew into a din. Chief Grantz looked around nervously.

"Let's go back to my office and talk, shall we?"

The chief gripped my father's arm and steered him back behind the counter. I followed, feeling dozens of pairs of eyes trailing me as I went. We skirted a few neatly kept desks in the center of the room, and then Grantz opened a door, waiting until we'd stepped inside before he closed it behind him. The chief's office was small and square, with a metal desk in the center and a huge JUNIPER LANDING PD emblem on the wall behind it. There were no filing cabinets, no high-tech equipment. Nothing but a phone and a coatrack with a jacket and one hat hung on it. In the center of the desk was Darcy's senior photo from school. My blood ran cold. How had they gotten that picture? No one on this island had that picture except maybe my dad, and if he had it, it was in his wallet. The chief saw me staring at it and shoved it into a drawer.

I glanced at my father, but he didn't seem to notice anything was amiss. In the next room, a pair of tense voices argued, but I couldn't make out what they were saying.

"There's no need to be alerting the feds, sir," the chief said quietly. "Your daughter has been missing less than an hour."

"But there *is* a reason," my father said, shooting me a wary, bolstering look as he wrung his baseball cap in his hands. "My family is here as part of the witness protection program. My daughter Rory was attacked by a serial killer named Roger Krauss just last week and as far as we know he was never caught. There's a possibility he has Darcy now."

The man stared at us. There was a long, drawn-out pause, and I felt like I could hear the gears in his head working through this information. "Sir, that's highly unlikely."

"I don't care how unlikely it is!" my father shouted. "I want them called in, now!"

The police chief took a step back and for once in my life, I was glad that my father was so scary when he was pissed off. In the next room, something slammed and there was a shout of surprise.

"All right. All right, then. I'll call my contact at the FBI." The man moved over to the desk and reached for the black phone sitting near the corner. The arguing next door continued, growing louder, tenser, but still unintelligible.

"If you'd please wait outside?" the chief asked, glancing at the wall between us and the fight.

"No. I want to be here for this," my father said.

"I understand, sir, but I'm afraid it's protocol," the chief said, his hand shaking slightly as he lifted the receiver. "I can't have civilians in the room while I discuss a case with the FBI."

My father blew out a frustrated sigh but yanked the door open. He let me through first, then slammed it, causing another stoppage of noise in the lobby. I saw a few people staring at us over the counter and turned my back to them. Inside the office, Chief Grantz began to speak in low tones.

"I'm so sorry, Rory," my father said, rubbing his brow with one hand and sitting down on a bench outside the office. He looked up at me, his eyes heavy. "I'm so sorry I didn't believe you."

"It's okay," I said quietly. "I didn't even know what to believe. Until now."

He reached for my hand and held it. "If I lose her . . ."

"I know," I said, my voice full. "We can't even think about that." I took a breath. "Dad? Can I see your wallet?"

His brows knit, but he reached for his back pocket. "Why?"

"I just want to check something," I said.

I flipped open the soft leather billfold and reached into the pocket where my dad kept family photos. Out came my sophomore picture, my bangs too short and my smile too big, and right behind it was Darcy's photo. It was still there. He hadn't lost it. Darcy hadn't taken it and given it to Joaquin. No one had stolen it to make copies. So how the hell had the cops distributed it?

The door behind us opened, and the chief came striding out. "Good news. It's not Roger Krauss."

"What?" I breathed. My father stood up, still clinging to my hand. The voices in the next room escalated.

"I just spoke to an Agent Lawrence with the FBI," the chief said, drawing himself up straight. "He says this Nell character took off for Canada, and they're following several leads there. They seem to think they're closing in on him. They want you to stay here for a few more days until they've brought him in, but they assured me that the man is nowhere near Juniper Landing."

I let out a breath, relief flooding through me. Canada. Darcy was all right.

"Thank goodness," my father said, relaxing slightly. "But then where's Darcy? Where's my daughter?"

"That's what the search party is for, sir," the chief said, placing his hand on my father's back and leading him toward the counter, away from the quickly escalating argument behind closed doors. "Every now and then, one of our visitors gets lost on the beach or turned around in that nasty fog and we have to go out and find them. We've done this before, and we've always been successful. So if you'll just let us go about our business . . ."

"Well, we want to join the search party," my father said forcefully. "Rory and I can help."

Someone nearby coughed, and the police chief tugged on his ear. "That won't be necessary," he said.

"Why not? The more people looking for her, the better, right?" I said.

"Well, yes, I suppose, in theory, but I think it's better if you two wait for her back at your house. You never know. She might just come walking through the door, and if no one's there, we have no way of knowing about it."

My father looked at me, considering the logic of this. I could tell he felt much better, much more secure, knowing that Steven Nell or Roger Krauss or whatever we were calling him was out of the picture. I wanted to feel that way, too, but I couldn't shake the feeling I'd had all week that something was off.

"Okay, fine," my father said finally, putting his arm around me. "We'll go home. But you'll let us know the second you find anything?"

"Of course," the chief replied solicitously.

An office door behind the counter flung open and angry voices echoed through the room.

"What makes you think you know more about this than I do?" a familiar voice shouted. I turned around just in time to see Joaquin, his face as red as blood, shout back over his shoulder into the office. "Who the hell do you think you are?"

He stormed toward the back of the building, not noticing me or my father, and slammed through a heavy metal door. One second later, Officer Dorn stepped into the doorway of the office, looking shaken—like he'd just taken a scolding.

"Who the hell was that?" my father asked me under his breath as we moved toward the front door.

"That was Joaquin," I replied, my legs quaking.

"The boy Darcy likes?" he asked, holding the door open for me. "Wow. He seemed really upset. He must like her, too."

"Yeah," I said vaguely. "He must."

But had my dad not registered what he'd said, what we'd just seen? What was Joaquin doing, telling off a police officer? What did he mean "Who the hell do you think you are?" And what, exactly, did he know more about than Dorn did?

THE SEARCH

I sat on the back deck of our house two hours later, facing north, watching as the search party of locals bobbed into view up the beach, the beams of their flashlights weaving and dipping across the ground and sky. I'd been waiting all night to see it in action, and now, here they were, a whole, long line of about two dozen, walking shoulder to shoulder along the sand. The line stretched from the dunes all the way to the water, and they walked slowly, their eyes cast down, scanning the ground beneath their feet with their flashlights. In this way, I supposed, they were ensured they wouldn't miss a thing. But as I watched as they approached my house, I felt a twist of discomfort deep in my stomach. Why were their eyes trained on the ground? Were they looking for my sister or searching for a body?

I took a deep breath and looked up at the sky. The fog had rolled out as my father and I walked back to the house, and now millions of stars winked merrily overhead, clearly oblivious to the torture I was experiencing under their watch.

Where was Darcy? If Steven Nell truly wasn't here, then where had she gone? Why had I heard her scream?

Off to my left, I heard raised voices. There was a white tent set up on an outstretch of land between the next two houses, a sort of makeshift headquarters for the search. Floodlights illuminated my father's face as he argued with the two cops stationed there. One of them was Officer Dorn. The other, I didn't recognize.

Then, in classic Dad fashion, he snatched the clipboard out of Dorn's hands and flung it out over the beach, where it flew like a Frisbee for a good one hundred feet before skidding into the sand. He stormed off, and moments later our front door opened and slammed. He joined me out on the deck, and I could hear him laboring to get his breathing under control.

"They still won't let me join the search," he said finally, standing next to my chair. "Even though I told them you'd be here. What's with these people? It's like they're some kind of insular clique. Like heaven forbid they let someone from outside the town inside in any way."

I said nothing. All I could think was that the FBI could be wrong. Steven Nell was brilliant, that's what Messenger had said. He very well could have led them on a wild-goose chase and come here while they were distracted. He could have Darcy somewhere on this island right at this very moment, and all we were doing was sitting here, waiting for her to come home.

A cold breeze lifted my hair from my neck. I glanced out at the water and froze. Tristan was standing on the beach down below, wearing a black sweatshirt with the hood up to cover his hair, gazing right at me.

"I'm going to go get a sweater," my father said, rubbing his hand across my back. Still facing the oncoming search party to the north, he hadn't noticed our lurker. "Do you need anything?"

I looked up at him and forced a smile, just wanting him to go so I could talk to Tristan. "No, Dad. Thanks."

He looked at me sadly, kissed my forehead, then went. I got up, throwing the blanket off my legs, and raced to the guardrail facing the water, my heart pounding, dozens of questions crowding my brain.

But when I looked down at the sand again, Tristan was gone.

HELP

Thorns tore at my ankles. A wet branch whipped my cheek. I fell to my knees, a sharp rock piercing my skin. But it was all nothing. Nothing. Nothing compared with what Steven Nell was going to do to me.

When I tried to get up, my knee buckled and all I could do was crawl. If only I knew where I was. If only I could just see where I was going, but it was so dark. So very, very dark.

Then something caught my eye—something white and smooth looming in the darkness. Whimpering, I leaned forward for a closer look. White fingers with chipped nail polish. Darcy's hand. Her arm stuck out at an unnatural angle from beneath a holly bush, the sleeve of her cheer-leading sweatshirt soaked through with blood. Shaking, I pushed the branches aside. Darcy's eyes were open, lifeless, the back of her head smashed in.

"Darcy!" I screeched. "No!"

I scuttled backward on my hands. Steven Nell had killed her, and I was next. I opened my mouth to scream again, and a gloved hand clamped over my lips.

"No!"

I opened my eyes and found myself staring at the ceiling of my room. I was still alive, but Darcy . . . The moment I remembered everything that had happened earlier, I sat up straight and screamed. Someone was sitting in my desk chair, dressed in head-to-toe black. His knees faced my mattress, his hood was up to cover his face, and his posture curled forward as if he was in mourning. As soon as I screamed, he looked up, the hood falling back from his blond hair.

Tristan.

"Shhhh!" he whispered, bringing a finger to his lips.

My chest heaved as I struggled for breath and tried to make sense of what was happening. I looked down and realized I was wearing nothing but a thin tank top with no bra, and I yanked my blanket up to cover my chest.

"What the hell are you doing?" I demanded. "How did you get in here?"

"We need your help," he replied, ignoring my question. He leaned toward me, resting his forearms on his knees and rubbing his hands together before clasping them. I saw the woven leather bracelet peeking out from the cuff of his sleeve. His blond hair fell forward, grazing his cheekbones as he looked me dead in the eye. "Steven Nell has your sister somewhere on the island."

"What?" I shrieked, jumping up, still clutching the blanket. My pulse raced so fast I was about to pass out. I brought one hand to my head and tried to focus. "I knew it! I knew—"

I paused and looked down at Tristan. He eyed me with a sort of reluctant expectance. Like he was waiting for me to realize what I was slowly realizing.

"How do you know about Steven Nell?" I asked, trembling. "Did the police tell you? Did they tell Joaquin?"

"It doesn't matter how I know," he said, standing. "I just do."

I blinked, completely confused. "Chief Grantz said he'd gone to Canada. He said the FBI—"

"Chief Grantz lied," Tristan said flatly.

"What?" I breathed. "Why?"

He blew out a sigh, looking at the floor as he shook his head. "It's a long story."

I paced in front of him, holding my head with one hand.

"Okay, okay," I said, my brain working hard to process all this. "How do you know he's here? Did he contact you?"

"No," he said, shaking his head.

"Tristan, you're giving me nothing here. What's going on?" I asked, growing more frustrated, more desperate, by the second. "What do you mean, you need my help?"

Tristan moved over to the north-facing window and leaned his elbow against the upper ledge on the lower pane. He closed his eyes and pressed the heel of his hand into his forehead, as if my questions perturbed him. As if he didn't know how to answer.

"All I can say is, you're the only one that can find her," he said, turning to look at me, his blue eyes pained.

Then he gazed out the window in a way that made my heart skip a beat. He was looking at something or someone down below. My breath short and shallow, I walked over to join him, my long blanket swishing behind me. At first all I saw was the glow, but as I approached the window, the crowd came into focus. There were at least a dozen of them gathered in a close-knit pack in the sand. Each of them wore a hooded sweatshirt, and each carried a black flashlight. I could see Joaquin, Lauren, Krista, Fisher, Bea, and Kevin, plus a few others I'd noticed around town. They were all there, and they were all gazing up at me in grim silence.

"Will you help us?" Tristan asked quietly.

I swallowed hard. My throat was dry, my heart was pounding, and white-hot adrenaline warmed my skin from the inside out. I knew I should go wake my father. I knew I should get him to contact the police. Nothing about this made sense. And there was no way I should be going out with a pack of strangers, a pack of kids, to try to take on a serial killer. But when I looked into Tristan's eyes, I knew there was only one answer to his question.

"Of course I will," I said. "She's my sister."

THE CLUES

The sand was soft and cold beneath my bare feet as Tristan and I made our way across the beach to his hooded friends. Every one of them watched my approach as if I were some kind of prophet. As if I were going to start glowing from within and spout the meaning of life. I held my running shoes to my chest, grasping them in my sweaty palms.

This was really happening. Steven Nell had found us.

"Rory," Joaquin said in a deep, no-nonsense voice. "What do you know about Steven Nell?"

"Not a lot," I said. "I thought he was just a regular math teacher until he attacked me in the woods near my house.

I'm not actually from Manhattan," I clarified, remembering how Darcy had filled Joaquin in on our faux history. "I'm from New Jersey."

No one even blinked.

"Go on," Tristan said, touching my back briefly.

"Well . . . it turns out he murdered fourteen girls all across the country, and I was the only one to get away," I said. Tristan and Krista exchanged a grim look. "The FBI agent who put us into witness protection told us Nell had never failed before, so there was a good chance he'd try to come after us, but that's all I know. I was hoping they'd caught him, until . . ."

"Until now," Tristan finished for me.

"Yeah." I gulped back a sob and looked down at the sneakers against my chest, knowing how terrified Darcy must be. If she was even still alive. "Until now. Why aren't the police here?" I asked, looking up again, sniffling back a tear. "Shouldn't we be talking to them about this? Or at least tell some adults?"

"The adults are useless," Joaquin said with a scoff. "They're all in denial."

"They think it's impossible for this man to be here," Krista explained. "They refuse to believe us."

I glanced at Joaquin, whose jaw was set. Was that what he'd been arguing with Officer Dorn about?

"But you think he's here?" I said. "Why?"

"Because nothing like this has ever happened before," Lauren piped in, her voice shrill. "Ever."

Tristan and Joaquin shot her an admonishing look, and she bowed her head, blushing.

"Nothing like what?" I asked. "Someone going missing? But Grantz said this happens every once in a while. That they always form a search party and . . ."

My words died on my tongue. Tristan was looking at me like he was waiting for me to catch on already.

"Oh," I said, my heart turning to stone. "That was a lie, too."

But why? Why would the police chief lie to me and my father? Was he in on it? Did he know Steven Nell somehow?

"What I don't get is why he took Darcy," Joaquin said, clenching a fist in front of his mouth. "If he's so pissed off he failed, why not just come after you again?"

"Because he's messing with me," I said, hugging my shoes even tighter. "He wants to make me pay before he—"

I couldn't finish the sentence. The crowd shifted on their feet, murmuring, whispering. I looked at Tristan.

"Has he contacted you since you've been here?" he asked.

I thought of the note he left on my bed back home in Princeton. "No," I said.

"Are you sure?" He squared off with me, toe-to-toe, and reached for my right hand. He held it lightly in his own for a second, then squeezed. "Think, Rory. You haven't received any messages from him of any kind?"

I looked into Tristan's eyes, and all of a sudden it hit me. It hit me so hard it knocked the wind out of me. The laughter, the humming, the song on the jukebox. The scrap of fabric, the messenger bag, the lighthouses. Maybe they hadn't been coincidences. Maybe they hadn't been taunts or reminders. Maybe they'd been messages.

"'The Long and Winding Road,'" I breathed.

"What?" Joaquin asked.

"The song. 'The Long and Winding Road,'" I said, my brain racing as I clutched Tristan's hand. "It's his favorite song. I heard someone humming it my first morning here, and then it was on the jukebox at the Thirsty Swan."

Joaquin looked at Tristan. "'The Long and Winding Road.' What could that mean?"

"I don't know," Tristan said, still looking into my eyes. "What else, Rory?"

"There was a scrap of fabric that looked like it had been torn from his jacket," I said. "It had two patches sewn on it. I think they were flags like you see on a sailboat."

"Can you draw them?" Krista asked, breathless.

"With what?" I asked.

"The sand," Joaquin suggested, gesturing down.

I tugged my fingers away from Tristan, dropped my shoes, and fell to my knees on the cold beach. The whole pack of locals gathered around me, their hoods shadowing their faces as they pointed their flashlights at a single spot in the sand. Shakily, I managed to draw the two flags.

"This one was blue-and-white checks, and this one was blue, white, and then red in the center," I said, looking around at them.

"They are signal flags. That one means *N*," Kevin said, pointing to the checked one. "And the other is *W*."

"Northwest," Tristan added.

Another murmur went through the crowd. All the tiny hairs on the back of my neck stood on end. My stomach turned, and I had to hold my breath to keep from vomiting on someone's feet.

"Dryer's Way," Lauren said. "That's a long and winding road."

"And it ends at the northwest point of the island," Joaquin added.

I stood up, dusting the sand from my legs. Another wave of nausea hit me, and I instinctively grabbed for Tristan's arm. I took a breath, cleared my throat, and let him go to stand on my own.

"There was one other thing," I said. "His messenger bag.

He left it hanging on my fence, and it was full of tiny light-houses."

Joaquin blinked. "There's no lighthouse on Juniper Landing."

I felt my heart start to fall. I'd thought we were getting somewhere.

"There used to be," Tristan said.

Everyone turned to look at him.

"What do you mean?" Joaquin asked.

"It was situated at the northwest point," he said, looking startled but resigned. "They took it down because people . . . visitors . . . kept getting hurt up there. But the foundation is still there. And so is the lighthouse keeper's cottage."

"How did I not know this?" Joaquin asked.

Tristan fiddled with his bracelet. "We never go up there. Unless we're going to the bridge," he said, glancing at Krista. All the friends exchanged knowing looks. Clearly, this meant something to them.

"He wanted me to find him," I said, shaking. "He was planning this all along, and now he has his bait."

Tristan took a step forward. "But he didn't plan on all of us coming with you."

I looked around at them. At Lauren and Krista, Fisher, Bea, and Kevin, all the others whose names I didn't know. Even Joaquin. All of them were willing to help me—to help

Darcy. All of them were willing to risk everything to save her. I didn't understand why, but I was grateful. Standing in their midst, I felt safe. I felt like it was still possible that everything could be okay.

I glanced over at Tristan hopefully. His eyes were determined but somehow sad.

"Well, what are we waiting for?" Joaquin said. "Let's go get her."

THE KILLER

We drove to the northwest point of the island in silence, me wedged in the front seat of an old, rusty pickup truck between Joaquin and Tristan, with Krista's sneakered feet on my thigh. Joaquin was driving, and Krista sat sideways on Tristan's lap. Three cars full of the others trailed behind us, their headlights occasionally catching in the rearview mirror, blinding me at random intervals.

The light filled the car. The jarring crunch as the truck slammed into our bumper. Darcy screaming. My dad desperate at the wheel. Then the weightlessness, the pain, the terror. My father dead splayed on the ground.

"Take a left here," Tristan said.

I slammed back into the present. I realized I was clutching Tristan's arm, and I slowly released my grip. He looked me in the eye, but not in a disturbed or judging way. He looked at me as if he understood.

Joaquin leaned over the steering wheel, squinting into the darkness through the windshield. "Where?"

"Right there!" Tristan said, raising his voice for the first time since I'd known him.

I spotted the dirt road at the exact same time as Joaquin, and then the truck veered left and the tires squealed, kicking up sand and dirt behind us. I gripped Tristan's shoulder as we made the turn. Krista's head banged against the passenger-side window.

"Ow," she said plainly, rubbing at it.

No one asked if she was all right. Everyone was too focused on the small, wind-battered cottage bobbing in and out of view as Joaquin navigated the bumpy road. My sister was inside that house. Alive or dead, she was there. I was sure of it.

The fog clung to the bay like the meringue on top of a lemon pie, and a few fingers of mist curled around the base of the house. Off to our left was the bridge, a tall, coppery structure with two towers, leading from the island off into the fog. It was even bigger than I'd thought, hovering over the water like a massive alien structure.

"Stop here," Tristan said. Joaquin hit the brakes, parking just around the bend from the cottage, the car camouflaged by a huge forest of overgrown reeds.

"Kill the lights," Tristan instructed. Joaquin did as ordered.

Behind us, the other cars cut their lights as well and rolled to a stop. Several car doors popped. Within seconds, the rest of the group had gathered around our truck, hoods drawn, flashlights off.

"What do we do now?" Fisher asked, his voice deep. His nostrils were wide, his jaw set. He looked like he was ready to rumble.

"We go in." Joaquin started to open his door, but I felt a surge of panic and grabbed his shoulder.

"No."

"What do you mean, no?" Joaquin snapped. "We're wasting time."

"Hear her out," Tristan said.

Joaquin exhaled loudly through his nose but sat back, the springs under his ancient vinyl car seat squealing.

"This guy is a genius," I told them. "He traveled the country killing girls and managed to elude the authorities for ten years. He baited me into coming here. Going inside could be a trap."

"So what do you want to do?" Krista asked quietly.

I pressed my lips together. I could just see the top of the roof over the reeds.

"We make him come to us," I said determinedly.

I gestured for Joaquin to get out of the truck. I slid out after him, and my knees almost buckled when my feet hit the dirt. I took a breath to steel myself and walked to the front of the car, the crowd of locals parting around me. My feet crunched on pebbles, sand, and broken shells as I tromped down the lane toward the house. I stopped ten feet from the door, Tristan behind my right shoulder, Joaquin behind my left, the rest of them gathered around like a small army.

In my mind's eye, I saw Steven Nell's dry hands as they grabbed me. Felt his breath against my face. Saw the watery film in his eyes. Every inch of me was shaking, but I curled my fingers into fists. I had to do this. I had to save my sister.

"Steven Nell!" I shouted at the top of my lungs.

Dead silence. There was no wind, no waves, nothing.

"I'm here! I did what you wanted!" I screamed, my voice breaking. "Now let me see my sister!"

We waited. I breathed in and out, counting the beats of my heart. *Onetwothreefourfivesixseveneightnineteneleven twelve—*

The door creaked open. My breath stopped. Tristan took a step closer to me. I felt his chest against the back of my shoulder. The shaft of light grew wider. Wider.

"Rory Miller!" Steven Nell's reedy voice called out. "Won't you come inside and play?"

Bile rose up in the back of my throat. Tristan took my hand, his warm fingers lacing around mine. "No! I want to see my sister first."

"You'll only see your sister if you come inside," he taunted, still hovering out of sight.

My heart slammed in my chest. My pulse pounded in my temples. Never in my life had I felt this terrified, this cold, this unsure. But I had to save Darcy. I'd come here to save Darcy. I took one step forward.

"What're you doing?" Joaquin whispered. "You said yourself going inside could be a trap."

"Let her go," Tristan said, releasing my hand.

"I don't know about this, dude," Joaquin said. "I don't like it."

Something inside of me snapped. I was sick of them talking about me like I wasn't there. Deciding what to tell me and when to keep me in the dark. This had nothing to do with them. This was about me and my sister. "I don't care if you like it or not," I said sharply. "Darcy's in that house, and I'm going in there to get her."

Joaquin and Tristan looked at each other. Neither one said another word. A light breeze kicked up as I approached the squat white building. Light shone through one cracked window. The roof sagged at the center, and the whole front porch leaned to the right. The boards let out a loud wail as I stepped up toward the front door, and the wind lifted my hair off my neck. I glanced back once at Tristan and Joaquin. They were as still as statues. Then I turned and stepped over the threshold. Darcy jumped up from the floor and lunged at me.

"Rory! Oh my god! Rory!"

I pushed her tangled hair back from her face, tears streaming down my cheeks. "Are you okay?" I whispered. "What did he do to you?"

She shook her head. There was dirt all over her pink tank top and blood on her shoulder, but otherwise she looked okay. Terrified, but okay.

"Nothing. He said he wanted you," she sobbed. "He said we were just waiting for you."

"Where is he?" I asked, shaking as my eyes darted around the small room. There was a tiny wooden table with two broken chairs around it. A hot pot sat on the floor in the corner, and there was a blue couch by the wall with a huge hole torn into the back of it. Slowly, Darcy's eyes shifted to the right. I started to turn, just as Steven Nell emerged from behind the open door. He grabbed Darcy's arm and yanked her out of my grasp, flinging her outside like a rag doll. She was still screaming when the door slammed in her face.

And suddenly I was alone with my worst nightmare.

"Hello, Rory," he said, a thin smile creeping across his lips. "I knew you'd come to me."

He tipped his head to the side, looking me up and down with a covetous, hungry expression. All at once I wanted to rush him, wanted to tackle him, wanted to pummel him into oblivion.

"I was going to have your sister, but then I thought that wouldn't be fair to either of us," he said, making my skin crawl. "You were always the one I wanted, Rory. Only you. The unsung star."

He took a step toward me and reached out his hand. I flinched as he stroked my hair with the back of his fingers.

"Let's finish what we started, shall we?"

With that, he lunged at me and turned me around, locking his arm around my neck. I was about to scream when an excruciating, piercing, burning pain sliced right through my gut. At that exact moment, Nell screamed and released me, staggering back against the wall and sinking to the ground, but I was in so much pain I was barely aware of him. I doubled over, gagging, coughing, wheezing for air. My hands flew out, but my face still collided with the wood floor. Suddenly, the door flew open, and Darcy's knees hit the ground next to me.

"Rory? What's going on? Are you okay?" Darcy was on

top of me, shaking me. The pain was so horrible the images in front of me bent and swayed. I turned my face slowly, my nose scraping against the splintery wood planks, and looked toward the wall.

Steven Nell was writhing on the floor as well. Screaming. Begging for mercy.

"What is it?" Darcy asked me desperately. "What's wrong?"

I coughed and closed my eyes. I just wanted it to stop. I just wanted the pain to stop.

And then, Darcy was gone. I heard her screeching, but someone had pulled her away. A hand touched the back of my neck, and a warm, comforting hum filled my body. Slowly, the pain began to subside. It cooled to a dull throb. I tried for a breath, and sweet oxygen filled my lungs.

"It's okay," Tristan whispered in my ear. "You're okay. Everything's going to be fine."

I opened my eyes. The world slowly slipped back into focus. Carefully, I sat up, Tristan's fingers still cupping the back of my neck. He sat down in front of me, our legs crooked to the side, and looked me in the eye.

"Breathe," he said. "Breathe."

So I did. Over his shoulder, I saw Kevin and Fisher dragging Steven Nell off the ground as he squirmed and screamed between them. Together, they moved for the door, but Nell staggered sideways, his knees giving way as he spit and sobbed and flailed. Somehow they managed to get him outside. Managed to drag him away.

"Look at me," Tristan ordered. "Rory. Look at me."

I did as I was told. I looked into Tristan's eyes.

"You're ready," he said, breathless. "You're ready now."

"Ready for what?"

But even as I said the words, it was happening again. A pinprick of emptiness began inside my chest and widened, widened, widened to engulf me. I reached out and clung to Tristan's arms as I felt myself start to slide backward, start to lose gravity and form, start to slip. Panic took hold of my every pore, squeezing out the air, blacking out the sky overhead.

But no, that was just the fog. Just the fog closing in.

"Look at me, Rory," he said firmly. "Trust me."

His eyes were so blue. The color so real, so true, so beautiful.

"I can't, Tristan," I heard myself whimper, squeezing my eyes closed.

"Yes, you can. It's time," he told me, holding on to me. "You can do it, Rory. It's okay. Just. Let. Go."

I took a deep breath and let it out. Suddenly, images came rushing in on me. My mother pushing me on the swing in our backyard. My dad blowing out birthday candles in our old kitchen, before Mom remodeled it. Darcy laughing at me over her shoulder as I chased her in a game of tag. The turtle I'd had for three weeks in fifth grade. The first science award I'd ever won, being hung around my neck. My mother in bed, so fragile and small, squeezing my hand and saying good-bye. Taking third place at regionals last year. Winning the ribbon at the science fair and Samir's grouchy face as he looked on. Christopher kissing me in his bedroom. Steven Nell grabbing me in the woods. Messenger telling us we had to go.

And then my father splayed out on the road. Darcy's head bashed in. The blood, the tears, the scream. The slice of a knife.

I opened my eyes, and the world slammed into focus. Tristan's fingers were tight around my arms, his eyes locked on mine, the fog growing thicker around us. And just like that I understood.

"Rory?" Darcy called out, breaking away from Joaquin. She fell on the floor next to me and grabbed my hand. "Are you okay?"

I cleared my throat, still looking at Tristan. There were tears in his eyes as he studied my face.

Darcy hugged me, breaking off the contact between me and Tristan, and I hugged her back as hard as I possibly could, not wanting to ever let go.

Outside, Steven Nell shouted one continuous, keening wail, as Kevin and Fisher lifted him like a rag doll and tossed him into the back of Joaquin's truck with a bang. Tristan rose to his feet. He helped me up, and Darcy supported my right side as together the three of us walked outside. Krista hovered near the door of the cabin with Joaquin and Lauren while Nell banged around in the bed of the truck, making enough noise to wake the dead.

"Take him," Tristan said to Krista.

She nodded, jogged over to the truck, and got in behind the wheel, alone. The guys stood back as she slammed the transmission into gear with authority and took off toward the bridge, kicking up sand as she went. The truck was about half a mile away when the fog suddenly enveloped the taillights, and abruptly, the screaming stopped.

AMENDS

It was still dark out when we arrived back at the house.
My senses were heightened. I felt every thud of my heart.
Smelled each note of the flowery air. Everything looked
different to me. The ocean water was too perfect. The
flowering trees seemed fake. It was all like something off
a movie set.

"I'm too wired to sleep," Darcy said as we approached the
front door. "Let's go out back."

We walked around the side of the house and up to the
deck, where we sat for a long time, watching the waves
roll onto shore. With every crash of the surf, my heart felt

heavier and heavier. I had ten million questions, but there was no one here to ask.

"I'm so sorry," Darcy said suddenly.

"For what?" I asked. She had nothing to be sorry for. If I had my way, she'd never feel bad about anything ever again.

"For not believing you. For fighting with you. For being such a bitch these last few months," she said, looking down at the dirt under her fingernails. "I shouldn't have taken it out on you. Christopher's the jerk."

She laughed bitterly and sniffled, wiping her nose with the back of her hand. There was a streak of mud on her face, and her hair was a mess of tangles.

I'd never thought of it that way, but he kind of was. No matter how much I liked him, no matter how much he liked me, what kind of guy broke up with a girl then kissed her sister that afternoon? I turned and looked at her. "You're right."

Darcy and I both laughed. "Too bad we can't call him up and tell him," she said, hugging her knees to her chest and resting her chin atop one. "Maybe when we get home."

My heart thumped, and tears filled my eyes. I looked away, toward the water, not wanting her to see.

"I'm sorry I kissed him," I said, biting my lip. "I'm sorry I took that stupid shortcut and got us sent here."

I squeezed my eyes shut against a flood of emotion and pressed the tears back.

"Rory," Darcy said firmly, reaching for my hand, "it's not your fault that psycho attacked you. You know that, right?"

I nodded, unable to form a word.

"And you know what? Aside from the terrifying kidnapping by a serial killer, I kind of like it here," she added.

I swallowed back the ball that had formed in my throat and nodded. "Yeah, Juniper Landing is okay."

Darcy yawned hugely and stretched her arms over her head. "I'm starting to crash. I think I'll go take a shower and go to bed."

"Maybe you should wake up Dad first and tell him you're okay," I said.

"Good point," Darcy said with a laugh, shaking her head. She started to go but paused near the door. "What do you think the cops will do with Mr. Nell? Do they even have a jail on this island?"

Probably not, I thought. I looked at her, feeling conflicted. It was almost sad, how she knew nothing. But I also envied her.

"I'm sure they'll turn him right over to the FBI," I said.

She nodded, accepting this. "Good. Then his ass will be out of here for good."

"Yep. I think that's the idea."

"Good night, Rory," she said.

"Good night."

Then she turned and walked inside. I sat back on the cushions and stared across the endless ocean. When I was little, I used to watch the waves and imagine I could see all the way across to the foreign lands on the other side of the world. I'd imagine visiting all these exotic places one day and standing on their beaches staring back at the spot where I'd once stood. Now I wondered what was actually out there. Did it go on forever, or did it end somewhere? I felt a chill that had nothing to do with the breeze and hugged myself as tight as I could.

"Rory?"

I whirled around, nearly jumping out of my skin. Aaron was tiptoeing around the side of the house, looking up at the deck.

"What are you doing here?" I asked, leaping to my feet. "It's three o'clock in the morning!"

"I know!" he said, looking up. "I couldn't sleep. Did you find your sister?"

My heart thumped extra hard. He was so sweet, unable to sleep because of me. Such a good person. A person who didn't deserve this. I felt a fresh wave of tears and shook my head at myself. Was everything going to make me cry from here on out?

"Yeah. She's back," I said simply.

His smile nearly broke my heart. "That's great! Can I come up?"

Part of me wanted to say yes. Wanted to hang out with him and chat and feel that sort of comfortable, safe, uncomplicated feeling I had when I was around him. But I couldn't just hang out. Not now. Not when I was feeling so raw.

"I'm really tired, actually," I told him. "I think I'm just going to go to bed."

Aaron had already made a move for the stairs and stopped in his tracks. "Are you sure?"

"Yeah. I'll see you tomorrow," I told him.

Hopefully, I thought.

"But thanks," I added. "For coming to check on me."

"Anytime," he said with a smile. "That's what friends are for."

He lifted his hand in a wave, then turned and walked back toward the street. I watched him until he dipped out of sight, morosely wondering if I'd ever see him again. Wondering if by tomorrow Darcy would have forgotten who he was.

THE TRUTH

After a while, I walked down the steps and out onto the beach, sitting down in the cold, freshly smoothed sand. Dawn was rapidly approaching, and I wanted to watch the sun come up. It was something my mother, Darcy, and I used to do together when we were little, down in Ocean City. She'd wake us up when it was still dark out and cuddle me into my stroller, then carry Darcy down to the water while she pushed me ahead of them. I'd doze off on the way, but she'd always wake me just when the sky began to turn pink. Then we'd both crawl into her lap and nestle there as we watched the first light creep toward us over the water and up the beach. Watched the gift of a new day opening at our feet.

That's what she'd always called it. A gift. I'd never realized how right she was until now.

Had my mother ever been to Juniper Landing? Had she ever watched this particular sunrise?

I took a deep breath and let it out. A tickle skittered down my spine as I felt Tristan approaching. His feet stepped up next to me in the sand.

"You want to talk about it?" he asked.

I shook my head and hugged my knees to my chest. "Not yet."

He dropped down next to me, pulling his legs up to his chin. I listened to the rhythmic sound of his breathing and stared down at his leather bracelet, his hand pressed into the sand near my hip.

"Is he gone?" I asked after a while. "Steven Nell. Is he really gone?"

"Oh, he's gone," Tristan said, lifting his chin a bit as the first haze of pink appeared on the horizon.

"What about Olive?" I asked. "And the singer from the park?"

"They've . . . moved on," Tristan said carefully.

"And the guy with the hat?" I asked.

"Him, too." He didn't even pause. He knew exactly who I was talking about.

"So when Mrs. Chen said Olive had sent for her stuff . . ."

"That was a lie," Tristan said frankly. "Krista messed up. It happens. Rarely, but it does. Of course, usually there's no one checking up on the visitors so . . . you made things a little more complex."

No one checking up. That's why Darcy forgot her. Why Aaron forgot her. Why the locals remembered her. It made it simpler. But then, why did I remember?

"She was still there that day, when you came by with Aaron," he said. "Joaquin went over there with her, and they were almost done cleaning out her stuff when you got there, but Krista was still in the room. She told me she hid in the closet until you left."

I knew it. I knew someone was in there.

I turned in the sand to face him, and he turned to face me. I crossed my legs just like his, and our knees touched.

"I need you to say it, Tristan," I said, my voice cracking. "Just tell me. Just say it out loud. Is this what I think it is? Am I . . . ?"

I couldn't make myself utter the word that clung to the tip of my tongue. I couldn't force it out. It was too unbelievable. Too surreal. Too wrong.

Tristan reached for one hand, then the other. He held them both between us, his fingers warm like the sun that was now bursting forth from the horizon.

"I'm so sorry, Rory, but yes, it's exactly what you think," he said. "You, your sister, your father . . . all of us here on the island . . . we're all dead."

Turn the page for a look at

the breathtaking sequel to *Shadowlands* . . .

THE TRUTH

The morning sun rose over the ocean, streaking beautiful hues of pink and purple and orange across the sky. I sat in the sand with Tristan Parrish, his hand clutching mine, and stared down at his worn leather bracelet while I listened to the sound of his even breathing and the rhythm of the waves rolling onto shore. On any other day, this would have been the most romantic moment of my life. But this was today. And my life was over.

Focus, Rory. Focus and breathe.

"So that night on the highway . . . that wasn't a nightmare," I said slowly. "Me, my father, and my sister . . . we all died."

Tristan's clear blue eyes shot through with pain. The callus on his thumb pressed into my palm. "Yes."

I was numb as I spoke the next few words. "Steven Nell killed us."

"Yes."

His grip on my fingers tightened, and suddenly a sucking void opened up inside my chest. I gasped, clinging to him as a barrage of images assaulted me one after another, like a film projected on a screen. Mr. Nell charging me, his watery eyes wild with hunger. The knife blade buried deep in my stomach. The bloodstain seeping through my shirt. The tree branches gnashing overhead. My last, choked breaths as I slowly slipped away and everything grew cold.

My heart twisted painfully and I bent forward, struggling to breathe.

"I'm so sorry," Tristan said again. "I had to show you the truth."

He squeezed my hand once more, and his gorgeous, chiseled face zipped into focus. If this had been any other day, I would have been obsessing about what he was thinking. Why he was still holding my hand. Whether it meant he liked me as much as I liked him. I'd be worrying over whether my palms were clammy, if I had morning breath, or if my hair was doing that insane frizz thing around my forehead it so loved to do. These were the things a sixteen-year-old girl was *supposed* to be obsessing about. I was not supposed to be obsessing about how I'd died.

Overhead, a fat crow cawed, swooping in and out before settling atop the roof of the white-and-blue beachfront house my family had been living—no, not living . . . *existing*—in since we arrived in Juniper Landing exactly one week ago. We'd been forced to flee our home in Princeton, New Jersey, when my math teacher, a serial killer who'd already killed fourteen other girls, had set his sights on me.

We'd followed the FBI agent's directions to a T, driving through a torrential downpour to our new location, our new identities as the Thayer family in tow. We thought we'd made it safely down to South Carolina, but we hadn't made it at all. Mr. Nell had found us on a lonely stretch of highway and finished what he'd set out to do. He killed my dad, then my sister, Darcy, then me.

Suddenly, I shoved myself up, spraying sand everywhere in my haste.

"Where are you going?" Tristan scrambled to his feet and reached for me, but I flung his hand away, shaking from head to toe.

"I have to tell my sister. I have to tell my dad," I said, my voice thick with tears.

"No. You can't," he said vehemently. "You can't do that."

Tristan got in front of me and blocked my way. Behind

him I could see the windows of my father's room. The room where he slept, oblivious to the fact that his life had ended. That his attempt to protect his daughters by leaving the house we'd grown up in, the house where my mother had lived and died, had failed.

"What? What do you mean, I can't?" I shouted. "They're my family, Tristan."

I tried to step around him, but he grabbed my arm, his grip so tight it sent a shock of alarm through my chest. I tried to wrench myself away, but suddenly a soft, soothing sensation sprang up inside my wrist and slowly traveled up my arm and into my chest. He clung to me, and my heart stopped slamming against my rib cage. My breathing returned to normal. I felt suddenly, oddly, calm.

I looked into Tristan's pale blue eyes. They were . . . victorious.

A thump of fear obliterated any sense of serenity. I yanked my arm out of his grasp, his fingernails scraping my skin.

"What was that? What did you just do to me?" I demanded, backing away in terror.

His face paled. "Rory—"

"No!" I shouted, betrayal clenching my gut. "You can't just mess with my mind like that! What *are* you?"

Tristan's face turned to stone, and his eyes flicked just past my shoulder. I felt the presence of someone behind me two seconds before I collided with something solid and unyielding. A pair of strong arms closed around me, locking my limbs against my chest and picking me up off the ground, all while Tristan looked on calmly.

I screamed as loudly as I could. The only response was a seagull's bark.

"This hurts me more than it hurts you," a low voice whispered in my ear.

My chest constricted, tighter and tighter, until I couldn't breathe and the world around me went gray. Tristan stepped forward slowly, looking into my eyes, his mouth set in a grim line.

"Why?" I gasped, trying to cling to consciousness. "Why are you doing this to me?"

"I'll explain everything when you wake up," he said gently. "I promise."

Then his handsome face contorted and blurred, and everything went black.

DIFFERENT

I came to on a dusty couch in a room that smelled like mold mixed with beer and sea salt. My chest ached and my short fingernails had cut painful grooves in my palm. Nearby, someone laughed.

Tentatively I opened one eye and took in my surroundings. I was in a wood-paneled, windowless basement. The room was decorated with green and orange shag rugs, a dim overhead lamp that looked like a sea urchin, and several saggy plaid couches. Milling near a marble bar with ugly, torn-up vinyl stools were about a dozen kids my age, sipping coffee from paper cups and chatting with one another as if my kidnapping was an everyday social event.

I recognized several of them as Juniper Landing locals, year-rounders in what I'd previously assumed was a vacation town. There was Bea McHenry, an athletic redhead, whose wet hair was slicked back into a ponytail, as though she'd just come in from a swim. Kevin Calandro, whose fire tattoo peeked out from under the arm of a dirty white T-shirt, eyed me curiously over the plastic top of his coffee cup. Next to him was Lauren Caldwell, whose black hair was held back in a plaid headband. Two girls and a guy I'd never seen before hovered in the corner, eyeing the rest of the group as if they didn't want to be there.

A door on the far side of the room opened, and Joaquin Marquez, the boy who seemed so intent on breaking my sister's heart, slipped out, followed by Tristan. One of the girls in the corner, a wispy emo chick with a short blond Mohawk, followed him with her eyes, an expression of longing I instantly recognized. It was exactly the way I used to look at Christopher Kane in the halls of Princeton Hills High, back when he was still with Darcy.

Fisher Morton was the last to step out of the back room. He closed and locked the door behind him quickly, then joined the rest of the party, turning his massive shoulders sideways to slip through the tightly knit group.

My lashes fluttered involuntarily. Why had he locked the door?

"You guys, she's awake," Krista Parrish announced, emerging from the crowd in a pink-and-white sundress. Her blond hair, the exact same shade as her brother's, was pulled up in a high ponytail, her blue eyes expertly lined as she frowned sympathetically down at me. Ignoring the pain in my chest and head, I sat up straight, taking in the whole room now. Behind her was a set of stairs leading up. An escape route.

I scrambled to my feet, my heart thumping. "What's going on?" I asked, edging away from them toward the stairs. "Where are we?"

"Don't worry," Krista said gently, putting out a hand as if trying to soothe a rabid dog. "No one is going to hurt you."

"I'm sorry it had to happen this way," Tristan said, the edges of his mouth curving down. I remembered how he'd looked at me right before I'd passed out, and averted my eyes. "We're in the basement of the police station."

"You kidnapped me and brought me to the *cops*?" I blurted.

Mohawk Girl laughed loudly.

"We didn't kidnap you," Joaquin said, rolling his eyes. "We saved you. You and your family."

Krista, Lauren, and Fisher looked at me so earnestly that all the tiny hairs on the back of my neck stood on end. I felt as though I'd suddenly landed in the middle of a cult.

"Well, if I'm not kidnapped, can I . . . leave?" I said, taking another step toward the stairs.

"Sorry." Fisher shook his head.

My heart nose-dived. That was the voice. The voice of the person who'd grabbed me on the beach. I took an instinctive step back and crashed into the wall. My pulse thrummed quickly in my veins.

"Will someone please tell me what's going on?" I demanded.

"We couldn't let you tell your family," Tristan replied.

"Excuse me?" I exhaled sharply. "You tell me we're all dead and expect me not to tell my family?"

"You can't," Tristan repeated. There was all this emotion in his eyes. Longing and pleading. Like he was just trying to help. Like he needed me to understand. But at that moment, I didn't trust it. I couldn't.

"Try to stop me."

I turned toward Fisher and jammed my foot down as hard as I could into his instep. He cursed and doubled over, giving me enough time to dodge past him, grab one of the wooden spindles that lined the stairs, and swing myself around and up the first two steps.

"Rory, no!" Joaquin shouted. Footsteps sounded behind me.

I tripped but hauled myself back up and kept going. I could see the light framing the doorway at the top.

"Stop!" Lauren called out. "Rory, they'll—"

I flung myself forward, reaching for the door.

"If you tell your family, they'll be damned to the Shadowlands!" Krista cried.

"Krista!" someone hissed.

"What? She was leaving!" Krista replied in a whine.

I paused with my fingers on the doorknob. My chest heaved with each breath. *The Shadowlands?* As I turned around, Tristan stepped into view at the bottom of the staircase. I stared down at him, barely able to make out his face in the dim light. Behind him on the wall was an old-fashioned painting of a sunset, the golden glow forming a halo around his head.

"What is the Shadowlands?" I asked.

"Will you please come back down here?" he implored softly.

"Not until you tell me," I insisted. "What's the Shadowlands?"

"Come down and we'll tell you everything," he said, reaching out with one hand. "You're safe here. I promise."

I glanced behind me at the door, but my curiosity got the better of me. Ignoring Tristan's outstretched hand, I edged past him down the stairs and walked to the center of the room, trying to look more confident and in control than I felt. Stone-faced, stoic, shrewd. But inside, everything quivered. Tristan hesitated, clearly thrown that I passed on the opportunity to touch him. Well, good. He deserved it for letting his friend knock me out.

"Okay," I said. "I'm listening."

"Juniper Landing is an in-between," Joaquin began, crossing his arms over the chest of his formfitting red T-shirt. "A limbo."

"One of many," Bea added.

"It's a place where people go to work through any unfinished business they have from the other world before they move on," Tristan said. "They arrive on the same ferry you did and stay until they're ready. Once they move on, there are two possible destinations. There's the good, which we call the Light."

"And there's the bad," Joaquin put in, a shadow passing over his handsome face. "The Shadowlands."

"Which was why we had to stop you on the beach," Tristan implored. "We couldn't risk your dad and Darcy being sent there."

"And you couldn't think of another way?" I demanded.

Tristan's cheeks turned pink. "I tried, but you kind of called me on it, remember?"

The warmth. The calming warmth. I realized now that

I'd felt it twice before—yesterday morning, when I was on the verge of a nervous breakdown about Olive's disappearance, and again last night when I'd started to realize the disturbing truth about Juniper Landing. Both times Tristan had used his touch, his power, whatever it was, to bring me back from the abyss.

"So why bring me here?" I asked. "With all of you?"

"We wanted to tell you about what we do," Krista replied. "We're the ones who usher people to their ultimate destinations."

"We call ourselves Lifers," Lauren said. She held up her arm to show me her leather bracelet, which slipped down almost to her elbow. One quick look around the room revealed that every one of my captors wore one. I'd noticed the bracelets when I first arrived on the island and assumed they signaled some kind of club or secret society. I'd had no idea they'd meant *this*.

"Lifers," I repeated, feeling an odd sense of déjà vu. I'd heard that word somewhere before. "So you guys decide where people end up?"

They all laughed. Even Tristan.

"Uh, no," Lauren said, placing her coffee cup on the bar. "Do we look like gods?"

"Well, some of us do," Joaquin said, turning his hands up.

Bea narrowed her amber eyes and shoved him so hard he almost fell over.

"That's *not* what we do," Tristan reiterated. "We simply act as ushers to the next realm. When someone's ready to move on, their Lifer gets a coin," He produced a gold coin from his pocket and held it out to me. It gleamed even in the duskiness of the room. I plucked it from his hand and turned it over in my own palm. It was heavy and thick, blank on one side with a sun on the other.

"We take the visitor up to the bridge, hand them their coin, and send them on their way," Tristan explained. "The coin knows which way they're supposed to go and leads them there."

The bridge. Of course. The events of last night filtered through my brain. Mr. Nell screeching and writhing as Fisher and Kevin tossed him into the back of a pickup truck. Krista getting behind the wheel and speeding off into the fog toward the bridge on the north end of the island. His screams cutting off abruptly and the eerie silence that followed. She'd ushered him to the Shadowlands. Right there in front of me. And I'd had no clue.

I studied the coin. How could this little hunk of metal know where I was destined to spend all eternity? With a sudden flinch, I tossed it back to Tristan. Not that I had any doubts, of course. It wasn't like they were going to ship me off to the bad place, right? Me, my sister, my father . . . we were all destined for the Light. We had to be.

Tristan stared at me, his eyes suddenly sad, and I felt the mood in the room shift, as if everyone had stopped breathing as one.

"Why are you looking at me like that?" I asked Tristan. The others suddenly became very interested in the crappy oceanic art on the walls. "Tristan, why are you telling me all this? If I can't tell my family, then why . . . why can *you* tell *me*?"

Tristan took a deep breath. He closed the distance between us and reached for both of my hands. I instinctively froze, waiting for that odd warmth, but this time, I felt nothing. Nothing other than the pounding of my heart.

"You know how you've felt all along that something was different about the island?" he asked.

My head went weightless. "Yes," I replied.

"And you asked why you remembered Olive and the musician from the park after they were gone, while Darcy didn't?" he said.

I blinked, thinking of my first friend on the island who'd disappeared last week without a trace. Where was he going with this?

"Yes."

"Well, that's because you *are* different," Tristan said

slowly, firmly. "You're not like the other visitors on Juniper Landing."

My chest constricted. "Different how?"

Tristan gazed down at my fingers for a long moment before looking me in the eye. There was no one else in the room right then. No one else who mattered. "You're a Juniper Landing Lifer. Like me."

"Like all of us," Joaquin put in.

"What?" I breathed. "What does that even mean?"

"It means you won't be moving on," he said quietly. "You're staying here. With us."

My fingers slipped out of Tristan's grip, and I pressed the heels of my hands against my eyes. I had just started to adjust to the fact that I was going to some ethereal place called the Light. That I would never see home again. Would never graduate from high school or go to college or med school or do anything that I had spent half my life planning to do. And now . . . now I was stuck here? Forever?

"Why?" I demanded, dropping my hands. "What makes me so special?"

"You died an unnatural death," Joaquin told me, his voice suddenly gentle. "At least, that's the first requirement you have to meet to become a Lifer. And in the last moment of your life, you achieved the second."

The room swam before my eyes, a wash of browns and

yellows and greens. "The second? What's the second?"

"You have to prove your selflessness. Either in the other world or once you're here," Tristan told me. "You used your last seconds of life to rid the earth of a sadistic killer. Even as you took your last breaths, you managed to make the world a better place."

One last image came spiraling back to me. A slow-motion reel of me, yanking the knife out of my stomach, turning it on the man who'd murdered my family and so many others, the look of shock on Nell's face as the blade arced toward his chest. A strangled sort of cackle escaped my throat.

"My selfless act was killing Steven Nell?" I said, aghast. "That wasn't selfless; that was revenge."

Tristan's brow knit. "Maybe on some level, but—"

"This has to be a joke," I said, looking around at the rest of them. Waiting—hoping—for one of them to crack. To start laughing and shout "gotcha!" But no one moved. "You're kidding, right? Tell me you're kidding."

"I wouldn't joke about something like this, Rory," Tristan said. "I wouldn't do that to you."

The room blurred in and out around me. The coffee cups scattered on the bar, the plaster cast of a jumping dolphin suspended over one of the couches, all the faces staring back at me—curious, pitying, concerned. I pressed one hand against my forehead and forced myself to focus on Tristan.

Only Tristan. His perfect lips, his strong jaw, his kind eyes. Right now he was the only thing that made sense.

I took a breath.

"So what you're telling me is, this is it," I said, the air catching in my throat, making my eyes sting. "This is where I'm going to stay."

"Yes," Tristan replied, his eyes shining. "This is your new home. Forever."

ACKNOWLEDGMENTS

This book would not have come to fruition without the endless hard work and patience of the dream team: Lanie Davis, Emily Meehan, Sara Shandler, Josh Bank, and Sarah Burnes. It's been a crazy ride, and it's only just begun!